About the Author

Leticia is a fifty-three-year-old US Army veteran and business owner from Alabama. She has spent her life as a storyteller through music and writing. Her album, *Do You See Me,* was released in 2011, featuring original music. She is a wedding planner and photographer. She earned her BA in marketing with a minor in German in 1993 from Troy University. She currently resides in Tuscaloosa, Alabama, with her husband of thirty years.

The Love of the Taymni

Beseeched

Tecia McLaughlin

Beseeched

Olympia Publishers
London

A CIP catalogue record for this title is
available from the British Library.

ISBN: 978-1-80074-664-0

This is a work of fiction.
Names, characters, places and incidents originate from the writer's
imagination. Any resemblance to actual persons, living or dead, is
purely coincidental.

First Published in 2023

Olympia Publishers
Tallis House
2 Tallis Street
London
EC4Y 0AB

Printed in Great Britain

Dedication

To my husband, Ken, and my daughter, SaVanna. Thank you for
being the best part of my life in every way. I'm proud to say
that the two of you are mine. I love you with all my heart.

Acknowledgements

Thank you, Lisa Dutton Hayes, for being so committed to the editing process of my manuscript. I look forward to many more novels with you by my side. Your eye for detail, professionalism, and creative charm is truly unique. Love you to the beach and back!

Chapter One

Sela Barnes walked aimlessly in the direction of her new apartment. It had only been an hour since she left, but already she had grown restless with the morning. Not having anything to do when she got home, or anyone to call for company, she moved noticeably slower than those around her. She had thought it would be a good idea to relocate to Charleston, South Carolina, but somehow she had been unable to adjust to her new life as quickly as she had hoped. It had been the longest three weeks of her life. The life she had left behind was all she could think about.

Leaving her fiancé, a successful attorney with a very promising future, back in Corpus Christi, Texas, was probably the dumbest thing she had ever done, but she felt she needed to get away. Too much had happened in the last year, and her responsibilities at the multi-million dollar ranch had begun to close in around her. Thoughts of her family engulfed her as she neared the place where boxes were carelessly stacked in corners. Her suitcases weren't even fully unpacked. She felt so alone in this town where no one knew her name.

Ten steps behind Sela, a man in a gray and white jogging suit followed undetected. He didn't know her. He had only been given a picture of her. He didn't care why she had been chosen as his target; it was a paying job. As the light turned green, Sela stopped at the corner and waited for her signal to walk. She didn't see the faces of those around her. They were strangers in a strange town. The signal changed and everyone moved fervently.

From behind her, a hand reached quickly and snatched a gold locket from her neck, and with the other hand grabbed her purse and shoved her to the ground. It was all too sudden to react. The man was yards away before she finally let out a yell.

"He just stole my purse! Right there!"

Her finger shook as she pointed, and her voice sounded weak competing with the traffic and sounds of downtown. She saw only the back of the small figure running madly down the street, disappearing behind a building. She didn't see his face, but his hands indicated he was a tanned male. He wore a hat, but his black hair could be seen. If she had to guess, she would say he was Hispanic. She watched him disappear without a chase. She expected somebody to attempt a pursuit. Nobody moved toward him. Instead, they seemed to move faster away from her, more eager to get away than help.

"Did you get a good look at him?" The elderly woman who spoke looked genuinely frightened.

"No. I didn't see his face, really. I think he was a Mexican guy, though."

She heard a few strangers around her asking if she was all right. She felt a hand on her shoulder, patting gently.

"I'm fine. Just a little shook up." She brushed debris from her hands and knees.

"It's really not common for someone in this area to be robbed in broad daylight." She could now see that it was the elderly woman's hand she felt on her shoulder.

"I wouldn't know. I'm not from here. I don't even know where the police station is." She could feel her insides shaking. It was a delayed reaction. Her legs felt weak.

"You really should file a report. If you're not afraid to ride with a stranger, I'll take you there." The lady smiled.

Sela looked at her small frail body, "I'm not afraid. Thanks."

"My car is two blocks up on the right. My name is Mrs. Harper. Ruby Harper. I've lived here all my life."

"Sela Barnes. It's nice to meet you." She smiled at the little lady who could more than likely barely see over the steering wheel of the car.

"So where are you from, Sela?"

"Corpus Christi, Texas."

"What brought you to Charleston?"

Sela didn't know if the woman really wanted to know or if she was making polite conversation to distract her and calm her nerves, but it didn't matter. It had been three weeks since she had spent time with anyone and she longed to just have a conversation.

"I came here to get away from some responsibility that has been dumped on me." She hated using the word dumped the minute it came out of her mouth. "You may have heard of my family. My dad is Charles Barnes." Sela slowed her pace a little, realizing her stride was twice as long as Mrs. Harper's.

"Yes, of course. Your family once owned the largest percent of the oil industry in North America." The lady nodded vigorously. Her voice became excited and enthusiastic. She had heard all about the late Texas tycoon and his family.

"Well, then you probably heard he was killed two months ago on a rig off the coast of New Orleans. It was a freak accident and three people were killed. Nobody knows exactly what happened. He was there on a routine check of something. I don't even know what. Something near his sleeping quarters exploded, they said. It's still being investigated."

"I did hear about the accident. I am so sorry."

"It still hasn't soaked in. Fifteen years ago, my mother died of breast cancer and that leaves my sister Charlene, and me the sole heirs. It's a lot. I guess I should be extremely grateful, and I am, of course, but with the money comes a lot of responsibility. Daddy always said that."

"So what are you doing here in Charleston?"

"I don't know. I just feel kinda lost. Trying to regroup without all eyes on me and the money."

Mrs. Harper nodded. Sela continued.

"It's not the money alone that's the huge responsibility. It's so much more than that. I have nearly two hundred children who live on our ranch. They have no family to take care of them. Only the people who work on the ranch. Families come and live on our property and take these kids in to be their own, but it's not long-term. They are rarely adopted by the families, but every bit of food and love they get comes from our ranch. I feel honored to be a part of it, but at the same time, it's overwhelming. Finding good employees and house parents is a tremendous job. My fiancé cares nothing about getting involved and I'm not sure I can handle all of it yet."

The woman was easy for Sela to talk to. She felt safe expressing her thoughts and feelings. It felt good to be expressing exactly how she felt to this stranger.

"I've read all about the good work your family has done for all the orphans at the ranch. I have always wanted to get involved in something so dynamic and see the lives of people changed. It's really inspirational what your mother started there. Not many people have that sort of opportunity. Most of us dream of helping a few children in our lifetime, but we don't have the means to help as many as we'd like."

Sela smiled. It felt good to hear someone speak of her

mother. When her mother came up with the idea of opening up a home for orphans, it was praised as a good gesture. No one thought she had the energy to actually go through with it, though. After the third home was built, she gained national recognition as year-by-year, one orphan after another was sent to college and became more than just a homeless kid trying to survive. She provided them with love and a family. She gave them a birthday and a Christmas to remember.

"My mother was amazing. She was so strong, even on her weakest days." Sela felt awkwardly ashamed of what she had left behind.

"So you don't want to pick up where your mother left off?"

"I've worked with the kids for years. I like it, of course. I'm just not sure if I want to commit to it for the rest of my life. This is not a business you leave at the office. Every child has needs around-the-clock. When dad died, life hit me in the face. I realized I was an adult. I'm making all the decisions now. With the help of some very loyal employees, of course."

"Here we are." Mrs. Harper pointed to the parking deck and directed her to the side elevator. "So you just felt the need to relocate and take a little break?" Her accent was sweet and southern. Only ladies from Charleston could speak with this gentle accent.

"Yes, ma'am. I guess that's it." She suddenly realized she had unloaded more than the woman probably wanted to hear. Everything had just gushed out of her. Maybe it was nervous energy. She now felt embarrassed at giving the woman so much detail in less than five minutes. It was so unlike her to talk about her personal life so readily.

Sela got into the long, plush Cadillac.

"Mrs. Harper, if you don't mind, will you just run me by my

apartment? I don't have a description of the guy, and I don't imagine the police can do anything without it. I'll just call and report it when I get home. I need to get my credit cards canceled as soon as possible."

"Are you sure? It's really no trouble at all."

"I'm sure. Thank you, though. I feel like it will be a waste of time."

"Okay, then. Just tell me where I need to go from here."

"It's just around the next block and two streets down."

"Is it Harbor Heights?"

"Yes, ma'am."

✶ There was a long silence, and then Mrs. Harper began to speak. It was like the words of a prophet soothing the soul. Like breast milk on the lips of a hungry baby.

"Dear, you have a load on your mind and heart that you don't have to carry alone. Let God lead your heart and direct you to the place you need to be. No more running. No more confusion. Let the windows of heaven pour fresh water on your soul and rekindle the burning desire in you to find the truth and true meaning of your life."

Sela felt a calmness come over her as she listened to these warm words of wisdom. She sounded so much like her mother, it was crazy.

"Thank you. Thank you for everything. Can we please keep in touch?"

They exchanged addresses and Mrs. Harper smiled as she waved goodbye. Sela had made her first friend in Charleston. She felt in her pocket for her keys. She normally dropped them in her purse, but today she had stuck them in a deep pocket in her loose-fitting khakis. "Good thing these were in my pocket," she mumbled.

16

robber

(Ruez) dialed a Corpus Cristi number. "I haf de purse and de locket. Now what?" His English was good, but his Spanish accent was thick. He had been living in the US for the past six years. In fact, he had made quite a living scamming and carrying out the dirty deeds of anyone who could pay him the right price. It had been a lucrative job so far, with few, if any, mistakes.

"Do what you want with the locket but bring the purse to me."

"Sure thing, Boss. Anything else you need before I head back?"

"Did anybody see you?"

"Nobody came after me. It doesn't matter. I'm wearing a disguise."

"Good. Then head home. Do me a favor, though. Don't call me on my cell number unless it's an emergency. You have my work number."

"Gotcha."

Ruez stripped off his disguise and walked quickly to the closest pawnshop. He slipped the picture of Sela and her father out of the gold locket. He turned it over and read the inscription: "Always Daddy's Baby Girl, but Sweet 16." Sela had been given the locket on her sixteenth birthday, and she was rarely caught without it. Ruez was given fifty dollars cash for the hit without any questions asked.

The phone rang, and Sela was jolted from a light slumber.

"Hello?"

"Were you sleeping?"

The soft whisper of her fiancé, Matthew, in her ear was a perfect way to be awoken.

"I guess I dozed off. I've been waiting for you to call, though. I left a few messages on your cell. Did you get them?"

"No, I haven't checked it yet. I'm still working. We have got so much going on right now, and I just can't seem to catch up."

"Are you still gonna come up this weekend?"

"Of course. I wouldn't miss your birthday for anything! Big twenty-four."

"Don't say it too loud. Changing the subject, but have you heard from Charlene? I've only talked to her once since she arrived in San Francisco. It's been nearly two weeks since I've heard from her." Charlene and Matthew weren't close, but they would sometimes text.

"No word here. Maybe she's been so overwhelmed with the city and her work that she just forgot to call."

"Not a chance. Don't forget this is my sister we're talking about. She's never been overwhelmed a day in her life." Charlene was the free spirit. The one who could go with the flow. She had taken the news of their father's death surprisingly well, holding it together for her big sister's sake. Sela wished she was more like Char.

"I talked to Lily this morning and she hasn't heard from her either. She isn't answering her cell or home phone." Lily was their life support. The one stable and constant piece of life that remained.

"You worry too much, babe. She's a big girl in a big world. She's fine. I wish I was there to soothe a little bit of that worry away."

"I know. I do, too. I just can't shake this feeling, though. Get your booty up here quick. I'm getting lonely. Oh! I was mugged today." She suddenly remembered her shocking day.

"You were what?"

"I was mugged."

"And you say it like it happens all the time?"

"Well, I was pretty upset at the time. Such a freak thing that could have happened to anyone. It's just that I was the one chosen for today's act of crime, I guess. I've already canceled my credit cards and notified the bank. A sweet lady helped me through it."

"What happened?"

"This guy just grabbed my locket and my purse and took off. He shoved me to the ground in the process."

"The one your dad got you?"

"Yeah. I'll check around at some pawnshops tomorrow. Maybe the thug got some quick cash for it."

"Were you hurt?"

"No. Just shook up for a while."

"I want you home. There is no good reason for you to be there."

"I think you're right. I still think about Dad every day, even though I am away from everything that reminds me of him. It doesn't matter how far away from everything I get. He's still in my heart and that's where the pain is. Pretty sure running was the wrong move."

Matt smiled. "That's what I've been hoping to hear for three weeks. I guess my prayers have been answered. You and I are going to have a weekend together that's going to change your life."

"Oh, really?"

"Yes. I'm going to convince you that moving here and marrying me is the best thing you could ever do."

"I don't know how you have been so patient with me all these years, but thank you. I do love you so much." Being away these three weeks had made her think more about settling down and starting a family.

"I love you, too, and I'll see you at the airport Friday evening. Do you have the flight information?"

"Yep. I'll talk to you before then, though."

"Sleep tight. I love you."

"Love you, too."

She knew she loved him, but she had been unable to give herself to him completely. Something inside her kept him at a distance while everyone else said she was crazy. They said he wouldn't keep waiting on her forever. Her father hadn't cared for him much, and in her gut, she was afraid he had legitimate cause that maybe he had never shared with her. Matthew was stable, successful, and extremely attractive. And he loved her with all his heart. What else could a girl ask for?

Matthew hung up the phone and chuckled.

"What's so funny?"

The tall blond lady stood in her short, silky bathrobe with her hair wrapped in a towel. Her long, tan legs were freshly-shaven and oiled to perfection.

"I've got her right where we want her. She actually agreed that running wasn't the answer, and she'll more than likely be moving home real soon."

He grabbed the woman's slender face and kissed her lips. "This is what we've been waiting for, baby. Let's celebrate." He reached for a bottle of whiskey and two glasses.

The woman was not so optimistic. She removed the towel and shook her blond hair free. He stared at her plump lips as she spoke.

"Let's wait until it happens this time. She's been on the verge of marrying you for two years now." She scowled skeptically at her longtime lover.

"Yes, but we're closer. You know just how to burst a bubble, don't you?" He threw back his glass of whiskey and winced at the taste.

"You know it's true, though. She's been 'threatening' to marry you for three years now and it hasn't happened."

"No, but she's madly in love with me. I know that much is true." His confident smug smile drew her in.

"Aren't we all." She slapped him on his behind and walked down the hall to the bathroom. "All I'm saying is that I'm not going to get my hopes up just yet. That's all."

Sela stared at the phone. Charlene had always been the responsible one. She was always together. She never missed sending out birthday or thank you cards. She was just like their mother. When she made a promise, she followed through with it, even if it meant a great sacrifice to herself. She had usually called her sister three or four times a week to chat. Now two weeks had passed by and there was still no word from her. Sela had been opposed to Charlee taking a job so far away, but it was something her sister really wanted. The company was based out of San Francisco, but her work would be all over the continental United States. She was an archeologist and loved her job with a passion. Sela admired her sister's responsible side. She admired her ability to do her own thing and reach her goals. She dialed Charlee's cell number again, but there was no answer. She felt a sickness in the pit of her stomach. Something just wasn't right.

Back at the ranch, Lily sat in the den reading a book. Occasionally, she checked her watch to see if it was late enough in San Francisco to call Charlene. She dialed the number. Still no answer. She decided to call Sela.

"Hey, honey. I'm sorry to call you this early."

"Thank goodness you did. I fell asleep on the couch and when I woke up, I wanted to call you, but I was afraid you were still sleeping. Have you heard from Charlene?" Both ladies spoke the words almost simultaneously.

"No. That's why I am calling. I was hoping you had." Sela could tell from Lily's voice that she was worried. It was Lily, a tall slender black woman, who had raised her and her sister from the time they were babies. After her mother's untimely death to cancer, it was Ms. Lily who helped them through the troublesome years of adolescence. It was Lily who taught her algebra and Lily who sang her to sleep when her father was out of town. It was Lily she had cried to when her best friend had moved away or when she needed answers to adolescent questions. She was a spiritual rock that Sela loved as her own mother.

"Something's wrong. I'm going to call the police." Sela felt her heart race as she spoke the words. Her chest tightened and she breathed as deeply as she could to get air. She couldn't stand the drama any longer. "This is just so unlike Charlee."

"Listen. Just stay calm, honey. If we don't hear something by tomorrow evening, I'll call and get the apartment manager to check. I'll call the work number she left us, too. Have you tried her at work? It's probably no big deal. But when I do get in touch with her, I'm going to make it a big deal." Lily tried hard to sound convincing, but she knew as well as Sela that this was so out of character for Charlee. "How's it going up there anyway? Are you settling in okay?" Lily wanted to change the subject and take Sela's mind off Charlee. She felt an uneasiness that she didn't want Sela to hear. She knew in her heart something bad had happened.

"Not really. I think I already regret the move, and I haven't even unpacked completely."

"Have you made any friends?"

"None. I've met a few serious swimmers at the country club, but I haven't really gotten to know them. Other than that, it's been just barely okay here."

"Do they know you won a gold medal as a national finalist and trained for the Olympic swim team?"

"No, but they know I can outswim all of them." She smiled. It was her true talent and passion in life. "I really thought I was going to get involved in organizations, church, and whatever else came my way, but I just can't get motivated. My mind keeps going back to the kids at the ranch, Daddy, and now Charlee being so far away. I thought this would help me figure some stuff out, but I'm even more confused. I just can't get focused anymore. Matthew is coming up this weekend. Maybe I should just marry him, start a family, and settle down the right way."

"These kids miss you, girl. They ask about you every day. Keep the letters coming. It's bragging rights in the cafeteria to get a letter from Miss Sela. You do what you feel in your heart is best. If you want to come home, then pack it up. About Matthew: pray hard, girl. That's a big step."

"I know, Lily. There was something about him Daddy had never liked. I wish he would have told me what it was."

There was something about him Lily didn't like either. He was somehow shady. She couldn't quite put her finger on it, but he wasn't sincere. The children never cared much for him either. She couldn't tell Sela she didn't like her fiancé, though. She would need to find out for herself.

"Your daddy wanted you to figure it all out for yourself. I'm gonna let you get some sleep. We'll talk tomorrow. I love you."

"I love you, too, Lily. Tell the children I miss them! Bye."

She didn't want to tell Lily about the attack. There was enough for her to worry about.

Sela lay there thinking of the smiling faces that so often cheered her up. She felt awful for abandoning them on such short notice. They had been deserted all their life and now she was doing the same thing to them. She felt tears welling up in her eyes. She cried silently for the children, not her own insignificant problems.

Sela spent the next day at the pool. She swam long and hard. It was her only source of relief from the pain and grief she felt over the loss of her mother and father. The pool was her safe place. Elegantly and effortlessly, she swam lap after lap. When she got back to the apartment that evening, there was an envelope balanced on the doorknob. She knew no one who would leave her a letter. She shuddered momentarily at the thought of her assailant finding out her address and coming to her home. Maybe he had gotten her address from something in her purse. She reached for the letter slowly. She looked around and saw no one in the halls. She opened it and read.

"I'm inside. I just couldn't wait until Friday. SURPRISE. Love, Matthew." Her heart leapt. She fumbled excitedly for the keys. It was truly a great surprise. Only one of many he had planned for the weekend. Sela opened the door quietly and saw him from a distance, sleeping on the couch. His brown curls were tousled recklessly, and his mouth was slightly parted, allowing deep breaths to come in and out. He was a very handsome man. He and Sela had been friends since grammar school. In high school, it was her best friend, Beth, who had fallen in love with him. The three of them were inseparable.

She and Beth had been complete opposites, but somehow so perfect for each other. Beth was tall and blond, giving off that perfect Victoria's Secret model look. She was more outgoing and loved a crowd, while Sela was of average height, with long, thick dark hair and an athletic build. She was strong and more reserved. For three years, Matthew and Beth were the couple of the year! They were homecoming king and queen, prom couple, and everything else that included a vote of the students. Midway through their senior year, Beth's dad got a job in Atlanta and they moved rather quickly. The letters from Beth came regularly for the rest of the year, and the three of them made plans to attend the University of Texas together. Just before registration, Beth said she had decided to go to the University of Georgia and was breaking it off with Matthew. The breakup left him heartbroken and sick. The letters and phone calls stopped and eventually all contact with Beth ended. Matthew Kinsley, "Matt" as he was called, went his own way and they seldom saw each other in the four years she was at UT. After graduating, Sela took a cruise to the Bahamas with some friends and Matt was on the ship. They hung out and realized that they still had a great deal in common and enjoyed each other's company, even without Beth. They began seeing each other regularly and that was three years ago.

She watched him as he slept. He was a successful man with a lot of enthusiasm. Well-respected. Charismatic. He made her smile, and he made her feel secure. Why did she feel so unable to love him completely? They had not had sex yet. She was waiting until she was married to have sex, and she sometimes wondered if it was the lack of complete intimacy that kept her at a slight distance. He respected her wishes, although he often complained. He described himself as a gentleman, able to wait on the woman he loved. She touched his face lightly. He smiled.

"I've been waiting for you." He rolled over and reached for her, beckoning her to lie next to him.

"I've been at the pool, down at the country club."

"I'll bet you had everybody's eyes poppin' out of their heads." He hugged her close and kissed her cheek.

"I don't know about that. I doubt it." She never really saw her beauty. She felt average, based on the media's beauty standards. She climbed up next to him on the couch. "How long have you been here?"

"Since around two, I guess."

Matt smiled a teethy grin. God, she loved his smile.

"So what have you been doing with yourself all this time?"

"Just watching the door and waiting for you." He smiled and pulled her close and squeezed her tightly. "I have big plans for us this weekend."

"Well, we don't have to wait for the weekend now."

"You are oh-so-right."

"Are you hungry? I know this great little restaurant I've been dying to go to. It looks so cozy and romantic. There's a jazz band Wednesday through Friday."

"Let's do it."

Sela stood up and handed him the remote. "I'll be ready in about forty minutes. Make yourself comfortable."

After showering, Sela put on a white V-neck sundress with white sandals and slicked her thick dark tresses back in a tight bun at the base of her neck. Her tanned body looked radiant against the white cotton. Her lips were candy apple red, and her blue eyes were heavily lined with brown eyeliner to accent her long black lashes. She and Matt would be the envy of both man and woman wherever they went. Not only was she beautiful, but she was loved by everyone, young and old alike. Her personality filled any room she entered.

Matt knew that this night would be the turning point. She had already said that she was ready to be his wife. Now all he had to do was play on those feelings immediately and get her to the altar as quickly as possible. With his finances in shambles and his reputation of being a fraud at risk of exposure, he needed this marriage more than anything he had ever needed. He would romance her and embrace her as if she were the last woman on earth. His whole life depended on her.

Matt pulled into the parking spot. He opened the door and quickly moved around to open her door.

"My lady." He reached in and took her by the hand, kissing it lightly.

"Thank you." She looked at him bashfully. He never opened her door in this fashion.

Taking her by the arm, he escorted his bride-to-be into the restaurant.

"Reservation for Kinsley." The hostess looked through the names. "Yes, here. Follow me."

Matt took her hand, and he could feel the stares of many eyes as they waltzed through the crowd of people. They were seated at a small table near a window with a view of the ocean.

"Thank you. This is so nice."

Matt pushed her chair underneath her and took his seat.

"Sela, I want you to remember this night for the rest of your life." He reached across the table and took her hands. "I want us to both remember the feeling and the love that we share this night. Together, we can build on it and make tonight the first night of the rest of our lives."

He looked passionately into Sela's eyes. She felt his love. She leaned over the small table, avoiding the candle in the middle, and placed her mouth on his, oblivious to anyone around her.

"I will always remember this night. I will always remember this night because, Matt Kinsley, I am ready to be your wife." The words were foreign to her mind and heart, but somehow felt okay in the moment.

"I promise to make you the happiest woman alive." He kissed her hand and breathed a sigh of relief. He could finally breathe easy. Everything was going his way. He was home free. She had rejected the ring he bought several times before, but now she would finally become Mrs. Kinsley.

It was near midnight when they arrived back at the apartment. Everything had gone as planned. It was a lovely evening of dancing in the moonlight, special requests played on the saxophone, and a dinner fit for royalty. They sat in the park looking at the river and talking for hours. He did love Sela, just not the way she thought he did. He had hoped to top the perfect evening off with a night of lovemaking to ensure the final loose end was tied, so to speak, and her heart was completely snared. He knew it would mean total commitment on her part.

"You looked so beautiful tonight." He stroked her hair and face as she lay beside him in a pair of silk boxers and top to match.

"Thank you. This was such a perfect night."

"I know one thing that could make it even better." He rolled her on top of him and they kissed madly. She felt his hands slowly pulling on her shorts.

"Matt." It was all she needed to say. She had said it so often before. She had waited this long; she may as well wait a little longer. She worried about the sex part. What if he was awful? What if he had no idea how to satisfy her? She wanted so badly just to give in. If the sex was awful, it would be devastating for both of them to back out.

"We're practically married. It isn't wrong anymore."

"Says who?"

"Says the whole world. We're about to be husband and wife."

"I don't care. God forbid, you had a terrible accident before the wedding and we never married. If we do it now, I wouldn't be able to give that special gift to my future husband-to-be. That's something I've made my mind up to do. Wait until marriage."

"Where do you come up with this stuff?"

"You've waited this long. What's a few more months?"

"How many months? We need to set a date. I need to know when I'm going to get all this." He made a sweeping motion with his hand.

Sela laughed. "You can handle it. Just think about how good it will be when it happens."

Matt rolled over and settled in for a good snuggle. It didn't matter anyway. She was just a stepping stone to the real good life.

Morning came with great excitement for Sela. For the first time, she felt totally and completely in love with Matt. She relished the moment. She had longed for those feelings, and now he had convinced her that he was really the man she wanted to spend the rest of her life with. She woke him with a kiss. "Good morning."

"Good morning." He stretched long and deliberately.

"Did you sleep good?"

"Next to you, I always sleep good."

"Well, I'm ready to spend every night sleeping next to you." She smiled shyly.

"You're serious then? It wasn't just a dream I had last night?"

"I am. I'm ready to leave here and become your wife."

"Then let's pack. You haven't unpacked much around here anyway." He sat up in the bed. The quicker the better for him.

"Well, what about the big weekend we had planned here?"

"It will be a bigger weekend for me if it means helping you pack and get back home." He held her face softly. She touched his hands.

"I want to show you some of Charleston. When will we ever get back up this way?"

"Charleston Schmarlston. I'm ready to head home and start planning."

"We never discussed our actual wedding day. But I imagine a big wedding with all the children and horses and…"

"Cattle and pigs. Forget all that. All we need is a small wedding for us. It's not for the kids."

"No, but they've been a big part of my family and I want them to be there. Lily will want me to have a big wedding that will include the kids." She could feel a little friction, even though he was joking.

"Lily, Lily, Lily. Charlee, Charlee, Charlee. What do *we* want?"

She remembered that she still hadn't heard from her sister.

"I want to have a nice wedding, even if it isn't very big. I'll be wearing a great big white gown and doing all the stuff a bride does before a wedding. A girl only gets one wedding, you know."

"I'm sorry. I know. It's just that I'm so anxious to make you my wife. We could take one of the yachts out for our honeymoon."

"Sounds perfect. We could hire our own private band, cooks, whatever, and just cruise around the Pacific until we feel like coming home." She had spent many summers on the water with her family.

"I don't think so. No bands, no cooks, no maids. Just me and my wife soaking up all of life and love together, without any interruptions. Spending days in the nude if we want to."

"That sounds pretty good, too. Swimming in the ocean!"

"Pretty good! Come on, Sela."

"I mean that sounds great. And you still have your boaters license and can drive something that big?"

Sela had grown up driving boats. It would be no problem for her.

"Well, the sooner we leave here the sooner we start on the wedding plans. Right?"

"You have a point."

The phone rang and Sela climbed across Matt to the other side of the bed to answer it. Matt held his breath. He lay still next to her, wondering if this could be the call.

"Hello?"

"Hello, may I speak to Sela Barnes?" The voice on the other end was deep but soft.

"This is she." Sela knew that no one had her number and she wondered who this stranger could be.

"My name is Jake Caraway. I'm a very good friend of your sister's. She arrived here in San Fran two weeks ago. But three days ago, we all went up near Washington on a study and she didn't show up at the meeting place. I've tried calling her over and over, but there's no answer."

Sela sat there, momentarily unable to speak. Charlee had always wanted to be an archeologist. This had been a dream position she had worked so hard to achieve. There is no way she would have just not showed up. She thought about what he was saying.

"Jake, yes, I've heard my sister speak of you often. Never arrived? What do you mean? Did she not report to work at all? I know she was looking forward to the project. It was the last thing we talked about. She said it would last about eight days, so I was hoping she had been tied up somewhere on the dig and was unable to call. Are you saying you haven't seen her at all in a week?"

"More like two weeks. She and I met up when she first got here. I showed her around for a few days. She was excited. She got here on a Wednesday. We unpacked a few boxes and did some shopping for her place. We hung out some over the weekend. I texted her the following Monday and she didn't answer. We're on different schedules, so I'm not sure about whether she checked in at work. I called her cell phone and her landline at the apartment repeatedly, and then I went by there. The door is locked, of course, and the manager wouldn't let me in, nor would she go check on her. I should have called you earlier, but I've been so busy."

"I've been trying to reach her night and day, as well. I'm afraid that something very bad has happened to her. Charlene would never make us worry by not checking in. If she had to pull over and use a gas station phone, she would do it. Dear God. I know something has happened." Her voice began to shake. Her lips were quivering.

"I was afraid of that, too. As her sister, you may be able to get the manager to open the door for me to see if there are any signs of foul play."

"I've got the leasing agent's number here. Let me get your number."

"912-344-5689. I'll be waiting to hear from you."

"I'll call you right back." Sela hung up the phone and burst into tears. Her hands were shaking violently as she dug inside the drawer next to the bed to get the name of the apartment Charlee was staying in.

"Calm down, baby. We don't know whether something has happened or not. Charlee is young. She's in a new town. Maybe she got out there and decided she didn't want a job and took off up the coast to go sightseeing." He patted Sela's back with affection.

"No. You know Charlee as well as I do. She is so responsible. She would never do something like that. There's not an impulsive bone in her body. Everything she does is calculated and with great planning. Unlike me." She felt a bit of self-pity rising up inside her.

She dialed the number of the apartments.

"Ski Lodge Apartments. This is Betty. May I help you?"

"Yes, ma'am. This is Sela Barnes. I'm calling from Charleston, South Carolina. My sister recently rented an apartment from you. We haven't heard from her in about two weeks and I'm afraid something really bad has happened. A friend of hers is on his way there to check out the apartment. Will it be okay for someone to let him look around?"

"Yes. That's possible in this situation. What is his name?"

"Jake Caraway."

"Oh, yes. He's been by a couple of times already. There's something else. I need you to call the police and have them escort him in." Her orders were direct.

"If you think it's necessary."

"It is."

"Then I'll call and tell him that someone will let him in. I'll be on the next flight out of Charleston, heading your way. I'm telling you, something has happened."

"Okay. I'll call the police and wait for them to get here. I have your number in Charlene's files. I'll call you back with any information."

"Thank you. I'll be waiting. Mr. Caraway will be representing the family until I can get there. If you have any questions, I'm sure he can answer some of them."

Sela hung up the phone.

"Are you sure you need to go to San Francisco, just like that?" He snapped his fingers.

"Yes, I'm sure." She gave him a sideways glance. "Why are you not taking this seriously?" Her irritation with Matt could be heard in her voice. She dialed Jake's number.

"The police are going over to Charlene's, but I'm not sure when. The manager said she would wait for them before she opens the door. I just wanted you to be there to answer any questions. I also want to make sure that they don't go fumbling around in there and mess up anything that could lead us to her whereabouts. You know, this is a newsworthy story. Charlee is a very rich girl. She could be kidnapped or who knows what?"

"I understand completely. I'm on my way."

"I'm on my way to San Francisco, Jake. Is there any way you could meet me at the airport later this afternoon?"

"Of course, I could. Just let me know when and where and I'll be there."

"Okay, then. I'll call you back with the flight info."

"I'll be waiting by the phone."

"You know I won't let you go to California alone, don't you?"

"Thank you. I could use a little support right now."

"Of course, you could. We'll get to the bottom of this together."

Matt hugged his future bride until she pulled away. "We've got to get packed and get to the airport."

Jake stood next to the officers as the apartment manager unlocked the door of Charlee's apartment. He had called them and reported a missing person, and they were happy to be there to check out the place with him. As the door swung open, the stench of rotting flesh filled their nostrils. Jake held his shirt over his nose as he followed the officers into the room.

"Call homicide. We've got a real doozy here."

The other officer called for backup. Charlee lay facedown at the table with a gunshot wound to the chest. Her body was stiff and swollen. Dried blood surrounded her chair and clung to her body. Her eyes were open with desperate pain and a note lay on the table beside her cup of tea.

The officer carefully picked up a pistol that was lying under her chair.

"Well, here's why no one heard a gunshot. There's a silencer on it."

He placed it in a bag and began dusting for fingerprints.

"Looks like we have typical suicide. Possibly another rich chick that couldn't cope, by the looks of this place." He hadn't meant for Jake to hear the words he was speaking to the other officer.

Jake spoke, quick and harsh. "This was no suicide. I'm telling you. This girl could never commit such an act. Note or no note. She didn't do this. The truth will come out soon enough."

The officers had heard it all. No one wants to believe their loved one could do such a thing as this. But for them, with no prints or evidence of foul play, it seemed to be an open-and-shut case.

The body was loaded up and taken to the morgue for an autopsy and forensic study. Jake followed them and filed a report, as he had witnessed it.

Chapter Two

By the time Sela arrived in San Francisco, her nerves were shot. She clung to Matt's arm as the airplane wheels touched the ground. She knew she was headed into something over her head, but she was prepared to pay any ransom and do whatever she needed to do to get her sister back. She had already resolved in her mind that Charlee must have been kidnapped.

She had never met Jake. She had never even seen a picture of him. As she stepped from the boarding ramp into the waiting area, she scanned the crowd quickly and her eyes locked with a set of compassionate dark eyes like she had never seen before. She had heard her sister speak of these eyes so many times. He was a man of domineering stature that commanded attention. A powerful physique and a welcoming smile that lured her in. He moved in her direction, never removing his gaze from her. She approached him with ease and they exchanged hugs. She felt the tension in her muscles slightly dissove and the lines on her forehead slowly soften at his touch. She wanted to linger in his arms a little longer, though she didn't know why. His voice flowed through his white teeth and pink lips ever-so-softly. She found herself mesmerized, even at such an inappropriate time. She was embarrassed at the blushing of her cheeks. Such a man had never crossed her path before. She knew he shared her anguish, and in that way, they were immediately bonded.

"I'm sorry we had to meet under these circumstances. This has been very troubling these last few weeks. I wanted to call sooner, but I just didn't want to worry anyone." He took one of her bags, offering a "hello" to Matt. Matt felt immediately awkward with Jake carrying Sela's bag. He had not realized she was even carrying her own bag. He squirmed at this stranger's forwardness and charm.

"This is my boyfriend, Matt."

"Fiancée," he corrected. They shook hands.

"Sorry." Sela raised her eyebrows to Matt to ask for forgiveness and turned back to Jake, dismissing Matt in an unintentional way. "So did you go to the apartment? Did the police ever show up?"

"No, they didn't. They'll be there around eight this evening." Jake had to lie. He couldn't tell her what they had found or what he had seen. Not yet. He tried to hide his pain.

"Well, this worked out perfectly then." Sela's attempt at being upbeat was falling flat.

Matt walked a few steps behind, studying the tall sandy blond male. There was something about him that he immediately disliked. Maybe it was the way Sela seemed to fall into his arms. Maybe it was the assuming way that he took her bag and barely offered him a hello. Maybe it was the fact that he was so good-looking.

It was a long walk to the parking deck and when they reached the car, Matt smirked. Now this is attractive, he thought. It was a very old Toyota, at least ten years old. It had been well taken care of, but it had over 200,000 miles on it. Sela smiled at the sight of it. She could not remember ever riding in something so old. She wondered if her sister had ever offered to buy him a new car, or if he was uncomfortable with taking charity from his girlfriend. She wasn't really sure what their relationship was. She had heard Charlee speak of Jake so many times, but they'd never actually met. She'd asked Charlee what their official title was, but had never gotten a straight answer.

"Sorry I don't have something better to drive you in."

"It's fine. As long as it'll get us there."

"It will do that."

Matt scowled as he placed his luggage in the back seat and eased onto the faded leather seats. Sela sat in the front with Jake. He started the car and turned the air conditioner on full force.

"Listen, I didn't want to say this in the airport, so when you asked me if the police had been there, I lied. They were there earlier today." He breathed heavily. In the back seat, Matt braced for the worst. He knew what they had found.

"They found your sister. She had been shot in the chest. She was slumped over at the table with a cup of tea in front of her. They found a suicide note, too. It said that she was so tired of life and its expectations and sick of everyone sucking the life out of her. It also said to tell her family and friends that she was sorry she was not stronger. It was her signature at the bottom." Jake didn't believe for a moment that it was a suicide. He had pictured the moments leading up to her death over and over in the last few days. He shook his head to clear the thought.

"Dear God, no! No! Not Charlee! Jake, no!" She sobbed the words over and over. Jake pulled her close and she laid her head on his shoulder. Matt seethed in the backseat. He should be the one with his arms around his fiancé at this moment. Minutes passed as she cried. Jake cried too.

Matt patted her shoulder from the back seat. Not exactly the manly thing he had planned in his mind. He could never have dreamed that Sela would have found out this tragic news while he was stuck in the backseat of a rundown Toyota.

Matt would have to wait his turn. He seethed at the sight in front of him.

"Something is wrong here and you know it. Charlee would never in a million years kill herself! She was sick of people? Sucking the life out of her? She surrounded herself with good people! She is a multi-millionaire, for God's sake. She could never go broke. She had you. She had me. She had Lily. She had a career and friends! She loved life and everything about it. She loved her job. No. This was not a suicide. What else did they find?" Her words were broken with sobs as tears fell down her hot cheeks.

"They're still looking. They were there when I left. They have no signs of foul play, Sela. There was no forced entry and no fingerprints anywhere. They found only Charlee's prints on the gun. They found only her prints throughout the entire apartment. I don't know who pulled off such a thing, but it seems so odd. It feels off. Everything about this seems too perfectly planned. Maybe they knew she was coming to San Fran, and when she would arrive. It had to be at a time when she was alone, so maybe they knew her schedule."

"I know in my heart that Charlee would never have done this. Never." Her throat ached with the lump that had formed.

"We will get to the bottom of this. We will find her killer." He stroked the back of Sela's head.

Matt cringed in the back seat. Who did this guy think he was? He didn't need him arousing suspicion and putting crazy ideas into Sela's head. It was a suicide and that should be the end of it.

"But who could be that evil? Who would Charlee know that was that evil?" Her words could barely be heard. They were only whispered. She could feel herself slipping away. Then everything went dark.

Later, Matt watched as they loaded Sela onto the hospital bed. This was about to get messy if Jake continued putting thoughts into Sela's head. He would find out real quick how evil things could get if he didn't mind his own affairs and let this go.

When Sela awoke, she was lying on her back in a white hospital room. She slowly opened her eyes and saw Matt sitting in a chair off to her left. She couldn't raise her head, but she could speak. She could hear beeping and the low rumble of machines. Matt immediately buzzed for the nurse.

"Hey, baby. I'm here. You blacked out." Matt held her hand and rubbed her fingers.

"Tell me I've had a bad dream. Tell me something that will make sense. How long have I been here? Where is my sister?" She could faintly remember something about Charlee. Her words were barely audible.

"Just rest and we'll talk later."

"No, Matt! Tell me how long I've been here and where my sister is. I don't want to rest."

"Sela, your sister committed suicide. You don't remember? She shot herself in the chest."

Sela stared at him, unable to speak. His words felt cold and emotionless. "You've been here for two weeks. You're back in Texas. The doctors called it a psychogenic coma which can be caused by hysteria."

"No. My sister did not commit suicide." Her words weren't powerful enough. She spoke louder. "She was murdered. Do you hear me? She was murdered!" Matt squeezed her hand.

"I hear you, baby. It's okay. I'm here for you."

She remembered someone else being with her. Jake.

"Where is Jake? I want to see Jake." She didn't know why

40

she wanted to see him. She just knew, somehow, that he could give her more answers than Matt. Matt clenched his jaw until his temple muscles bulged. He had waited for so long, anticipating the moment when Sela came to, only to have her ask to see another man the second she woke up. He spoke as calmly as his body would allow. He repeated the account of her passing out and arriving at the hospital.

"Honey, you passed out when Jake told you about Charlee. We were in his car. He should have never told you like that. You went into a coma. The doctors said it was shock. We thought it would last only a few hours, but when you showed no signs of recovering quickly, I had them move you back home where Lily and I could look after you. Jake is still in San Francisco. He left as soon as you were taken to the hospital." That wasn't true and he knew it. It had just flown out of his mouth before he could stop it. She would not be happy to know it was a lie.

"Where is Charlee?"

"Charlee was cremated. It was Lily's decision. Everything has been taken care of. I assure you of that."

"Was there a service for her?"

"No. You know I wouldn't allow that to happen. We were waiting for you, babe."

"I need to talk to Jake."

"About what?"

"About my sister, Matt!"

"Jake can't help you."

"What? Why are you acting like this?"

The nurse came in and saw that Sela was visibly upset.

"Let's check your vitals."

"If everything is looking good, when do you think I'll be able to go home?"

41

"I'm not the doctor, but if your vitals remain good over the next day or two, I'm sure that he will release you." She looked at Matt. "Do everything to help keep her calm. No stressful conversations, please." She left the room.

"Don't you ever say that my sister committed suicide again? Never! Do you hear me? She did not. She did not! What is wrong with you, Matt? Why are you so intent on believing that she killed herself? You are not acting like you're on my side."

"Baby, I am always on your side. But there was a note, Sela. It was Charlee's handwriting. Please, let's talk about something else."

"There was a note. That's it? There was a note? That makes it a legitimate suicide? What if every murderer in the world started forging suicide letters? Would they stop investigating homicides? I don't think so. Understand me. I will not rest until I see the person who murdered my sister die!" Her eyes pierced him in a way that he had never seen in Sela. Her vow of determination was fierce enough to send a cold chill down his spine.

She pressed the button for the nurse.

"May I help you, Miss Barnes?"

"Yes. I need something for my nerves."

She turned her face away from Matt so that he couldn't see the anger in her eyes.

Sela was released from the hospital and settled into her ranch home two days later. Lily worked hard to help her regain her strength. Sela sat in bed reading a magazine. Now and then her mind would wander off to the handsome man she had met in San Francisco. Had he given up so easily on Charlee?

She didn't know much about him, but he seemed so passionate and certain that it had been a murder. She shook her head as if to shake the thought from her mind. Her focus was to regain her mental and physical strength and go from there.

"Sela, do you feel like talking on the phone?" Lily's voice was soft as an angel's.

"Who is it?"

"It's Jake Caraway." She placed her hand over the phone so he couldn't hear her speak. "He has called to check on you every day since you went to the hospital. I called him to let him know you were home with me. He wants to talk."

Sela couldn't believe what she was hearing. He had checked on her every day? Sela felt her pulse quicken. Matt made her believe that Jake had left and never looked back again. She picked up the line in her room and heard Lily hang up.

"Hello?"

"Hi, Sela. It's Jake."

"Hi, Jake. Thanks for calling."

"So how are you?"

"I feel better already, now that I'm at home."

"Did Matt tell you I came to see you a few times?"

"No, he didn't. When did you come?"

"I was there three times." He would've gone everyday if he could have. He'd already spent so much on plane tickets and a hotel room and had even missed work for Sela.

"Are you kidding me? You flew all the way from California to visit me?"

"Yep. He didn't tell you?"

"No." She didn't want to tell him what he had actually said. "Jake, I still believe that Charlee did not commit suicide. Do you believe me?"

"Of course, I do. Lily and I have been talking about it. She paid the rent for Charlee's apartment for the next year. We've hired an investigator, too."

"Really? She and I haven't had a chance to talk about those things yet. She's trying hard to keep me calm about all this. Thank you so much for everything. So I guess we'll be staying in touch while working together on this, in a way, kinda?" Why did she sound so awkward talking to him? In a way, kinda? She breathed deeply, trying to chase away the butterflies she felt.

"Yes, in a big way. Until the very end. Until we find out what happened to your sister, I'll be right here for you." He spoke with genuine feeling.

"Thank you for everything. This may be a long and difficult road, but I'm prepared to travel it at any cost."

"I feel sort of strange saying that I'll be right there with you if you need me, when we don't even really know each other. But I truly mean it." He did mean it.

"I have a feeling I will need you. My fiancée seems to believe that Charlee's death was indeed a suicide. He is not going to be much support." Fiancé. She suddenly felt less enthused at the idea.

"How long have you been engaged?"

"Well, only one day before I went into the coma. But we have dated for years."

"Do you love him?" He said the words before he could stop himself. Nothing could have been more inappropriate, but something in him had to know the answer. The words rang out into the atmosphere. Do you love him? Do you love him?

Jake's query seemed almost like a trick question, yet the answer should've been the easiest one of her life. She felt her mouth go numb. She couldn't speak.

"Sela? I'm sorry. It's really none of my business."

"I'm sorry, I thought I heard Lily speaking to someone. What

44

were you saying?" She needed a few more seconds to gather her thoughts.

"I just asked if you love Matt?"

"Of course, I do. I'm marrying him soon. It just took me three years to realize that I love him." It sounded and felt forced.

"I don't think it would take me that long to realize that I love a woman with all my heart. It happens in your heart and not your mind. I could never be persuaded to love someone."

"That makes sense." She felt a little uncomfortable talking about something so personal. "Anyway, I guess we'll be in touch as soon as either of us hears something about the investigation."

"Do you mind me calling you on this number? Or do you want to give me your cell number?"

She wanted to say no, she didn't mind, but her gut told her that something confusing was taking place.

"How about I call you with any news and you call me with any news?" There. She had kept it "official business" without giving him a direct yes or no.

"That sounds good. I look forward to hearing from you." His disappointment in her not saying it was okay to call was as thick as fog.

"Bye, Jake."

"Goodbye, Sela."

She felt her energy surge. "Lily?" she called. Lily came from somewhere down the hall.

"Yes, baby girl?"

"How do you like Jake?"

"I love him. We've really gotten to know each other over the past few weeks." Lily sat on the end of the bed.

"Really? How?"

"We've spent a lot of time on the phone. We've talked about

Charlee and you and the ranch. He is so genuine and caring. He just makes me feel warm all over when I hear his voice. He reminds me of your father in so many ways."

Sela knew what she meant. Even though they had not spent any time together, she knew he was a kindred spirit. She felt a connection with him like she had never felt before.

"How do you feel? Your cheeks look like they're getting a bit more color in them."

"I feel good." She felt good knowing that Jake had been to see her. She felt good having him on her side.

Her recovery was quick and her resolve unmovable.

She was on her feet in no time, with plans to head back to San Francisco. She couldn't understand why Matt was opposing her efforts, but it really didn't matter. She knew Jake was behind her and would be until the killer was caught. Her mind was made up and her flight was scheduled.

"I don't know why you're doing this." Matt sat at the airport with her.

"And I don't know why you don't understand why I'm doing this. Someone has murdered my sister for no reason at all. I want to find out who did it and why. Is that so hard to believe?"

"Sela, I have waited on you for so long. You always have another excuse why we can't get married. I'm running out of patience. I have a life. I'd like for it to include you and a family of my own. But so far, you've managed to come up with every excuse known to man not to marry me. All I'm saying is that maybe it's time to put yourself first and start a new life with a new purpose."

"Every excuse! I wouldn't call my father dying just an excuse. I was in no mood for marriage at the time. And now, for

God's sake, Matt, I've been in a coma for two weeks. I didn't plan it. It just happened. Last year, I didn't have an excuse. I just didn't love you enough to marry you. My father didn't like you and I had reservations because of that. There. I said it."

There were a few moments of silence. Matt did not respond to any of what she had said. He had pushed a trigger button and didn't want to do any more damage with his woe-is-me tactics. He didn't care if the old kook liked him or not. He was dead now.

"Why didn't you tell me that Jake had been to see me every week while I was in the hospital? You made it sound like he left and never looked back."

"Who told you he was there every week?"

"He did. Lily did. What did you expect?"

"When did you talk to him?"

"He called the other night."

"Why?"

"To talk about Charlee's murder."

"For God's sake! He's the one filling your mind with all this nonsense." It slipped out before he realized it.

"Nonsense? Are you crazy, Matt? Do you not remember the person we are talking about? Charlee. Do I need to refresh your memory? Just get away from me!"

"I'm sorry. I didn't mean nonsense in the way you think, okay? I do believe she was murdered. I just didn't want you to take this any further for your health's sake. I'm thinking of you, baby."

"Then support me and stop hindering me. Now, why didn't you tell me that Jake had visited me?"

"He didn't ask me to tell you. I didn't even think about it, really. I was the one who was there every day." Maybe she needed to know that.

47

"How could you not have thought about it when I asked to call him?"

"Truthfully, I didn't want you to call him. I was afraid he would start upsetting you again about the suicide. I mean murder. I'm sorry. I wanted to be the one to comfort you. That is what a husband is for. Is that so wrong, to want you for myself?" He placed his hand on her knee. "I'm sorry. I didn't mean to imply that you were making up petty excuses not to marry me. I want to spend the rest of my life with the woman I love, and things just keep getting in the way."

"Okay, Matt. Just please support me on this. That's all I ask."

"One-hundred percent. If there's anything I can do, just let me know."

"Thank you. I'm sorry I keep losing my cool. I'm just on edge these days."

"No problem. I understand completely."

She leaned onto Matt's shoulder and rested until it was time for her to board.

"I'll see you in a few days." She kissed his lips.

"I'll be waiting."

Her arrival in San Francisco was once again welcomed by the compassionate smile she had heard her sister so often speak of.

"First things first," she was giddy with excitement. "I want to do something for you and please don't tell me no. It's something from the bottom of my heart that I want to do as a thank you. This is not an offer of charity and it's not because I feel sorry for you."

"Huh?"

"I want to buy you a new car. Whatever you want. The choice is yours. A brand-new car." Jake smiled. "You know, those are almost the exact words Charlee said when we were in South Dakota at the beginning of the year. I never let her buy me one because I didn't want anyone to have an excuse to say that I was using her. You know?"

"So will you accept my offer?"

"I will, because I do believe this is just a special gift from a special woman."

"Then let's go."

Jake and Sela drove to Charlee's apartment in a new Mercedes M-Class. Now that the fun was over, there was work to be done.

The phone rang directly into Matt's office. "Hey, Bossman. A little bit to report. Not much. They just left the Mercedes lot in a new M-Class. The old car was left at the lot. Looks like they're headed toward the Presidio. Thought you might be interested."

"Thanks. Keep an eye out." Matt fumed over the purchase. In all their years of dating, she had never offered to buy him anything of such significance. His Yukon was two years old, and he was up to his ears in debt with it. He knew Sela was a charitable person, known for giving, but this guy really got under his skin. He could feel the chemistry oozing between Jake and Sela.

Waiting in the parking lot of the Ski Lodge Apartments was an old friend of the family and private investigator, Teddy. He was a big burly man with gray bushy hair. Fairly athletic in his day, but that day had long since passed. His eyes still radiated concern. His leathered features expressed his deep compassion. He had investigated the death of her father without any luck of finding foul play. That was a good thing. No one could explain how the explosion had occurred. It had been described as a combination of faulty equipment that needed maintenance, coupled with highly explosive petroleum. A spark had been ignited, resulting in the death of five people on board the rig and serious injury to several others.

Sela hugged his thick neck. "It's good to see you, Teddy." The last time they had spoken, he had been giving the final report on her father's investigation. She remembered their phone call well. He felt as if he had let her father down because he couldn't give her exact answers, just a general report.

"It's good to see you, too, girl." His large hands nearly covered her back.

"This is a very good friend of Charlee's, Jake. He's been sort of my support lately. It seems he and Lily are the only two people who believe that Charlee couldn't have done something like this." There were many others who believed this wasn't a suicide, but Jake and Lily were the two closest to her.

"Well, with me that makes three other people." He extended his hand to Jake. "Nice to meet you, big guy."

"Likewise."

"I'm glad to be of service. I went by the police station and introduced myself. I explained that I'd be doing some private investigating and asked to see any reports they may have on the place. They gave me a copy of them and a copy of the autopsy. There wasn't anything unusual in the reports. They had it as an open-and-shut case. Looks like they did a thorough sweep of the place without any signs at all of an intruder or guest. It's going to be up to us to find whatever we can to nail this killer."

"Lily paid the lease up for the next year, so nothing has been disturbed. The lady in the office made sure of that. I know it's been a few months, but whatever's in there is still there."

"That's right. Let's go take a look." Teddy was an expert. He knew if there were any clues there, that he would not stop until they were tracked back to their originator.

Sela opened the door and one-by-one, they filed in. It was her first time in the apartment. From the looks of it, her sister had not been there more than a few days. There were only enough things unloaded from the boxes to get by. The furniture had been set up by the movers, but was awkwardly placed. There were a few dishes that had been unpacked, too.

"I need for everyone to put these gloves on, but I would ask that you not touch anything, just the same. If you see something that you think is of interest, let me know and I'll place it in the bag to be analyzed. It doesn't matter how insignificant you think it may be. Let me know."

Sela and Jake nodded. Sela looked around the kitchen first. The place was covered in fingerprint dust. Every inch of the kitchen had been covered. The only prints found there were Charlee's.

"Sela, would you mind walking down to the office and asking the manager when the last time was that anyone had been in the apartment? We need to know when maintenance was last there, who they were, and what was done."

"Sure, Teddy. I'll be right back." Sela walked over to the office.

"Hello, Ms. Betty. We have just a few questions we're hoping you can answer."

"I sure hope I can."

"We need to know who cleaned the apartment before Charlee moved in and if maintenance performed any routine checks or anything. We need to know who they were, too."

"Well, I can certainly answer all of those questions. Just a minute and let me see who was on duty and who made out the report on that one." She left and returned with a file. "The maintenance check was done by Roger Pugh one week before Charlene moved in. He checked to make sure all that the faucets were in order, that the air and heat were working properly, that the fire extinguisher was present and full, that all window and doors were functional, and that all the locks worked. He also changed the air filter and replaced the garbage disposal in the kitchen. Ms. Linda Hernandez did the cleaning. It was done after the previous tenant moved out. She's responsible for all the apartments in that building."

"Can I have a copy of that report? I have a private investigator working on my sister's murder case and every little detail is important to him."

"I understand. Of course, you can."

Sela was given a copy of the report and she returned it to Ted.

"This is great."

"What does it tell us?"

"It tells us that your sister was murdered and that she did not commit suicide. The person who killed her was careful enough to wipe all fingerprints from the kitchen and off the doorknobs. There should have at least been prints from maintenance and housekeeping somewhere. If maintenance was the last one here, especially. It's quite possible your sister cleaned them away from the sink, but not the doorknobs. I sincerely doubt she would have removed all prints from the doorknobs. It's not going to help us catch a killer, but it strengthens our belief that it was a murder."

"Hey, come see this." Jake was standing at the end of the table, pointing to the edge of the rug. Ted leaned over and spotted what Jake was pointing at. He took out his camera and took several pictures before picking it up and placing it in an evidence bag. It was an earring. A silver earring that dangled from the lobe, with a large turquoise stone in the middle surrounded by black onyx. Sela stared at the earring.

"That is not my sister's earring." It was a fact she knew for certain. "My sister has never in her life worn an earring like that, nor would she ever. She kept a diamond stud in the top hole and a very small loop in the bottom hole. She never took them out. She said they matched whatever she was wearing and that was it. She didn't even have a jewelry box! She wore one ring that Daddy gave her and a locket that she seldom took off." Sela thought of the locket that had been stolen.

"She's right. I knew Charlee for a year and she never changed her jewelry. I know this because I almost bought her some earrings for her birthday. She said she never changed her earrings. She picked out a purse instead."

"Okay, then this was either left by a previous owner, which is unlikely since housekeeping would have certainly seen it on a bare floor, or it was left by someone who was visiting Charlee. That means the killer would most likely be a woman. One thing's for sure; whoever she let in was someone she felt comfortable with. She had a cup of tea in front of her. It's my guess that she was probably sharing a cup of tea with her killer when they pulled a gun and shot her. They then wiped the gun clean and placed it in Charlee's hand. They put on some gloves, cleaned the cup, and were careful to wipe down the doorknobs going into the bathroom, and anywhere else they could have touched while visiting. It could have been an overnight guest. Let's check the back bedroom."

The back bed was stripped and searched, but there were no signs that anyone had slept in the bed. Ted's eyes were obviously trained for this type of search and he took great care not to miss a spot. On the edge of the carpet leading into the bathroom, was a single blond hair. It was about six inches long and nearly platinum blond. Ted picked it up with a pair of tweezers and placed it in a bag.

"Ladies and gentlemen, we may have our first serious clue. This could be the beginning of our search."

"What is it?"

"It is a blond hair. Now all we need is someone to match it. Someone who can explain why their hair is in the back room of Charlee's apartment. We'll find out what color hair Ms Hernandez has on our way out. Something tells me it isn't blond, with a name like Hernandez. In the meantime, if you can think of any friends or co-workers with this color hair, or that could have had this color hair, let me know."

After searching every inch of the apartment, they said goodbye to Teddy and wished him luck.

Sela and Jake drove to his apartment. She would be spending the night at his place rather than at a hotel. The thought of seeing Jake walking around shirtless in his Adidas shorts suddenly became very exciting. This was so new for her. She loved Matt, but was now struggling with why these mental images of Jake bringing her coffee in the morning was making her so giddy. It had to stop. She would return to Texas in the morning. She would be much more clear-headed once she could put all this behind her. Charlee's murder was clouding every aspect of her life.

Matt picked up the phone and dialed Beth's number. He let it ring once, then dialed again. He let it ring once more, hung up, and called her back. She knew it was him. It was the way they had always done it.

"Where have you been?" She asked, without saying hello.

"Hello to you, too."

"Hello. Now, where have you been?" Her mood was playful but to the point, and she was clearly irritated.

"I've been busy. Maybe you forgot. My fiancée has been in a coma? I'm doing my best to keep these wedding plans going, and this guy Jake is throwing a kink in my plans."

"What kind of kink?"

"He keeps insisting that Charlee was murdered, and Sela is just feeding off him. They've hired an investigator, and she's in San Fran as we speak, going through Charlee's apartment."

"So they think it was a murder. So what?"

"So I don't want that hanging over my head for the rest of my life. Wouldn't it bother you to know that someone is determined to put the killer behind bars?"

"It was a clean murder. There's nothing there to link either of us to the crime. You were accounted for, and I'm not even in the picture."

"You're right. I can't help but worry, though."

"Just relax and keep Sela happy for the next few weeks. Get a ring on her finger, do whatcha gotta do, and get the hell out of there. I don't know how much more of this suspense I can take."

"I've had a few setbacks and things have not gone exactly the way we planned, but we are almost there."

"Yeah, we are. When are you coming to see me?"

"As soon as I get all of this madness under control and Sela settles down a bit."

"She's always been high maintenance."

"You're one to talk." Matt hung up after a long goodbye.

Jake sat on the end of the couch, watching Sela sleep. She was kicked back in a recliner with a blanket pulled up to her neck. He had lit candles and ordered some Chinese food. Now he would just wait for her to wake up. A ten thousand dollar stereo system breathed soft jazz music to every corner of the room. Sela slept like a baby. He wanted so badly to wake her. He fantasized about waking her with a soft kiss on the lips. The reality was that their time together was limited, and he didn't want to waste another moment.

"Sela?" He touched her arm.

"Oh, how long have I been sleeping?"

"I thought I should wake you so you wouldn't be restless later tonight."

"Thanks. I only meant to grab a catnap anyway."

"Are you hungry?"

"A little."

"I ordered some Chinese. Do you like cashew chicken?"

"It's my favorite."

"Stay put and I'll get you fixed up."

Sela looked around the dimly lit room. It was so romantic. She couldn't explain her feelings or what this man did to her. She felt as though she were cheating on Matt. She *was* cheating, emotionally. She had never been a dishonest person, but right now she felt like the biggest loser there was. Jake returned with tea and a hot plate of food on a TV tray.

"Maybe we could rent a movie later if you're up to it."

She wanted that more than anything right now. To just watch a movie and feel the peace that she had longed to feel for so long. That same peaceful feeling she had lost after her daddy died; the feeling she now felt in Jake's arms. But she was an engaged woman, and this was nothing more than a scandalous affair of the mind that would move into something physical if she would

56

allow it. And she would not. She could not.

"Can I be really honest with you, Jake?"

"You shouldn't even have to ask that."

"I know. The better part of me says I shouldn't get too close to you. I feel like I'm cheating on Matt. I never, in a million years, would do something like that to him. Honestly, sitting here with you, I feel emotionally unattached to him, and I know that's wrong. I realize we don't really know each other, but I feel I know you so deeply because of your connection with Charlee, I guess."

She felt a stabbing pain in her chest as she spoke the words. Words she should not have said.

"I understand completely. Sela, I'm not asking you to cheat on your boyfriend." Boyfriend. It sounded so trivial. So high school. Only in high school, Matt's girlfriend was Beth, one of her best friends.

"I am only asking you to watch a movie with me. You don't even have to sit on the same couch as me. Would that make it better?"

"I guess so. I'm sorry for insinuating that you were making me cheat. It's not what I meant at all. I'm just all over the place right now. I think my mind is playing tricks on me. I'm so thankful for you at this moment, Jake. For so long, I've battled all kind of things in my mind."

"Like what?"

"Like what to do with my life, for starters."

"Hmm."

"Charlee knew what she was doing. Mom and dad always knew what they were doing. Me, all I have ever done is take orders. I've never had to really decide anything. I've worked at the ranch with the children, I've worked for mom and dad, but I have never set any long-range goals or tried very hard to achieve them."

"But you're a hard worker. That accounts for a lot."

"I guess."

"You guess? You are a brilliant athlete with the world at your fingertips."

"That's the problem. I've had everything given to me. I need to work at something and see the rewards of success."

"So what are you passionate about?"

"The children, of course. I feel like such a loser for letting them down when I moved to South Carolina. Matt doesn't want me involved too much because his dreams are to get out of Dodge as soon as possible."

"If you don't mind me saying, the one thing you feel so much passion for, Matt doesn't support you in. Isn't that a bit frustrating?"

"Exactly the word I am feeling. But Matt has been so stable in my life that it's been a comfort having him around."

Jake did not answer. He stared at Sela as she ate and waited for her to speak next.

"This conversation sure took a deep turn."

"I guess it did. I've had some hard times myself, Sela. When you get tired of wondering what to do next, turn it over to the good Lord, and let Him carry your burden and lead you to the path you should take."

Sela smiled. She had heard her father say the same thing so many times. She couldn't help but think about Mrs. Harper back in Charleston speaking those same words of wisdom.

"You know, Jake, I am tired of worrying. I'm tired of always being sad over my losses." She stared at her hands as they toyed with a piece of lint from her pants.

"I need a fresh start. That's why I went to Charleston."

"Then why don't we start now? Together."

The word "together" rang in her ears. Together. Me and you. Together. A fresh start.

"I'm making a new start beginning now."

"Me too." Jake nodded and choked back emotion. He felt something happening between himself and Sela, but he wasn't sure she felt the same.

"Now, how about that movie as soon as you are done eating?"

She could barely contain her excitement as she finished her food.

"Okay, I'm done. How about we just go see a movie?"

"If you're up for it. You have an early flight, you know."

"I can handle it."

The next morning Matt stood at the airport waiting to pick up his fiancé. When she arrived, she was radiant. She hugged Matt with renewed enthusiasm. She felt different somehow.

"I tried calling you all night." Although he tried sounding nonchalant, he was completely irritated that she had not checked in once since she had been gone.

"I'm sorry, Matt. I was busy during the day, I took a long nap, woke up and ate. Then Jake and I decided to catch a movie."

As if he didn't know. She'd been followed the entire time.

"Well, next time I would appreciate a simple 'hello, I'm fine, and I love the man I am marrying' type of phone call, if possible."

"I know I should have called. It won't happen again."

"Good." Everything felt very formal all of sudden.

Sela paid particular attention to the fact that Matt never asked to carry her bag. She couldn't help thinking about what a gentlemen Jake had been.

Chapter Three

Lily sat at the table staring at the newspaper, sipping a cup of coffee. It had been so long since she and Sela had sat and talked. So much had happened, and she knew there was much to be said. There was so much grief. So much loss. For one girl, it was simply unbearable and there wasn't much she could do. She, too, had lost a dear friend in Mr. Barnes, and now the loss of Charlee was no less painful than her losing her very own daughter. She was numb with pain. She knew she must be strong for Sela. She prayed for the right things to say.

Sela entered the room and went straight to Lily. Lily stood up and the two embraced.

"Did you have a good trip?"

"Yes, I did, as a matter of fact."

"So tell me." Lily didn't need to explain what she meant.

"We found a blond hair and an earring that was definitely not Charlene's. I believe if I could find the person this hair and earring belong to, I would have my killer."

"You could be right, but it could just as well have been a friend visiting her."

"Ted is completely convinced that she was murdered, because the person wiped everything clean, including the doorknobs. There should have been some fingerprints somewhere."

"Good point."

Suddenly tears began to flow down Lily's cheeks, and no

words were necessary. She had held back the pain as long as she could. She never wanted to break down in front of Sela. They embraced, and there were no words to say what they were feeling. Their bond was deep and so very strong, that each one understood exactly what the other was thinking.

"Sit down, Precious." It was a pet name Lily had used for Sela since she was a small child.

Sela sat next to her and the two held hands.

"We have been through a tremendous loss, and we have a right to grieve. We can cry as much as we want, but we must never give in to self-pity. We have a right to be angry, but we must not be trapped in a life of revenge and anger. A bitter life is a useless life. You are my baby. I am here for you just like you are here for me. We will lean on each other and support each other all the way. But we cannot forget that God is our source of strength, and He is our avenger. Let Him work, honey. Let Him do his job. And let Him take care of you through all of this." Her words were soft, like that of an angel.

"I know, Lily. I am trusting. Believe me. Right now, more than ever in my life. I'm not bitter. I am angry, though. I'm so angry! I can't help that. God gave me this emotion!"

Lily listened in silence.

"You know what angers me even more is that my so-called fiancée isn't standing with me and helping me out at all. It's like he just wrote off the whole deal and that is that. Every time I even mention something about wanting to find out about her killer, he says I need to be rational, or I need to focus on healing and not dragging out a bad thing. I'm so sick of it. Do you know, he didn't even ask me what we found in Charlee's apartment? Why not?"

"Charlee wasn't his family. He's not hurting the way we are. He has a life that involves marrying the woman of his dreams and

61

starting his own family. He's waited a long time for you, girl. Now you're telling him once again that this is not a good time to get married. He's trying to pull you back on track, so that you two can resume a normal life together."

"I know, Lily. I know that. That's exactly what he said. But he acts like he doesn't understand what I am going through at all."

"He doesn't understand. He has never, on his worst day, been through the pain that you've experienced. This one thing is true, though; putting your life on hold is not the answer."

"I'm sure you're right. There's more, though. I honestly don't know if I love him the way I should. This is going to sound crazy, but I have always held back some of my feelings with Matt. I could never quite figure it out. I've never been in love before. Never. I just thought this was as good as it gets. But when I saw Jake at the airport and our eyes met, it was like they locked, and my body was electrified. I did my best to conceal it. I was ashamed, because for one, I was newly engaged, and secondly, it was my sister's boyfriend, for crying out loud. I couldn't believe how my body was ignited, though. Is that crazy?"

Lily laughed out loud. "No, it is not crazy at all. It's the passion of the heart at work. It could have been that you knew how much he loved Charlee and you felt the connection, or it could have been love at first sight. Whatever it was, it's got you thinking twice about marrying Matt. I can see that in your eyes."

"Is it really obvious?"

"As obvious as the nose on your face."

"When we were together this weekend, I made every excuse not to be alone with him too much, for fear I would cheat on Matt."

"You know what you need?"

"What?" Lily was always full of good ideas.

"You need a break. Maybe these new feelings need to be sorted out. You need to call an old friend and the two of you just go away together and regroup. Get your mind together. Talk about your feelings. Talk about Matt and Jake. Do the girl thing."

"You're probably right."

"Call someone who makes you laugh and makes you feel good all the time."

"The person I always had the most fun with was Beth."

"Why don't you look her up? It would give you a little project to do and put an end to all the guessing."

"That's not a bad idea. Although I did write her lots of letters that were never answered. She never once returned a call, either. That is just so strange to me."

"Okay, then you two have definitely got some things to sort out, too. Who knows why she didn't keep in touch. Maybe something really embarrassing was going on with her family. Maybe she was angry for leaving and took it out on everyone. Maybe she ran away from home and was never to be seen again. Look her up. Ted has the investigation under control. Find something to keep you occupied."

"I think I will. Matt has her dad's number, I think. It seems like he tried looking her up a few years ago. I'm not even sure where they're living now." There was a bit of excitement in the air all of a sudden. She missed her old best friend and they had a lot of catching up to do. "I'll call Matt later this afternoon."

Sela called Matt's office.

"Hey. Are you busy?"

"Not really. Just wrapping some things up. How do you feel today?"

"I feel better. I had a great swim this morning and a nice chat with Lily. She has talked me into a much-needed rest. These last few weeks have been really hard on me."

"I hope this rest involves me and a wedding?"

"Actually, I wanted to talk to you about that. I know I said I was ready, but if you could just give me a few months to wrap up this murder investigation and clear my mind, it would do us both some good."

"A few months will turn in to six months and then a year. What makes you think it's going to be wrapped up in a few months?"

"I just know I have the best detective in the world investigating and he has found several leads already."

"What kind of leads? Why haven't you told me about this before?"

"He has asked me to keep my mouth shut on this. We can't afford for anything to be leaked to the press and jeopardize this case in any way."

"This is your future husband you are talking to. Remember? The one you are supposed to share everything with from now until eternity."

"I'll tell you, I guess. Just not right now, okay? What I actually called about is this. I want to look up Beth. I think it would do me good for us to just get together and hang out. She knew me so well. She understood me in a way few people did. She makes me laugh. I just feel like seeing her. Don't you have her dad's number?"

Matt's stomach flipped. Why this? Of all the people in the world that Sela could have chosen to rekindle communication with, why her? Why now? It wasn't a good idea.

"Yeah, I have it somewhere, but why her all of a sudden?

Why don't you call Tracey or Denise?" He felt his palms sweating against the phone. Sela reconnecting with Beth would not be good at all. He needed to find a way to stop her.

"Lily suggested it. I guess because she brings back such good memories. Just innocent childhood memories of two girls being girls, when nothing else mattered and nothing was wrong."

"Look, why don't I book us a cruise? Somewhere exotic. Somewhere you have always dreamed of going. We can sail away, get married, and come back and start a family. Don't you think a new baby would lift your spirits?" His efforts were useless.

"Wow. You sure drive a hard bargain, but I still want to wait. Just a little while." She couldn't say that she had suddenly developed feelings for a semi-stranger in San Francisco.

"I know it's difficult to understand, and I should have broken it to you a little more gently. I just don't want to get married in the next few months. I want to wait and plan my wedding with a clear mind. I need you to understand that."

"I do, Sela."

"Good. Now, will you call me back when you get Mr. Garret's number?"

"If you weren't so worth it, I would just tell you I was sick of waiting on you." She had no idea how worth it she was. He knew his time as a 'successful' lawyer was quickly coming to an end. Over the last year he had managed to accrue $200,000 in debt and his clients were few and far between. He had placed his bets on marrying a billionaire's daughter and inheriting the family fortune, but things had gone a lot slower than expected. He kept only enough clients to have a job going. His free time was spent with Beth in Atlanta. She was always 'a big client' he was meeting somewhere across the country. He kept his clients a secret. Confidentiality was very important, after all. He didn't know how much longer he could take money from Sela's credit cards without her knowing it. Her accounts were all set up on an automatic draft system, and for someone with her worth, she never checked the balances. An accountant did all of that. No one ever questioned the withdrawals. He had been making purchases and drawing out money for nearly two years.

"Thanks for being so understanding, Matt. You're such a great man and I'm really thankful for your patience." Why did she sound like a recorded message?

Sela lounged in the den while waiting for the number of her old friend's dad.

Matt picked up the phone to call Beth.

"Bad news."

"What?"

"Sela has the bright idea that she wants to look you up. She's not taking no for an answer."

"So tell her you heard I left the country. Or just tell her you couldn't find me."

"Somehow, I don't think that will stop her. She's waiting on your dad's number now."

"Tell her you have no idea where he lives, and you no longer have the old number."

"That's not going to work. He's not going to be that difficult for her to find. I just wanted to give you a heads-up. If the two of you get together, it can only mean trouble for us."

"Not necessarily. So an old friend looks me up, we get together and discuss life. She talks about you, and I tell her how great you are and that she would be crazy not to marry you right away. This may actually work to our benefit."

"You may have a point. You could always persuade her into doing the craziest things. You could tell her how romantic it would be for us to just sail away somewhere together or something."

"I could tell her how great you are in bed."

"Of course, you could."

"So what time are you gonna be here tomorrow?"

"Not till late. I may not even be able to leave tomorrow. I haven't spent any time with Sela lately. She's been gallivanting back and forth to California every chance she gets, to meet with this detective guy and that surfer dude, Jake. I think I need to spend a nice evening with her alone tomorrow night."

"Whatever. I'll see you for sure on Saturday then."

"Right. So do you want me to give her your number or what?"

"Go ahead. I could always be a real bitch and make her never want to see my face again."

"True. But what reason would you have for treating her badly?"

"She's about to marry you! Isn't that enough?"

"She doesn't know you care. I like the other plan better. The one about how great I am."

"I'll play it by ear. I'm just so tired of this whole thing being dragged out."

"I'm just as tired as you are. I'm the one doing all the work, don't forget."

"Oh, real hard work having two women at your beck and call."

"Yeh, yeh. Be ready for her call. I've got some work to do."

"I'll talk to you later, baby."

"Bye. I love you."

"I love you, too."

Sela picked up the phone. "Hello?"

"Hey. I talked to Mrs. Garret. She gave me Beth's number. Said she would love to hear from you. She was really nice and said she missed all of us. I asked her if Beth ever talked about

67

us."

"What did she say?"

"She said no. She didn't know what had happened to Beth. After she graduated high school, she became reclusive and pretty much abandoned all efforts to maintain a connection with her family."

"That is so weird. Do you think I should try to call her? I'm even more curious now."

"That's entirely up to you. I wouldn't if it were me. But I know you are going to do what you want to do in the end, anyway. I just don't want you to be hurt. She walked out on your friendship, don't forget."

"I want to talk to her."

"Well, here's her number. Don't forget to mention my name and let her know what she's missed out on all these years." He chuckled mischievously.

"When's the last time you talked to her?"

"I guess it was my first year of college. We wrote some. We called back and forth a few times, and then she just disappeared. Anyway, it's a good thing she did because you and I would have never had a future together."

"That's true."

"Tell her I said hello and thanks for nothing."

"Yeah, right."

"Let me know what she says, though. Seriously."

"Of course I will."

He gave her the number and they said goodbye.

Sela stared at the number. After all these years, she was really going to call Beth. She felt shaky. She didn't know why. She missed her long-lost friend and her heart beat with pure excitement. She needed a glass of water before she made the call.

Chapter Four

It was close to 7:00 p.m. when Matt pulled up the long drive to the ranch. After buzzing through security, he drove down the winding brick road toward the house. He had a lot to accomplish tonight. He had to find out what leads Ted had on the case. That was a must. Then, he really needed to persuade Sela that the time was right to marry. Everything was at a standstill until they married. His life was a bogged down mess and there was only one person capable of throwing him a life vest. Sela. He needed to bug the house in order to stay informed on whatever else was going there, especially since the relationship between Beth and Sela might soon be rekindled. The more he thought about the idea, the more he didn't like it. It would be better for Beth to completely blow her off and be done with it. He hoped the contact had not yet been made and he could tell Beth to ignore her calls.

Lily greeted Matt at the door with a hug and kiss.

"Come on in. Sela will be right down." Lily had never been fond of Matt. Neither had her father. He always said there was something sneaky in his eyes. He didn't trust the boy. That had bothered Sela and she wondered if it was those comments that had kept her guard up with him. Lily kept her feelings to herself. She knew in the end Sela would see who she wanted to see, and hopefully make the right choice. In her heart, she sure hoped it wouldn't be the man in front of her.

"You are looking as lovely as ever, Ms. Lily. I can't believe someone hasn't snagged you and whisked you away to paradise."

Empty words from an empty heart.

"I have all the paradise I need right here. I stay too busy to get involved with anyone."

"You should never be too busy for love, Lily." He grabbed her hand and spun her around as if they were dancing.

Lily was already leaving the room when Sela entered.

"You two have a good night. I'll see you in the morning, Sela." She kissed her on the cheek as she passed.

"Love you, Lily." She turned to Matt. "So what do you want to do tonight?"

"I just want to stay here and be with the love of my life."

"Good. I rented some movies. You have a choice between Tom Cruise, Brad Pitt, or Mel Gibson." She smiled as he pulled her close.

"It's up to you."

"Are you hungry?" She was energetic but not because Matt was there. She just felt good.

"A little. Whatcha got?"

"Some leftover Chinese takeout from earlier. I got a bunch. Want some?" She thought about the last time she had eaten Chinese food with Jake. Much different scenario. Matt thought about the bugs he needed to plant and figured his chances of getting it done would be better if he knew where she was and what she was doing. This may be his best chance.

"I'd love some. If you don't mind, I'm going to run to the restroom and then just kick off my shoes and rest a minute. I've been running all day."

"Sure."

He made an exit for the hall. There were several separate phone lines that would need tapping. He could hear Sela moving around in the kitchen. It wouldn't take more than a few minutes to heat the food and fix the drinks, but that was all the time he needed. He stopped by Sela's room and hid a bug behind her bed, then he went back to the den and placed a small bug under the table. He went to the kitchen and placed another one underneath the cabinet. Sela stood watching the food spin around in the microwave. He stood silently, watching her. She was a beautiful girl. Such a loving and pleasant girl. There were times when he thought he was really falling in love with her. It would have all been so easy if he had just been patient and let life run its course. He would probably be married to her right now. He had thought she'd come running into his arms once her father was dead. He'd thought a lot of things that didn't happen. One thing that did happen was that Sela was now the sole heir to billions of dollars, thanks to him and Beth. Now he was standing in her kitchen, about to eat takeout with her. It was the closest thing to money he had ever known, but not nearly as close as he would be before too long. The waiting game had become unbearable, but he had to be careful not to scare her away. He had to be patient and not too pushy. It was a fine line he was walking.

Sela spun around with the food.

"Whoa. How long have you been standing there?"

"I just walked in."

"You scared me."

"Sorry. Here. Let me help you with that."

Sela poured the drinks. "It seems like forever since we've been alone here."

"It has been. According to my calendar, it's been nearly three months."

"It hasn't been that long, has it?"

"You forget you were in a coma for over two weeks. Since then, you've been pretty preoccupied. It's something I want to talk to you about tonight."

"Let's talk now." They placed their food on the table and sat down to eat.

"I'm sad, Sela." He figured he would start with his feminine side first and try to reach her that way. "I'm sad and tired. I have loved you for so long. So long that it has started to hurt that you apparently don't feel the same for me. Be honest with me. I'm old enough to take it. Do you just not want to marry me? Do we not have the same thing in mind for our futures? If not, then tell me so that I can move on with my life." It was time to move into another area of emotion. "You know, there are so many women out there who would die to have me as their husband. I've put my life completely on hold for you. I want a family. Kids. I want to wake up with you by my side. I'm not begging you to be my wife, but I *beseech* you, Sela, to take a long look at where our relationship has been, and where it's headed." He looked deeply into her eyes in hopes of seeing something he could read as promise. "Remember the night in Charleston when we vowed to be together? What do you feel for me now? I need to know the truth."

"Matt, you mean everything to me. You really do. I'll be honest with you. I have been afraid to marry you. Afraid of something, but not even really sure what it is. Being here with you tonight and hearing you say those things, well it really means something to me. I know that I've been selfish. I've made you wait long enough. I told you in Charleston that I was ready. I thought I was." She thought about the brown eyes that had locked with hers at the airport and the emotion that had risen inside her. That's all it was. Emotion. It wasn't love. Love is being with someone who knows you and wants to raise kids with you. Not lust for a man you've just met. She dismissed Jake from her mind.

"I will marry you without hesitation. We'll begin making plans tomorrow." She looked at the beautiful diamond ring she had been wearing for so long. It was time to set a date. "Do you have a favorite month you'd like to be married in?"

"Yes, this month."

"That gives us only three weeks. I can't pull it together by then. Give me six weeks. Seriously. I'll have a small wedding with just a few friends and the children." Her eyes begged him.

"Then you promise we'll leave the following morning on a voyage around the world?" He gave her the same sad eyes as she had given him.

"A voyage it is."

They looked at their now lukewarm food. "Do you want to stick it back in the microwave?"

"No, I'm way too excited to eat. You've really surprised me tonight. I love you so much."

"I know you do, Matt. I love you, too. Come on. Let's just eat later." Jake disappeared from her mind in that instant. Her decision would be based on a solid love for this man who had been by her side for so long.

Two out of three things, done in less than an hour. Matt was feeling hot. He never expected such a response so quickly. Now he needed to find out what leads they had found on Charlee's case. They carried their drinks to the couch. Sela put on some soft music and sat next to Matt.

"Let's talk about the investigation. I've been dying to know what they've found out."

"Well, first you have got to swear not to tell a soul. I mean no one. I know in your line of work you have to be able keep a secret, so I trust you."

"I hope so. I'm practically your husband, after all."

"Okay. We found an earring at Charlee's. It was a rather large dangly earring, and as you well know, she never wore earrings like that."

If that was the only lead they had, he was in luck.

"Wow. Whose earring do you think it was?"

"We think it was the killer's. Definitely not Charlene's. We also found a blond hair. It was about six inches long and was chemically bleached. The earring was big enough that there was part of a fingerprint on the stone. It was smudged, though. Basically, what we've figured out is that someone knew Charlee's plans. They phoned her and made arrangements to come visit shortly after she got to San Fran. It was someone she trusted enough to just let them walk in and sit down for a cup of tea. Whoever it was, was an expert. They cleaned up every spot that could have left a fingerprint. They actually cleaned too well. The doorknobs should have had fingerprints from maintenance and housekeeping, but there were none. There weren't even any of Charlee's prints on several of the doorknobs. The hair was sent for analysis. The DNA has been studied and an attempt was made to match it to any criminals in the FBI database. There were no matches. But at least we have something to go by."

"It's a real shot in the dark, huh?"

"Yeah. I guess you could put it that way. I have something going for me, though. God. I have really prayed over this. I pray about it every day. I believe God will somehow lead me to the killer. Some way. Somehow. I don't have any idea how, but I'm believing it just the same. It's all you can do in a case like this."

Beth was a professional, but she had left something behind that could end up being the death of both of them. He had seen enough criminal investigations on TV to know that one hair could link you to a crime and convict you.

"Her phone records indicate several phone calls from the Bay area. They were traced back to a local hotel. The room they originated from had been cleaned many times over. The name the occupant registered under was Olivia Grayson. She paid with cash. The desk clerk confirmed that she had blond hair just past her ears and that it was either natural blond or bleached. Said she was very attractive. A tall lady in her early twenties, perhaps. Dressed really snazzy. Had some sparkly nail polish. She remembered commenting on the color."

Matt had to get in touch with Beth immediately. If the two of them met now, after that description, she would be on death row by the end of the month.

"Sounds like you have a pretty good description of the lady."

"I have more than that. I have a composite drawing."

"You have what?"

"The police actually believe us now. They are working with us on this. They had someone draw us a picture based on the desk clerk's description."

"I want to see it." Matt was tense and his voice sounded frantic, he was sure.

"Sure. Just a minute." Sela left the room and Matt took a deep breath. He had to remain calm. Perhaps she would take his excitement as joy of the newly discovered news.

"Here it is." Sela was holding it in front of her as she walked. "Ever seen anyone who looked like this?" It was an uncanny likeness of Beth. She resembled Sharon Stone.

"She's very pretty. But I can't say I've ever seen anyone around here or anywhere near Charlee who looked like that."

"Me either. I just really haven't a clue. We're planning to have this picture posted on America's Most Wanted next week. Ted is doing the legwork now. Someone has to know something."

Matt felt his stomach flop. "Wow. You're really moving ahead with this. Good for you." He felt like he was about to throw up. "Will you excuse me for just a minute?"

He went to the bathroom and stared into the toilet. He didn't feel so good. If Beth was linked to Charlee and the investigation went a little deeper, it wouldn't be hard to link him to Beth. The trail was a mile long for someone with experience. He had to leave now. He needed to talk to Beth quickly. She would have to change her hair right away and somehow disguise her face, too! He washed his face and walked back to the den.

"Listen, baby. I don't feel so good. I don't know what's come over me. That Chinese food hit me like a bomb. I think I should go."

"Just lie down. Let me rub your feet or something. Go to sleep. I'll watch the movie without you."

He walked over to the couch to lie down. His call to Beth would have to wait. He felt too sick to drive.

Matt didn't know what time it was when he woke up. He had fallen asleep on the couch and Sela had gone on to bed. He put on his shoes and checked his watch. It was 3:00 a.m. and time for him to go. He remembered the evening's conversation and shivered. An unbelievable twist of events was actually causing him to think twice about his involvement in this scheme. It had not started out to be his idea. It was all Beth. She was the one who had been jealous of Sela's money for so long. It was she who came up with the elaborate plan to kill off the family one-by-one until all the money would be left to Sela. But he had agreed. Not only had he agreed, he had participated. He was in it up to his ears. He had come much too far to panic now. There would just be no way of connecting Beth to a long-lost friend's sister who had recently moved to California without some sort of real miracle. As long as Beth got busy and changed a few things about herself, everything would be fine. He drove into his garage and sat listening as the big metal door came down behind him. He shivered. "This is almost over. Hang in there until payday," he whispered to himself. "All I have to do is marry the girl. Beth is the one who killed Charlee. If it comes down to it, I'll deny everything and stick it out with Sela for a while. Sorry Beth, but you could be on your own if this goes any deeper."

Chapter Five

Matt set the alarm for six a.m. and lay awake until he heard it buzz. He had to talk to Beth. He called her up.

"Hey, it's me."

"Yeah, I know who it is." Her voice was scratchy and quiet. "What's wrong?"

"A lot, actually. Are you awake enough to grasp what I'm about to say?"

"I am now. What is it?"

"The investigator on Charlee's case has found one of your hairs in the apartment. A six-inch-long bleached blond hair. They also have an earring. It's one of yours, I'm sure. A dangly earring, they said. They are now certain it was a murder because of blah, blah, blah. The cops are working with them, and that's not all. They have a phone number traced back to the hotel where you stayed."

Beth interrupted. "So what, Matt? Every woman has earrings. Everyone has a few hairs belonging to someone else in their house. Especially at an apartment. So someone called her from a hotel. Big deal. What's the blah, blah, blah about?"

"Just listen. It *is* a big deal. Apparently, the front desk clerk remembered you so well that she was able to even describe your fingernail polish. They have a composite drawing of you, for crying out loud."

"They what?"

"They have a drawing of you! I've seen it, Beth. It looks a

whole lot like you. They plan to post it on America's Most Wanted next week. They also have a partial finger print. Do you hear what I'm saying to you?" His voice had gotten increasingly louder.

"Calm down. I can handle this. I'll change my looks. No one will miss the old me, I promise. I don't work, thanks to you, and I haven't seen my family in ages."

"Thanks to Sela, you don't work. She has no clue of the amount of money I've skimmed from her accounts. Anyway, someone will say they've seen you shopping at the local grocery store or mall. A neighbor will surely recognize you."

"I've been at these condos for less than six months, and I haven't met a neighbor or mailman since I've been here. As for the grocery store, I'll start shopping somewhere else."

"It's just all coming at a bad time, with Sela wanting to look you up and all."

"It's fine. I'll definitely be the last person on her list of suspects when she sees me."

"They described you as a snazzy dresser. A somewhat flashy lady. Very pretty. A Sharon Stone look-alike."

"That's nice to hear. Trust me. The next time you see me, you won't even recognize me. I'll be a Rosanne Barr look-alike. What else have you got?"

"Well, you wiped the door knobs clean of everyone's prints including the housekeeping and maintenance staff. Apparently, they figured out there should have been more prints in the place. After putting two-and-two together and checking her phone records, they suspect foul play. If we had waited a few months to let her get settled in and make some crazy friends out there, it might have looked less suspicious. You were in such a rush. Right now, they're busy trying to find the person who matches the hair!"

"Nearly impossible."

"But not totally impossible."

"Just don't crack up. You sound so rattled. How in the hell do you think that one piece of blond hair is going to lead them across the United States all the way to Atlanta, Georgia? Huh?"

"You should be a little rattled yourself. You're the one who's about to have her picture posted across national television."

"Well, I can't do anything about it so I'll focus on protecting my identity until you can get the money. I'll lay low and wait it all out."

"Some days I wonder why we ever got ourselves into this mess. We could be living in a four-bedroom house with a picket fence and a few kids, with no guilt right now. Instead, we're murderers who will probably have a heart attack before we can even enjoy the money."

"We did it to be wealthy and free. We did it so that we wouldn't have to work the rest of our lives and we could buy anything in the world we wanted. We did it so we could live in something more than a four-bedroom house, slaving our lives away to pay for a mortgage, a new car, and college tuition."

"I'm just so sick of all the hurdles."

"Just keep thinking about payday.

"I never quit thinking about payday."

"Keep me posted."

"I will."

"I love you."

"I love you, too."

When Matt hung up the phone, he felt better. Beth could always make him feel better. He fell asleep and slept soundly.

Sela was finally ready to make the call. She had thought about it for a few days now. Beth would be shocked to hear about her engagement to Matt. She wondered if she should even tell her. Would it be awkward? Yes, she should tell her. She wanted them to be able to share things together like they used to. If that was possible. She wasn't going to get her hopes up, though. She had been through that before. She dialed the Georgia number and heard the voice on the answering machine.

"Hi, this is Beth. Leave me a message and I'll call you back." Beep.

Her voice raised with excitement. Her body tightened. After all those years, there was her friend's voice.

"Beth, it's Sela. I've been thinking about you for a long time. I have so much news to tell you. Call me back, if you will. I really want to hear from you." She left her number and hung up the phone. What she wanted to say was, "why did you stop keeping in touch?" Still, she didn't want to push the issue if something really bad had happened. Maybe she was paralyzed in a terrible accident or something. Maybe she was disfigured and embarrassed.

Beth listened to the voice on the answering machine from the bathroom. She watched as her blond hair fell to the floor. She cut her hair very short and colored it brown. She added some mousse and pushed it behind her ears. She washed her face clean and put a little brown color on her lips. She took out her blue contacts and put on her glasses. She hated wearing them, but she knew it was necessary. She smiled at the image in the mirror. From fabulous to frumpy in just one hour. She put on some old jeans and a T-shirt. It would be hard to make her body look bad, but she would try. She needed some big loose dresses. Something that would hide her curves. A trip to Goodwill would provide her with the perfect wardrobe. She looked around her condo. It was a bit elaborate. Most of her furniture was new and had been given to her by Matt. Paid for by Sela without her knowledge. She passed a mirror in the hall and stopped to admire her work. "There is no reason why I should call Sela back. It will only cause problems. I don't need any more problems. I need Matt to get on with his end of the deal so we can get out of this country and have a real life." She listened to the message from her old friend again. No, she would not return the phone call. It was too risky.

Sela busied herself with community volunteer projects. She had been involved with United Way, Red Cross, and Girl Scouts for many years. She had been recruited to help raise money and volunteers in the different programs when she was just a teenager, and was featured on several commercials for the state in support of each one. She'd been favored over the other applicants because she had won the National Championship in swimming at the age of sixteen. She was also the daughter of a billionaire and had been a Girl Scout since she was seven years old. She enjoyed what she did and was glad to be back in the swing of things. She had tried running away from all that was familiar, but it didn't stop the pain. The pain was there and all the things that she enjoyed were not. It was such a relief to be occupied with causes that really did make a difference in the lives of others.

It had been a week since she had left the message at Beth's house, and still there was no reply.

Lily was sitting in the garden, next to the pond, swinging. Her glass of iced tea sat on the table next to her.

"Now, isn't this a pretty picture. Lily resting in the middle of the day."

"You caught me." She smiled her big smile. "You fixin' to

go for a swim, I see. I sure do wish I could swim. I just never learned."

"It's not too late."

"Oh, it's too late for me. I like watching a whole lot better." Sela sat next to her.

"I never heard from Beth. This is the weirdest situation I've ever seen. I mean, here is a girl who was my very best friend in the whole world. She leaves and we write letters for a year making plans to attend college together, then she doesn't show up and I never hear from her again. I don't understand it. It really bothers me. What could have happened that was so bad that she would never speak to her best friend again or even tell me what was wrong?"

"Why don't you do this? Get her address and go to Atlanta. Find where she lives and watch her house. If you see her go in, call her and tell her you happen to be in town and you really need to talk to her. Tell her you're very worried about her. Or forget about it and wipe her from your list of people to ever call again."

"If she doesn't call me back, she obviously doesn't want to rekindle the relationship. But it's one of those things that just eats at me. I can't explain why. It's just a feeling. I really want to just look her in the face and say what is wrong?"

"So go see her then. Just pop in like I said, and watch her place till you see her."

"I think if I could talk to her just once I could forget about her forever. What if she is living in poverty and is too embarrassed to tell me?"

"Then you could go see how she lives and if she's poor or in need somehow, you'll know what to do."

"I would give anything to her. You know?"

"Then go."

That's not a bad idea. A little sneaky, but I think it would work. I'm obviously not someone she wants to have a friendship with. But I want to know why. You know what? I have an even better idea. Why don't we go together? It would be less obvious that I was hunting her down. We could say we were there visiting some friends of yours."

"I thought of her as one of my own, too. You two were inseparable."

"Then you'll go with me?"

"I wouldn't pass up this little investigative caper for the world. I don't have a lot of excitement in my life, you know. Do you want to road trip or fly?"

"What do you want to do?"

"I think I would rather road trip. By the time we wait in lines at the airport and then get pushed back from a late flight, we could be halfway to Atlanta."

"Then road trip it is. Let's plan to stay a few days and shop for a wedding dress."

"This is getting better and better. Speaking of the wedding, we have only five weeks left. Are you excited?"

"It's soaking in more day-by-day. I love Matt and I am ready to start a family."

"Sounds very convincing. I'll leave it at that. I think we have everything ordered. The dresses for the bridesmaids will be ready in a few weeks. We'll get those shipped in. Invitations were sent yesterday, and the food for the reception will be done here. Have I left anything out?"

"I don't think so. You've done such an incredible job of organizing all this. Mom and Dad would be so proud of you for taking care of me." Sela held her hand and felt her squeeze.

"You are my only child, Sela. This wedding will be the only

one I participate in. I want it to be beautiful." Her eyes were brimming with unshed tears.

"All right now, let's don't get all teary-eyed in the middle of the day. There will be plenty of time for that."

"I'm gonna get my swim in and then let's plan the trip. We'll tell Matt that we're going to look for dresses in Atlanta and it won't be a lie."

Lily heard the kitchen phone ring. "I better get that."

"If it's for me, tell them I'll call back."

"Hello?"

"Hello. This is Jake. Is Sela there?"

"Oh, hello, Jake. Yes, she is, but she has just jumped in for a swim. Can she call you back later?"

"Sure. I don't have anything new to tell her about Charlee's case. I just wanted to talk to her a minute. See what's going on."

"I'll be sure to tell her."

"Thanks."

Lily didn't think returning the phone call would be a good idea for someone who was about to be married. Then again it might be the best thing for her. Her gut said she was making the wrong move marrying Matt. She stepped out into the hot sunshine, covering her eyes with her hands.

"That was Jake." She watched as Sela's face lit up.

"What did he say?"

"Just that he wanted to see what you were doing. No news from the investigation. He just wanted to talk."

Sela pulled herself up the ladder and grabbed her towel.

"I told him you'd call him later." She could see Sela's momentary lack of interest in the swimming pool.

"Okay. I'll call him later." She had a childish grin.

"What's that look all about?"

"What look?"

"That look like you're in first grade and someone just gave you a kiss on the cheek."

"Oh, Lily. I can't help it."

"Then maybe you shouldn't call him. You're practically a married woman. Or call him and call off the wedding plans."

"So I won't call him. You know there will always be other men out there. I've made a decision to marry the man I love and that is that." She did a cannonball into the water and splashed Lily. Lily screamed and jumped back, laughing.

That night Sela couldn't sleep. She lay awake thinking about Jake and her sister. She wondered if he would've been the one to marry Charlee. She thought about her wedding plans and her trip to Atlanta. Everything was racing through her mind so quickly. She had spent only a few nights with Matt lately. He had been so busy at the office. His trips out of town had become more frequent. He promised they would stop after he wrapped up these few big cases. He even promised to quit work if she wanted him to. She didn't know what she wanted. Maybe she and Matt could get involved in some charitable events together. Maybe he'd get involved in the ranch if he did stop working. After they were married, she'd start to feel more like they were on the same page together. Where would they live? In the ranch home? Would he be comfortable here? She had so many questions? It would be so great to set sail for a month and just do nothing but love on your new husband. She focused on the honeymoon. She imagined the blue water. Swimming in the early morning hours with the dolphins. But the water would be so cold. Matt didn't care much about swimming. Her romantic thoughts were sidelined by a picture of her swimming alone while he stood on the boat and watched. Oh, well. She wondered if Jake was a swimmer. His body was tan, so she knew he enjoyed the sun. She had heard Charlee talk of him surfing. At least he loved the water. She thought about his body. "What does it matter if Jake likes to swim?" She was irritated with the direction of her thoughts. "This is crazy," she said out loud. She tried to focus on her trip to Atlanta. She'd be leaving in two days.

Ruez listened carefully to everything that was going on in the house. The one phone call from Jake was nothing worth reporting. He popped a French fry into his mouth and sat just inside the edge of the woods. "Hey, Boss. As usual, nothing to report. A phone call from Chattanooga, Tennessee, from a bridesmaid and one from Huntsville, Alabama. It's been two weeks. Not one word from the investigator. There was a call from that guy Jake yesterday, but he told Lily there was nothing new."

"What did that little punk want?"

"Just wanted to talk to Sela. That was all. Asked her to call him back. She never did."

"Good girl."

"I heard a lot of wedding plans being made. They're going to Atlanta to do some shopping for a wedding dress, so I'm going to take a break. This is getting very boring." His thick accent was hard for Matt to understand.

"Then take a break. Sela told me they were leaving Monday. I'll be gone too. I won't be back until Sunday. I'll talk to you next week."

Ruez was not a cheap person to hire. He had been paid more than twenty thousand dollars over the years. His biggest job being the explosion on the oil rig, along with all the organizing and coordinating required to get Mr. Barnes there at just the right time. He had been promised fifty thousand dollars once Matt had his hands on the money. He had a contract in writing and could hardly wait. It was Ruez who had followed Charlee to her apartment day-after-day to learn her routine, and he had every step of the murder planned for Beth to carry out. His expert services had found someone to forge Charlee's handwriting perfectly and without any possible suspicion. He hung up the phone. "This better wrap up soon. I can't eat on a promise. Bossman's gotta pay up real quick."

Matt moistened his lips and cracked his knuckles.

"How ironic that we will all be in Atlanta at the same time."

Chapter Six

Sela and Lily packed their bags into the trunk and grabbed their snacks and ice chest. It would be a long drive, but they had made arrangements to stop along the way. They would overnight in New Orleans and spend Tuesday in the French Quarter, having fun. Thursday they would drive along the coast and stop off in Destin, Florida for a few days, then head up to Atlanta on Friday afternoon. There wasn't a cloud in the sky as Sela headed for I-10. With the windows rolled down and the music playing loud, the ladies sang along with Mick Jagger's *I Can't Get No Satisfaction.*

Matt booked his flight into Atlanta through Delta, as usual. He would arrive on Thursday and stay until Sunday. He actually did have some real work he had to get back to on Monday. He called Sela's cell phone.

Lily turned the music down so she could hear.

"Hello?"

"Hey. Have you gotten on the road yet?"

"We just left. Headed toward I-10 now. I was just fixin' to call you." She winked at Lily.

"Be careful. Make sure you check in with me."

"I will. You know where we'll be staying, but I'll call you along the way. I love you."

"I love you, too. Ya'll be careful."

"We will."

Lily turned the music back up "…and I try, and I try, and I try, and I try… I can't get no… dunn na naaa… I can't get no… dunn na naa…" Lily played the drums on the dashboard and Sela bobbed her head.

After several hours, Lily slumped over against the window with her pillow and slept. Sela thought of nothing but the road and the sky. It felt good to be road-tripping with Lily.

It had been four days since they had left Texas. Sela and Lily looked out over the balcony of their condo in Destin, Florida. They watched the waves roll in and back out again. There was only the sound of seagulls and water slapping against the sand.

"Let's stay just one more day. I need this. I really do. Let's charter a boat and go out on the water today. This might be our last big trip together, Lily. I'll be married soon and who knows what that will hold." Lily heard the longing in her words.

"Hey, I'm up for anything. There's nothing too important for me to get back to. The ranch is running smoothly and so is the business. We can do whatever we please. You know, I've never been on a chartered boat."

"It's settled then." Sela called a number listed on a brochure she had picked up. "I would like to charter a boat today for myself and one other person. We want the whole boat to ourselves. Is that possible?"

"Sure, it's possible." He knew money was not a concern when someone wanted the boat to themselves. He didn't bother quoting a price and she didn't ask.

"Meet me at Pier 25 at 10:00 a.m., if that's not too early. Do you know where that is?"

"No, sir."

"I'll have someone pick you. Where are you staying?"

Sela gave him all the information and her name. The arrangements were made.

Sela lounged at the front of the yacht in her leopard print bikini. The last time she was on a yacht, it had been with her dad and sister. They swam and fished together for hours. She thought about every detail of the trip. She'd forgotten what fun it had all been until just now. She had pushed so many things from her mind in the last few months, but now she found herself searching desperately to bring them back into focus. She remembered her whole family going out for weeks at a time when her mother was well. Her father had fixed a special room, just for the girls, in the bottom of their boat. It was their secret hideaway with a secret entrance that was next to the wall on the other side of the bed. She and Charlee had spent so many days in that playroom together. There was a TV, toys, games, a bed and a kitchen. They were on their own down there. And best of all, it was soundproof. It didn't matter how loud they got. She smiled at the thought of the two of them jumping on the bed with the music as loud as it could get. She yelled across the deck, "Lily. I'm gonna go for a swim."

"In this water?" Lily stood up from her table and laid her book down. A wide brim hat covered her face, and her sunglasses nearly covered her face.

"Yes, in this water. It's perfect!"

The boat had been stopped for nearly an hour. Sela slipped on her goggles and jumped in the water near the side with the ladder. Lily watched the water bubble. Minutes went by before Sela resurfaced.

"Good Lord, child. Don't scare me like that."

Sela looked genuinely surprised. "Scare you how?"

"You stayed under so long."

"I saw something down there, so I went to investigate. It was too deep. I didn't realize it until I got way down there. I'm fine, Lily."

"But those waves look so scary."

"I love the waves."

"I'm not letting you out of my sight, just the same."

"Suit yourself." Sela swam circles around the yacht for what seemed like hours. She dove and flipped like a mermaid. Lily watched in wonder at her talent.

It was very late Friday night when they arrived in Atlanta. They drove straight to the Buckhead area where Beth was living. They unloaded their bags at the hotel and fell into bed. Saturday morning they would get a map and ask for directions to her house.

"Come on, Lily. We need to get a jump on it. What if she has early Saturday morning plans?" The truth was, she had awakened early and couldn't go back to sleep.

"All right. Give me an hour to get myself together, at least.

"An hour!"

"It's only seven o'clock, Sela. I need some coffee and a shower."

Sela had already showered and dressed. She had waited this long. Another hour wouldn't hurt.

"I'll go get a map and some directions. I'll bring you some coffee and a bagel back from the lobby."

"Are you sure you don't want to shop first? That way we could say that we'd been shopping and had some time left and wanted to look her up."

"I'm too excited to shop. We'll tell her we came to shop, but that I wanted to look her up before we got too tired, or something like that. I don't know. Let's just find the place first."

Sela returned with directions to 1432 Franklin Drive East, a cup of coffee, and a bagel with cream cheese, as promised. She had already eaten hers. "Are you ready?"

"Don't I have a minute now to eat my bagel?"

"I'm sorry. Sit down. Take your time. Just not too long. Just kidding."

"Do you think she knows Charlee was killed?"

"If she watches any little bit of news, I'm sure she heard about it. Now that police suspect it was a murder, there've been regular updates. Plus, that composite drawing was made public last week."

"Yeah, you're right. She'd have to be living under a rock to not know something about Dad and Charlee."

Matt rolled over and snuggled up to Beth's back. She pressed herself into him. She'd been lying awake, thinking.

"You never said how you like my new look. Do I look anything like the drawing?"

"Not at all. You're still gorgeous, but nothing like the drawing."

"How much longer am I going to have to live this charade? It's getting so old you, know."

"It's getting old for me, too. I told you the wedding is only four more weeks away."

"But how long will I have to wait after that?"

"We've been over this. You know the plans as well as I do. Why all the fuss all of a sudden?"

"I just want to make sure the plans are fresh in your mind. You won't get a second chance, you know. It will be the only time you'll be with her alone on a boat in the middle of nowhere. If you blow it, and I have to sit around and wait for you to come up with another plan, or Ruez, or whoever, I am not going to be happy. I may even begin to think that you're stalling."

"You must be crazy. You are the only woman in the world for me. It's all set. It's going to be so easy. I've rehearsed it a thousand times in my head."

"I have something to show you." She eased out of bed and opened the top dresser drawer.

"These." She handed him two passports. They were perfect German passports with their faces, but different names. The name on hers was Beverly Glass and his was Timothy Glass."

"So you already got us married, huh?"

"I also got these." She handed him two driver's licenses. "You know a person always needs two forms of identification."

"Excellent." Looking at his new passport gave him a new sense of urgency. "There are still some loose ends I've got to tie up before Sela and I leave on our trip. Like making sure I'm the legal beneficiary of her estate, and that there aren't any little legal technicalities sprung on me later."

"If she dies, the husband gets the money, and that is that."

"Unless it's been willed to someone else, or some charities, or special instructions are given to specifically not give it to the husband."

"Better get those minor details in order, most definitely." She jumped back in the bed and squeezed herself as tightly to his body as she could.

"Remember, if you don't hear from me for a while after her death, it's because I'm a grieving widower and we can't take any chances once all eyes are focused on me and Sela. Just stay put until you get the signal, then meet me in Munich at the Marriott Hotel."

"I've heard all that a hundred times." She pressed her mouth to his neck. "But I love hearing you say it."

Sela and Lily drove to Beth's neighborhood. It was an above-average area of garden homes and condos. The yards were manicured and the cars in the driveways were Hondas and Toyotas. Nothing elaborate. They drove slowly through the string of homes looking at each address carefully.

"That's it, right there." Lily pointed to a brick home with white shutters. "1432 Franklin Drive East. It's right there on the mailbox."

Sela felt her heart pound. She passed it by and looked back over her shoulder.

"Yep. That was it, all right. There were two cars in the driveway, so she either has a roommate, overnight company, a boyfriend, or two cars."

"Probably her overnight company is also her roommate, which is also her boyfriend."

"Right." Sela was nervous.

"So call her." Lily handed her the phone.

"Do you think it's too early?"

"Now you ask? We are already here. You got me out of bed, nearly made me choke on my bagel, and now you wonder if it's too early? Call the girl." Lily handed her the phone.

Sela dialed the number.

The phone startled Beth and she reached for it immediately.

"Who's calling me this early?" Matt didn't have a chance to stop her from picking it up.

"Hello?"

"Hey, Beth. This is Sela."

Beth's tongue felt thick as she fumbled for a reply.

"Sela?" It was all she could get out. Matt lay motionless, holding his breath.

"I know this is sort of crazy, but I just need to see you." There was a long silence. "Are you there?"

"Yes. Yes, I'm here."

"I'm here in Atlanta with Lily doing some shopping. I don't know what's wrong. I don't know if I did something or if something so awful has happened that you think you can never face me again, but whatever it is, I just need closure here. I just need to know what happened with us."

"I understand. I um..." She fumbled for words. Sela interrupted.

"I have your address here, and if you don't mind, Lily and I were wondering if we could come over before we do our shopping. It would just give me some peace of mind. That's all. It's me, Beth." She tried to use her aggressive marketing skills so as not to give her a chance to say no.

Beth listened and thought. She needed to help Sela close this chapter of her life somehow. She looked at Matt with panic.

"I'm so sorry I didn't return your last phone call. I intended to, really. Of course, ya'll can come over. If you don't mind , would you give me an hour to clean up and get showered?"

"That sounds great. If it would be better for you, we could meet you somewhere."

"Actually, that would be better. I had some friends over last night and the place is a mess."

"Where do you want to meet?"

Beth couldn't think of anywhere to meet. She'd been

avoiding all her old hangouts since taking on her new look. Not that she had that many hangouts to begin with.

"Tell you what. Just come here. I'll cook us some lunch and ya'll can meet me here at my house around 11:30. How does that sound?" Beth gave the directions and Sela wrote them down as if she didn't know where the house was.

"11:30 it is. I can't wait to see you, Beth."

"Yeah. Me, too. We've got a lot to talk about. Tell Ms. Lily I said hello and I can't wait to see her, too."

They sat in the car looking down the road at the house.

"Don't you think we should go? It might be a little unusual for a black Jaguar to be parked on the side of the road at nine in the morning around here."

"They can't see us way down here. I'm just so close to her house, and I'm sitting here thinking that just like that, I'm here. I could have been here years ago. I would have done anything for Beth. Given her anything she wanted or made a way for her to have it. It's just so puzzling." Sela looked at her friend's home, just down the road. They had lost so much time.

"It didn't sound like she was mangled or paralyzed. I mean, she's planning to have us over for lunch, and she had friends over last night. What could it have been?" She stared at Lily as if she had the answer.

Beth's front door opened and out came a man wearing only his jeans and a ball cap. He walked down to the end of the drive near the street and picked up the newspaper. He stopped by his car and popped open the trunk.

"Dear God, Lily. That's Matt! Right there at that truck!" The hairs on her head tingled.

"Matt Kinsley? I can't be so sure from here?" Lily strained to see.

"How can you not be sure from here? I saw his face. I know his walk. His mannerisms. Look at that ball cap. Do you know anyone else with a green and blue cap and a chest like that? I gave him that cap. Look! What is he getting out of the trunk?" Sela was speaking fast. Repeating herself.

"Looks like he got his briefcase."

"That's exactly what he's got. His briefcase, Lily. That is Matt. My Matt! Going into Beth's house. Do you understand what's going on?" She trembled all over. Her throat ached. She could feel the hairs on her neck standing straight up. Her back itched and she suddenly felt lightheaded.

"Calm down, sweetheart." She could see Sela's body shaking.

"What is going on is that Matt has been coming here when I thought he was away on business. He told me he was going to meet with a client this weekend." Her voice was getting louder and faster. "Maybe Beth hasn't been able to keep in touch because she's seeing Matt. It all makes sense now."

"Slow down, Sela. How does it all make sense? Are we one hundred percent sure that the man walking in over there is Matt?" She grabbed Sela's arm to slow her down a bit.

"Lily, I have never been more sure in all my life. That man who just picked up that newspaper, with those curls poking out from under that green cap that I gave him two years ago, carrying a briefcase that he never goes anywhere without, is Matt! I would bet my life on it." Sela felt herself about to throw up. "I don't know if I can drive, Lily. I think I'm about to be sick"

"Just sit here a minute. That isn't Matt's car. I'm not saying you're wrong, but it's not his car." Lily was doing anything she could to create a bit of doubt that this was really him.

"This is just unbelievable. I don't know what to say right

now. I'm…" Her words trailed off for a moment.

"I don't know what's going on. Why would he ask me to marry him if he's seeing Beth? How long has he been seeing her, I wonder? This is just too crazy. What is happening here?"

"Well, you hear about people living a double life all the time. Maybe you should talk to Beth and see if she even knows ya'll are getting married. See how she acts when you tell her about him."

"Maybe I should go barge in on them. We certainly timed this right. I'm in total shock right now!" Sela leaned her head on the steering wheel and forcefully exhaled all the air in her lungs.

"You know, Sela, this isn't all bad. At least now you know why you haven't been able to truly love Matt the way you felt you should. It was that gut instinct that just said it wasn't right to give your heart away to this man."

Sela felt a sense of relief fill her entire body. Jake flashed across her mind in an instant. How could something so bad, suddenly feel so right. She was now free to fall in love with Jake. Anger turned to possibility.

"You have a point, Lily. I don't think I ever truly felt the way I should have towards Matt."

"I know, Sela. I could see it in your eyes."

"But you know, something tells me there's more to this little ordeal than meets the eye. Something stranger than just an affair is going on."

"We're going to have to get ourselves somewhere a little less conspicuous to continue this conversation."

Sela waited until she was sure Matt was inside and not coming back out, then she backed up and headed in the opposite direction. She wound her way out of the subdivision and parked in the back of a gas station at the edge of the neighborhood. Matt would have to pass it in order to leave. They grabbed a cup of coffee and waited. At 10:30, Matt pulled into the gas station across the road and pumped some gas into his rental car. They watched his every move.

"Now do you wonder if it was really him?"

"No, honey. It's really him." They watched as he drove off. "Are you all right?"

"I think I'm okay. After what I've been through, this is a drop in the bucket. Thank God I found this out before we were married. Now I've got to figure out what he's up to. Why is he so determined to marry me?"

"Your money and the Barnes name would be my guess."

"Maybe Beth can help answer some of our questions. Maybe not, though."

At 11:30, Sela pulled into the driveway. Beth walked to the door wearing a loose floral print dress and hardly any makeup at all. Her body was hidden behind the loose fabric. She had short brown hair and her glasses were thick. Sela could hardly believe she was looking at the beauty she remembered. She waved as Beth walked towards the car and met Sela at the car door.

"Wow. You have certainly changed." Beth looked her up and down. "You look like a grown woman. You finally got boobs!" She smiled and hugged her old friend and was immediately jealous of the time Matt had been spending with the not-as-attractive young girl she remembered.

Sela looked at Beth's homely appearance. Something was off, but she couldn't quite figure out what. How do you go from glamorous to frumpy so quickly? It was a complete opposite look from the Beth she knew.

"I guess I did change. It's been nearly six years. You have, too." Sela had missed her so much.

Beth knew she was thinking the worst. She hated looking like a wallflower, but it would have to do for now. She stared for a long uncomfortable moment, examining Sela up and down. So this is what Matt has been spending his extra time with. He had grossly exaggerated Sela's appearance. They would definitely discuss that later. He had said she was rather homely.

"How have you been, Lily? You look as lovely as ever." They hugged.

"Thank you. We have sure missed your smiling face around the ranch."

"Well, I have a lot to tell you about. You guys come in. How long can you stay?"

"We aren't on a set schedule. We're just flying by the seat of our pants right now." Sela glanced over at Lily who nodded in agreement.

"Is that your car?"

"Yeah. I got it for my birthday a few years ago. Dad picked it out for me."

"A Jaguar. You always wanted one of those." Beth led them inside and closed the door. "Have a seat here. Lunch is almost ready. I hope you like shrimp Alfredo. I thought I remembered you liking it."

"Yes, and it smells wonderful."

After so many years apart, Sela could not believe she was sitting here talking to Beth about shrimp Alfredo. She knew small talk was inevitable, but she was ready to get down to the nitty-gritty. She wanted to just tell her to spit it out. What's been going on?

"Well, I guess your curiosity has gotten the best of you and you're dying to know what happened to me."

Sela felt a little bit of anger rising, but it was easily controlled. Yes, her curiosity had gotten the best of her, to say the least. Sela got up and joined Beth in the kitchen.

"Yes. You meant a lot to me Beth. Still do."

Lily sat quietly, just studying Beth's body language from a distance.

"Well, at the end of my senior year, Matt came to visit me. I don't know if you knew that. He flew up and spent nearly the whole summer with my family. At that point we were all going to college together. That is, until I found out I was pregnant. I got pregnant in June and was really starting to show by fall semester. I was embarrassed. I felt like such a loser. I was fat, sick, and trying to figure out how I was going to raise a baby. I didn't want anyone to know." Her eyes were starting to water and her lip quivered. "Mom and Dad took it pretty hard. All of a sudden, I was going to be a mother. There wasn't any way they would take the baby and let me go to school. Matt wanted me to have an abortion, but by the time he found out about the baby, I was too far along. I was afraid to tell him. He had promised me that if I would get rid of the baby that there would be plenty of time for babies later. We would get married and start a family." She stirred the bubbling shrimp sauce without making eye contact and continued.

"I couldn't do it. I ended up being a nineteen-year-old mother with no future. I tried hard for about a year, but I just wasn't cut out to be a mother. I mean, well, I was just too young. I was very depressed. I got hooked up with the wrong crowd and started doing anything I could to make money, if you know what I mean. Sex and drugs are a deadly combination. Yes, drugs were involved. I hit rock bottom. I broke all contact with my family. I knew they were ashamed of me. I thought everyone was talking about me. I assumed Matt had told someone who had eventually spread it around that I was knocked up, and strung out, and wouldn't be going to college with you guys. I guess he can keep a better secret than I thought." Beth was proud of the lie she told with such conviction, and even managed to bring up a few convincing tears in her eyes. She turned quickly and looked as Sela to see her response.

"He has never said a word about any of that, Beth. I'm so sorry you went through all of that."

"It turns out he was a real sorry son-of-a-bitch. When he found out I kept the kid, he was afraid I would ask him for child support, so he cut off all contact with me. I tried to reach him after I gave the baby up for adoption, but he still wouldn't return my calls or letters."

Sela knew she was lying but wasn't' sure where the lies started or stopped. "So how did it end with you two?"

"What do you mean?"

"I mean did he forgive you in the end? He has to understand now that he is older."

"I don't know. I quit trying. It was over a long time ago and I only wish the best for him The baby is with a great family and is five years old now."

She turned to get the plates from the cabinet. Lily glared at Sela, and each knew what the other was thinking. What was going on?

Beth felt good about the way she had convinced them of her struggles. It was partly true. She did get pregnant and that was why she broke contact with Sela, but she had given the baby over to a foster family at Matt's request. She had felt ashamed for so long. She did go through a period of depression and not wanting to speak to anyone or see anyone. Depression was the reason she had not started school in the fall, and then it never worked out for her financially, so she had given up all thoughts of being college-educated.

"Beth, I have something to tell you. Matt and I are getting married in a little more than a month. He and I have been dating for over three years now." She waited for a reaction. Beth looked up from the table and focused her eyes on Sela firmly.

"You and Matt are getting married?"

"Yes."

"I don't believe it, Sela. You and Matt?"

"That's right."

"Well, good luck to you both. I hope he finds more happiness with you than he did with me." Beth had already thought about how she would end Sela's preoccupation with maintaining their friendship. It was time to act. "Obviously he had things going on in Texas that I had no idea about."

"Oh, no. We only ran into each other after college and started dating then."

Beth turned up the dramatics. "Oh really? I wondered why he was so quick to beg me to get an abortion if he loved me so much. I would have married him then. I had a feeling he was preoccupied with someone else. I had no idea it was my best friend." She slammed the pot of noodles into the sink. "He must not have wanted you to know that I was pregnant because it would have messed up his relationship with you! It's starting to make a little more sense now." She slammed a plate down on the table. "And you, my best friend! You were busy trying to snag my boyfriend while I was away. How long did it take you to sink your claws into him after I left? Did you know I was pregnant? You couldn't deal with a little bastard baby, could you? It might ruin your reputation." Beth was putting forth her best crazed theatrical performance.

Sela stood up and looked at Lily. Beth looked as if she would snap at any moment. She wasn't sure what to do. Lily stepped in to try to defuse the situation.

"You've got it all wrong. Sela and Matt…"

"I never want to hear his name again. I especially don't want to hear the name Mrs. Matthew Kinsley. He is a psycho. He is a cruel psycho who made me give up my baby! What did you do, come all this way to rub my face in it? You drove from Texas to tell me face-to-face that you're marrying Matt? What is wrong with you? You deserve each other!" Crocodile tears were streaming down her cheeks.

She was crying and hitting the table. The plates clanged as her fists came down hard.

"Is this what you wanted to see? Is this what you drove all the way to Atlanta to see? A broken-down girl who's lost everything she ever loved? Well, here it is! Now, go enjoy your life with the man I should have been with. Just get out of my house!" Her eyes were red with tears and her face was splotchy and distorted. It was a masterful performance. She pointed dramatically at the door.

Sela grabbed her purse and helped Lily up from the couch.

"I'm sorry it had to end this way. This is not what I wanted to happen at all."

"Did you think about what I may have wanted when you were cuddling up with Matt all those nights while I was trying to raise his baby?"

"I had no idea. Seriously, Beth. I'm sorry. How could I have…"

Lily interrupted. "Beth, can I use your restroom before we go?" The two girls paused momentarily and looked at Lily. It was such an inappropriate time for her to ask such a question. It took both of them off-guard.

"Sure. First door on your left down the hall."

Lily walked swiftly to the bathroom. Once inside, she carefully opened several drawers until she found one with hairbrushes inside. She carefully placed one of the brushes with the most hair in it inside her purse, then flushed the toilet. She washed her hands and met Sela in the car. She did not tell Beth goodbye on her way out. They drove off in silence. Once they reached the hotel, they sat in front of the door for a few minutes. Neither one was quite sure what had just happened. It had all happened so fast.

"Dear Lord, Lily. Can you believe that?"

"She was like a time bomb just waiting to explode, huh?"

"I got something for ya."

"What?"

"When I went to the bathroom. You didn't think I just couldn't hold it, did you?"

"I was wondering why in the world you were asking to use the bathroom at a time like that."

"I got a hair brush."

"For what?"

"I have a sneaking suspicion that one of the blond hairs on this brush might just match the hair they found in the apartment."

"You mean Charlee's apartment?"

"That's exactly what I mean."

"It never crossed my mind. Lily, you are a genius."

"Not only that, but I'm willing to bet you'll find a few of Matt's hairs in there, too."

"Oh, this calls for a celebration! You know what? How would you like to get on a flight and head back home?"

"Without you? What are you going to do?"

"I'm going to call Jake and see if he'll meet me here tonight. I want to tell him all about this. I want to see him as quickly as possible."

"Well, let's make the arrangements."

"Do me a favor. When you get back, order a wedding dress for me. I don't want Matt losing sight of whatever it is that he has planned. We'll continue to go along with this until we find out what's truly going on between him and Beth. I'll call him and tell him I ran into some friends here, and will be staying until next week."

"Sounds good."

"I'll turn this car in at the airport and fly back home."

"This may have been the most adventurous trip I have ever taken. No, without a doubt, it was!" Lily chuckled.

"I will certainly never forget it." They laughed, but felt the pain at the same time.

Sela waved goodbye as Lily boarded her plane. She drove back to the hotel and called Jake.

Chapter Seven

Jake lay on his couch, idly flipping through the TV channels with no real interest. He had waited a week for Sela to return his call, but it never came. He couldn't help but think of her. They shared so much chemistry. He knew that she had felt it, too. He thought about his relationship with Charlee. They had been best friends almost since the day they met. They had so much in common and really enjoyed being around each other. He wondered what Charlee had said about him. About their relationship. They were best friends. They loved each other, but they were not a couple. They were assigned projects together, they worked together, they spent their off-time usually doing things together with friends, but there was no mysterious love connection that kept Charlee on his mind. She was his best friend. Charlee knew that. Sela, on the other hand, had caused him to think. Her eyes had locked with his for a moment and everyone else seemed to be moving in slow motion around him. He knew she was getting married, but he wanted to see her just once before she did. If she was anything like Charlee, she would be loving and kind. Something told him that the guy she was marrying was not so kind. He had borne the brunt of several snide remarks and sarcastic accusations, none of which Jake felt the need to respond to. The phone rang, jolting him from his thoughts.

"Hellooo?"

"It's me. Sela."

"Sela. It's so good to hear from you." He hoped she hadn't

called only to report some news about Charlee. "What's going on with you? Did you get my message?"

"Yes. I want to apologize for not calling you right away. I really didn't think it was a good idea when Lily said you just called to talk. I mean, well, I did want to talk to you, but I was afraid that if we started talking..." She heard herself babbling.

"That if we started talking, you might enjoy it so much that you couldn't stop?" Jake finished her sentence for her. She laughed uneasily. She knew it was true. He was all she could think about.

"Well, I don't know what I was thinking, really. I should have just called. But here I am now. I'm in Atlanta, Jake. This is going to sound crazy, but will you meet me here? I need to talk to you about some things?"

"Why are you in Atlanta?"

"It's a really long story. If you'll come today, I promise not to leave out a single detail. I'll make all the accommodations for you. All you have to do is show up."

"What about work Monday? Can you write me a doctor's excuse, too?"

"No, but I can do better than that. I will offer you twice as much as what you're now making and give you your own place at the ranch if you will come and work for me. I need someone to help with the ten- to twelve-year-old boys. It's a very rewarding job. You'll play football and baseball with them. Listen to their problems and be a friend. The truth is, something has come up and I really need your help."

"So you're saying you want me to move to Texas and work for you at the ranch and just give up everything I've worked for here? Is that right?"

Sela sat silent. It was a crazy idea. She was a fool to suggest he leave his career for someone he barely knew.

"Sela, are you there?"

"Yes."

"Well, I don't think I've ever had a better offer. How could I pass up anything that involved spending time around you?" His voice was caressing the phone and she could feel it. Oh, how she could feel it.

"Jake, you have no idea what this means to me. We can talk more later. Pack only what you need. Whatever you forget, we'll buy."

"I always travel light anyway. I can't wait to see you."

"Same here. I'll call you back with flight information. I'll see you tonight!"

"Great! See ya soon."

Jake's big chest pounded under his dark blue tank top. He could almost hear it. What had he just agreed to do? His heart had gotten him into sticky situations before, but nothing as irrational as this. He tied up some loose ends with friends and phoned his boss.

"Hey, Cathy. This is Jake. This is really short notice, but I'm leaving town for a while. I'm not even sure how long yet. I don't have anything going on that will leave you stranded, do I?"

"No, you don't. But you'll be missed. There's not anything wrong is there?"

"No. A friend needs my help and I feel like I need to be there."

"How come I never had any friends like you?"

"You work too much!"

"You're probably right. Take care and keep in touch. Where are you going?"

"Texas, for a while."

last time they had spoken was just after graduation, sometime after she decided not to go to college with us."

"And there he was."

"Yes! There he was. We called her and explained that we were in Atlanta and that I really wanted to see her. We asked if we could come by, and she put us off long enough to get Matt out of the house. When we finally met and got around to the reason why she quit corresponding with me, she gave us this big story about getting pregnant and Matt wanting her to have an abortion, and so on. Said she hated Matt and that things ended very badly between them. She yelled and accused me of being the reason Matt left her and wanted her to get an abortion. I tried to explain, but it was useless. She just lost it. She was pounding the table and screaming that she never wanted to see or hear my name or Matt's name again."

"Seriously? Oh, this is really crazy! What the hell is up? Do you think Matt saw your car?"

"Absolutely not." They stared in silence at one another. Both hearts were pounding as they shook their heads.

"Something is really off here, Sela. Tell me, how did it end?"

"Pretty badly. We left without good-byes. She was ranting and raving like a lunatic."

"This is crazy!"

"I've had a few hours to think about this. I believe she intended on instigating the fight in order to keep me out of her life. Whatever she's got going on with Matt, she obviously doesn't want me to interfere with."

"You're probably right."

"Matt and I still have a wedding date set in four weeks. I'm not calling it off. I want to find out what kind of charade he is playing."

"Okay. Well, work on that southern accent while you're there." She tried a southern drawl.

"Yes, ma'am." He did his best to respond likewise. He'd been raised as an army brat and picked up accents from around the world. Depending on where he was, that accent seemed to show up. Mostly he just sounded like a Midwesterner. Pretty much without accent.

He didn't know if he'd be coming back home before heading to Corpus Christi with Sela, so he cleaned out his refrigerator and turned everything off. He'd just play the rest by ear.

Sela paced back and forth, waiting on Jake's plane to arrive. When she saw it touch down, her hands began to sweat. She had acted irrationally, asking someone she barely knew to come work for her and give up his job. What was she doing? Would it be possible to tell him she'd changed her mind? She thought he was probably just doing it out of sympathy anyway. She watched every face unload from the boarding area. When she saw Jake's face, everything within her being felt the most intense delight. She'd forgotten how wonderful his smile made her feel. He grabbed her like she was a longtime friend and hugged her tightly. She held him just as tight. When he released her, he stepped back and looked deeply into her eyes.

"Thanks for asking me to come." There was something that needed to be said between them.

"Thanks for coming." She couldn't think of anything else to say. There, in front of her, were those big brown eyes and those gorgeous lips, and all she could think of to say was 'thanks for coming.'

"These are my only bags, so I guess we can go." He pulled her hand in the direction he was moving. "I know it's late and you're tired, so don't worry about entertaining me tonight. We'll have plenty of time for that another day." He grinned. She felt like melting.

"Actually, I'm not that tired. I slept a while this afternoon so I'd be ready for ya when you got here. I've got so much to tell you, I don't even know where to start."

"I can't wait to hear it."

Sela had booked a large suite with adjoining rooms. It was bigger than anything Jake had ever stayed in.

"This is great." He had never even seen such a fine hotel room, except in movies.

"I don't normally stay in the rooms like this, but I figured since I had a guest coming and I had something to celebrate, I would go for the gusto."

"Something to celebrate?" He didn't quite understand what she meant. Celebrating his decision to help her on the ranch?

"Sit down, Jake. Can I get you something to drink? The refrigerator is loaded."

"I wouldn't mind an orange juice if you've got it." He sat down on the long plush animal print couch and waited for Sela to return with the juice.

She handed him the drink and plopped down in the corner of the couch. She slipped off her sandals and pulled her knees up next to her chest. "Let me start from the beginning."

Jake nodded.

"Lily and I decided to take a road trip. It was a very spur-of-the-moment decision. I was needing a pick-me-up and Lily suggested I look up an old girlfriend of mine, Beth. She was my very best friend from second grade through high school. After high school, we lost contact. But let me back up. She dated Matt for nearly three years of high school."

Jake interrupted. "So you're engaged to your very best friend's ex?"

"Yes, but it's not like it seems. We all lost complete contact with her. Literally nothing since we were eighteen. Matt and I actually talked very little while we were at college. We met accidentally on a cruise." As the words came out of her mouth, she almost felt as though it weren't an accident after all. Lost in thought for a moment, she remembered how he had traveled alone on the cruise, saying his friend bailed on him. Had Beth been with him then? Her mind raced until Jake spoke her name.

"Sela? Are you ok?"

"Yeah, I'm fine. Just started thinking about something. But anyway, I thought Lily's idea to get in touch with Beth was great, so I found her number, and called her. When she didn't return my call, I became very concerned that something was going on that she was trying to conceal from me, although I couldn't fathom what. I couldn't imagine what terrible thing could have happened to make her want to completely break contact with me. I became intent on finding out what it was. I have tried to contact her many times over the years. This time it was different, though. I needed to know why she wouldn't return my calls or answer my letters, so Lily and I decided to stake out her house and pop in on her."

"You what?" He laughed out loud. "You spied on her?"

"Yes, and when we arrived at her house, we found Matt."

Sela sat on the edge of the couch and leaned forward to Jake, repeating herself. "WE FOUND MATT."

"The Matt you're going to marry?"

"Was going to marry. Not anymore."

"And you are sure it was him?"

"Without a doubt. It was most definitely him. He told

"That's what we have to find out."

"I don't know why I wanted to drag you into this. It's just that you were the first person I thought of as soon as I was over the initial shock."

"You didn't drag me in to anything. I jumped in headfirst and willingly, and I'm glad I did. Have you told Mr. Ted about any of this? Does anyone know besides me and Lily?"

"No. We just found out today."

"Okay. good. This needs to stay quiet. Whatever he is up to, you now have the upper hand. It's all a matter of playing the game now, to see where he is headed. That won't be easy, but it's the only way to see exactly what's going on. Start listening for any signs of where he might be heading with this."

"I will, for sure. He's not going to be happy when he finds out that you're working at the ranch."

"Does he have to know? I mean, does he usually know the affairs of the ranch?"

"Not really. That's a good point. There's really no reason the two of you should ever run into each other."

"I'll be doing the 'undercover surveillance.' I think we should call Ted now. He may have some ideas about what we should do, for starters. He said it's never a bad time to call him." Sela reached over and grabbed Jake's hand.

"I am so glad I met you, Jake." The words sounded inappropriate since it was her sister's death that brought them together. "I mean, I wish it could have been under better circumstances... I'm sorry." She suddenly became choked up and couldn't continue." Jake picked up where she left off.

"I know exactly what you mean. I feel like I've stepped into someone else's life all of a sudden. My mind and body are doing things they've never done before. I've had thoughts and feelings that make me feel guilty because I know Charlee brought us together. But I choose to look at it this way: God brought us together. Now, the rest is up to us. I thought I was mistaken about you when you didn't return my call. I thought you were madly in love with Matt, and I didn't stand a chance." He squeezed her hand. "I knew the day we met there was something between us that needed discovering. I tried to block it out because of the situation, and you loving Matt."

"I knew it, too. But I also knew that I had committed to Matt."

"Now, here we are in Atlanta together, getting ready to share a romantic evening. There is absolutely no place I'd rather be."

He took her other hand and rubbed them both softly. He kissed both hands. At that moment, she wanted him so badly.

"Me too." The words were just above a whisper. Sela blushed at his touch. He leaned in and they kissed passionately for the first time. It was the first time she had ever really loved being kissed.

After a nice dinner, wine, and a live band, it was time to call Ted.

Jake listened again in utter astonishment at the whole thing. She also told him about the hairbrush Lily took.

She relayed her conversation with Teddy to Jake.

"Ted had some pretty good points. His first reaction was not disbelief. I guess he sees a lot of everything in his line of work."

"I'm sure he does. So what did he say?" He had moved closer to Sela, and she could feel his deep concern.

"He said that my father had always expressed concern with my choice of a boyfriend. He didn't like Matt from the beginning. He wasn't close to his mom, and that concerned him. He said his dad had served years in prison for insurance fraud. He said dad hated the way he would always talk about what he would do if he had money. That is certainly true. There was a time when he was obsessed with it. He would talk about winning the lottery. Or about being a famous."

"I guess he wouldn't have any need to wish for money when he's marrying a billionaire." It came out cold and harsh.

"Ever since he became a successful lawyer and started earning enough money to do whatever he wanted, he no longer obsessed about it as much. At least not that I have noticed. Ted did say it's possible that Matt may be trying to marry me for my money. Especially since I'm the sole heir to the fortune. He's questioning whether Matt may have had a hand in Charlee's death somehow. He thinks this could possibly go even as far back as my dad's death. I don't know. This is all too crazy. One theory he has is that Matt and his girlfriend plan to kill me and jolly away on my money."

"It could be possible, you know. Why would they both be denying that they've had any contact unless they had something to gain from it?"

"I can't believe that Matt would do anything to hurt anyone. Sure, he's a liar, but killer is a strong word. If the hair from Beth's hairbrush matches the strand we found at Charlee's, though, I think we've got our killer. The only problem with that is it's not a crime for an old friend to drop in on another friend. We need more evidence."

Jake looked at his watch.

"Try not to think about all this right now. We'll have plenty of time to talk later." Sela started to get up and Jake took her hand and eased her back to the couch and pressed his mouth against hers. She gasped. Her body was ignited, and her face was hot. She felt his tongue moving gently but passionately inside her mouth, and she knew she had not been loved before this. She wondered if her sister were watching them.

"I don't want you to stop, but I don't want to feel like I'm cheating on my sister either." It was such a weird feeling.

"Sela, Charlee and I were just friends. We were best friends. We shared everything with each other. I think she liked to talk about you as much as she liked talking about anything. She loved you. I feel I know you because of her. Sometimes I wondered if a person like you could really exist. Charlee made you sound perfect, and she was right."

"Really? You weren't lovers?

"No."

"I feel like I know you, too." Sela tried to recall anything in Charlee's conversations that would have led her to believe they were lovers. She couldn't. She had only assumed.

"So the two of you were not dating?"

"We went places together, but we were not a couple. There was no passion or lovemaking involved."

Sela turned away at his words. There had been little passion with Matt. It was as if they had been best friends. She felt the need to tell Jake more about her relationship with Matt.

"You know that Matt and I have dated for three years, but we have never had sex. I could never bring myself to do that with him. Guess my mom and dad taught me pretty good, huh? It's a good thing, too." It made her sick to her stomach to think how close she had been to giving in to Matt when they were in Charleston.

"No doubt it IS a good thing. That son-of-a-bitch doesn't deserve to be with someone like you."

He stroked her long dark hair and she began to relax and breathed deeply. She felt the familiar sweet peace sweep over her again.

"Do you like to swim?" she whispered

"It's one of my favorite things to do." He knew why she asked. Charlee had told him it was her passion.

She smiled. She knew her prayers had been answered. Her prince had finally come. Not riding a on white horse, but flying on a 747.

Chapter Eight

Per Ted's instructions, nothing concerning the case or their new information regarding Matt and his lover was to be discussed in the house, or over an unsecured phone. If they were somehow involved, they were professionals and had a track record of getting away with murder. He intended to find out how. He could not allow any information to be leaked about what was going on.

Jake had moved into his home at the ranch. With his newly grown mustache and beard stubble, he was easily disguised with a hat and glasses. His now had a nice two-bedroom, two-bath home situated in the middle of ten acres of land. Nearly all of the workers had a home on the ranch. They were well-taken care of and very loyal to the Barnes family. Many of them had worked their all of their lives and had raised their children in the homes provided to them.

Sela took Jake to one of the boy's homes where he would be working for a while. Surrounded by rolling hills and stables, a three-story house stood in pristine condition. He could hear many voices coming from the basketball courts out back, and could see a game of soccer going on in a distant field. Five boys greeted them at the door. The others were busy doing homework, watching TV, or playing games. There were twenty-four boys in that particular home and four mentors to oversee them. There were four homes on the ranch. Jake's job would be to provide a sports program for the boys, and eventually have intramural teams that would actually compete for trophies and bragging rights all year. She introduced him.

"This is Mr. Jake. He'll be the new athletics director here. He's going to get us some football and basketball teams going."

"I can play good basketball." A little boy with white blond hair and blue eyes smiled from ear-to-ear with excitement. He looked to be about nine. The other boys joined in.

"I can run real fast."

"Yeah, me too."

"I should be the quarter back. My daddy used to tell me I was born to be a quarterback!"

"Well, you will all have a chance to show Mr. Jake your many talents tomorrow. He has a few things he needs you to teach him in the next few days."

"Like what?" The boys were eager to please Sela.

"Like how to ride a horse. He says he doesn't know how to ride."

"You better learn, 'cause walking is hard work around here." The voice came from behind the couch where a black boy appeared to be glued to *Nick at Nite,* but was obviously listening in.

"I learned that the hard way. I didn't want to ride no horse. Then I realized really quick that if I want to eat while the food is warm, I better get my butt on a horse and get down here. It's easy once you learn."

Jake smiled. He was going to love this job. He could tell already.

"Well, Mr. Jake has a lot to learn from you guys, so you help him out. He's not from the south, so you may have to teach him how to dip a cornbread patty into a bowl of butterbeans."

Jake laughed along with the boys. One of them took him by the hand.

"I could show him some stuff right now if he wants me to."

"There will be plenty of time for that. Right now, we've got to get back to the big house for a little meeting. We will see all of you tomorrow, bright and early." Sela patted them on the head and squatted down to eye level. "Do I get a hug from anyone before I go?"

From around the room, boys came to give hugs to her. Jake watched as the little arms wrapped around her. He choked back the emotion he felt.

"I'll see you guys tomorrow." Jake waved goodbye.

"Bye, Mr. Jake. Good to meet you."

"Don't forget. I can run real fast." the little voice repeated.

"Oh, I won't forget."

Once outside, Sela began to tell Jake a little about the boys.

"The one that 'runs real fast' is Chad. Somebody left him in a dumpster about eight years ago. They left him to die and someone heard him crying. He was at Saint Mary's Home for nearly three years. We brought him here and he's been here for five years. He is so precious."

"Aren't there thousands of people out there wanting kids?"

"Yes and no. They want a certain kind of kid. Or they want only a baby, usually. Once they get to be a certain age, people don't want them anymore. They all have a sad story, or they wouldn't be here. The little guy who was born to be a quarterback saw his parents murdered. They were at a football game, of all places. He said they were walking to their car and someone came up with a gun and robbed them. Shot his mom and dad in the head over seventy dollars. He said the last thing he remembers his daddy saying as they left the game was 'Son, you keep working like you're working, and you'll be out there in about ten years.' He always reminds us that his daddy said he would be a quarterback one day."

"Have you ever seen him throw a football?"

"Yes, and he definitely has an arm on him. He spends his free time throwing at targets and with the other boys. He is very good."

"Maybe I can help his dream come true."

"It's a lot of pressure, Jake. We're trying to fill a hole that no one will ever be able to completely fill. Some of them are so angry and confused."

"Thank you for asking me to come here. My heart is already breaking for these kids."

"It only gets worse. One thing about it, though, every day you get your reward, and that makes it all worthwhile."

Jake and Sela sat in the den with eight other resident assistants that he would be working with. They had no idea their conversations were being recorded. Everyone answered questions and tried to prepare him for his new job.

"It may be hard to break through to some of them. They are all at different stages. Some have just gotten here. Some have seen their parents shot to death or killed in a car accident. Others never knew their parents and have been here all their lives. We are the only family they know." The man who spoke had worked on the ranch for twenty years. He had seen many kids come and go. "The truth is, nothing can prepare you for what you are about to experience."

Jake felt such a deep compassion for the children. He was ready for this knew and unexpected challenge.

As the sun began to set, Sela watched his house from her upstairs window. She wondered what he was doing at that very moment.

She would not be able to spend any time alone with Jake over the next few weeks. She was a very well-respected lady and did not want to do anything to jeopardize her reputation. It had already been three days and she had still not seen or talked with Matt. She knew she had to stop making excuses. She was never any good at lying, and now their relationship was going to be the ultimate lie. She would have to stay focused on the reason for the lie. She had to see what he was up to. Ted had given her a few ideas, one of which she planned to implement immediately. She called Matt at work.

"Are you swamped or can I come by to see you?"

"You' better come by. I can wrap this up within an hour. Have you gotten my messages?"

"I got one. We came in so late the other night that I didn't want to wake you."

"What was your excuse for the last two days?"

"Just been busy and tired. I did call you at work a few times and once at home, but I didn't leave a message." She hoped she didn't sound too aloof. "Do you want to just meet me at Carol's Place for lunch?"

"That sounds good. I can get out of here and be there by twelve-thirty?" She did her best to sound excited.

"That sounds good. I'll be there. I've missed you baby."

"I've missed you, too. How was your trip?" To Atlanta, she wanted to say. And how was Beth?

"It was a lot of work. I flew to Denver to meet with a client on Wednesday and then to Arkansas on Friday. It was pretty hectic, but the money will be worth it. I want to hear all about your trip and the dress." He wanted to take the attention off of himself.

She was shocked at his ability to lie so fluidly. She now

wondered how many clients he actually had. How successful was he really? Who was this man?

"I'll tell you all about it later. Why don't we both promise to stay in town until the wedding? I've missed you and I haven't been giving you the attention you deserve."

"My clients need me." He lied.

"Forget the extra client trips and stay home with me. I'll pay you whatever you miss from them unless you just like the work."

"No, I don't just like the work. I just find reasons to meet clients so that I can bill them for hours. People talk, you know,. So don't let it get out that you are paying me to stay home. I have a reputation to maintain. You don't want them saying I married you for your money." Beth would not be happy with this arrangement.

"It doesn't matter what other people say. I'm a billionaire. If you never want to work again in your life, then you don't have to. Remember that. Anyway, I'll see you at twelve-thirty."

"Yeah. I'll see you then."

The phone rang as she closed the door. She ran back in and answered it. It was Ted.

"Hi, Sela. We have a match."

"We have a match?" she repeated. Sela knew he was referring to the hair. "Only one?"

"Nope. We have two matches. We need more. We are a long way from solving this crime, but we now have DNA evidence. Beth was in Charlee's apartment and Matt was in Beth's. We have a lot of pieces to fit together. We've got to have patience, or we could lose our edge. Hang in there, girl."

"I'm doing fine."

"I'll call you later."

The phone conversation was brief. Straight to the point, with no extra details.

As Sela drove to meet Matt, she reached for her cell phone. She had left it at home. She wanted to ask Ted about the fingerprint. She stopped at Retro Gas, the only place she knew where they still had a row of pay phones, and called Ted back. She couldn't wait.

"Hey. I'm on my way to meet Matt. Was there anything else I needed to know besides the two matches? What about the earring and fingerprint?"

"No. Nothing else. Glad you called, though. Wanted to see if you had already arranged your meeting with Hanson?"

Hanson was the family attorney. He had handled her dad and mom's will, and was a longtime family friend.

"Yes. I'm going to meet him today. Oh, and here is Jake's new phone number." She rattled it off from memory.

"Where are you calling from?"

"I'm at a pay phone down the road. I left my cell phone at home."

"Did you notice anyone following you?"

She looked around and saw no one.

Ruez sat at the edge of the parking, lot taking notes.

"Don't take any chances. Someone could be watching your every move. After all, that's how they found out exactly when and where to kill Charlee, and possibly your dad. Where are you headed?"

"I'm on my way to meet Matt."

"Then do this. Call him from the pay phone. Tell him you're running late and that you needed to stop and get some things from the pharmacy. Tell him your cell phone is at home and that you're at a pay phone."

"Why?"

"Because if someone is reporting to him, he'll be aware of your pay phone call, and it won't send up a red flag. Be discreet. I have a strange feeling that you're in deeper than you know. Your home and phones could be bugged, Sela."

"Seriously?" The thought made her shudder.

"Let's not take any chances anywhere at any time."

Sela did as he said and called Matt from the payphone.

Ruez watched. He had heard her phone conversation with Ted in the house, but wasn't sure what it was about. He called Matt.

"Bossman."

"Go ahead."

"Your girl is at the pay phone at Retro. I just heard her on the phone with that guy Ted. He said they have two matches. Not sure what that means yet."

"She just called me from the payphone. Her cell phone is at home. She's meeting me for lunch and she's running late. Thanks for all the other info. I'll find out what the match is all about. Was that all that was said?"

"No. He said they had two matches. I'm not sure what kind of matches, though."

"Just keep your ears and eyes open." He had no idea what kind of matches they were talking about.

Matt was already seated when she arrived. He saw her and met her halfway across the room. He greeted her with a kiss. "I've taken the rest of the day off to be with my bride."

Great, she thought.

"Well, I feel honored, indeed." He pulled her chair out and she sat down. "Actually, I have some plans this afternoon that you may care to join me in." She was toying with him and she loved it.

"What's that?" He sipped his sweet tea.

"I'm meeting with my attorney concerning my estate and will." She tried to read his face.

"You know, should I die, every penny would be left to you if I haven't specified exactly where I want it to go. There are a few things I would like done with some of it. I spoke with Hanson earlier last week. He said it was absolutely necessary for me to come by and sign some documents."

"Well, I think it's important that I be there to support you and your decisions."

"He has advised me to get a prenuptial agreement. I mean, should anything happen to our marriage, God forbid. My family has worked very hard for generations to build an empire, and splitting it with someone just because they married into the family hardly seems fair. What do you think?" She sipped the lemon water that was placed before her.

Matt was stunned. He stared at his knuckles, watching them turn white as he squeezed his hands together.

"Excuse me? Did you say a prenuptial agreement? I hardly think that's the right way to start off a marriage. As a matter of fact, I would say that you've doomed us right from the start. I've proven that I can make a living on my own. You've never done anything on your own. I don't need your daddy's wealth. What have you done to deserve so much money anyway? You were born into it. So what if I marry into it? What's the difference? Neither of us earned it. It's being handed to us. Your daddy didn't make you sign a prenuptial because you didn't work for it. You're not saying 'until death do us part.' In your mind, this is a trial run. I'm sorry, Sela. It's all or nothing. I'll not have my wife putting me in such a position, as if I'm an experiment that may or may not work out. We should both be making the decisions together concerning our finances. This will lead to other problems. You'll not want me to invest or contribute to certain things because it's legally not my money to invest. It's a giant snowball effect."

Everything he said made sense. She would never actually consider a prenuptial agreement if she really loved the man she was marrying.

"And so what if I should inherit the money if something should happen to you? I should be the one person you trust to run things and the one person you would dearly love to give it to. Tell me how you want the money disbursed and I will do it."

The waitress arrived to take their order. Sela ordered her usual large grilled chicken salad without looking at the menu. Matt ordered a ribeye, medium rare.

"You're right. I'm sorry I didn't think of everything that way. Please forgive me."

"I'm upset, but I do forgive you. I'm a little surprised though." Shocked was what he felt.

"It wasn't my idea. It was Hanson's, our family attorney."

"I wonder what other great ideas he has up his sleeve to doom our marriage."

"Let's wait and see."

"How was your visit to Atlanta?"

"It was crazy, actually."

"What do you mean?"

She knew he already knew all about the visit. She was sure it was the reason he had not pressured her already.

"Well, we got there, and I decided to pop in on Beth." She gave him a moment to let it soak in. "So on Saturday morning I called her, and we arranged a meeting for lunch at her condo. Lily and I decided to drive by the place earlier. We got a city map and found her street. We drove by around nine a.m. and saw two cars in her driveway. One was a rental. We parked our car a good distance away and just watched her place for a minute."

"So you were spying on her." Matt could feel the sudden pressure in his temples. His palms went clammy.

"No, we weren't spying. It had been so long since I had seen her, and I hoped to maybe catch a glimpse of her getting her morning paper or maybe something out of her car. I wanted to see if maybe she was injured or disabled, or in a wheelchair. I don't know what I really hoped to see. I was just glad to be close to her."

"So how long did you stake the place out?" he asked sarcastically.

"Just about thirty minutes."

Matt tried to remember when he had retrieved the paper and his briefcase. Was it earlier or later than 9:30? Had she seen him from a distance and not recognized him?

"Finally, we left and came back at lunch. We didn't stay long, though. She started telling me about her getting pregnant with your baby and the whole story about the two of you. She freaked out."

"What? She freaked? Why did she freak?"

"I told her we were getting married and it came as a real shocker. She said you tried to force her to have an abortion."

"She what?" If Matt wasn't truly surprised, he was doing a darn good job of pretending.

"Said you got her pregnant the summer after graduation. She still loved you. Still loves you, probably. But she never wants to hear your name again. She said we were sneaking around on her and she hated me for it." Sela wondered if she should be acting

130

really upset about the whole thing. "Is it true about her getting pregnant?"

Matt was angry. She was supposed to have talked about how wonderful he was and what a great catch he would be to the lucky lady who married him. It was true, he had gotten her pregnant, but he didn't know if she was lying about keeping the baby or not. She had told him it was aborted. He would get to the bottom of that lie later.

"Sela, I'm sorry you found out like that. It's true about her getting pregnant. I wanted to move to Atlanta and marry her. Her parents talked her out of it. They said we couldn't support ourselves and that we were way too young. She became very bitter and crazy. They were the ones who were trying to force her to have an abortion. She left home and they didn't know where she was. That's why she never answered any letters and they never contacted us. They were embarrassed about the whole ordeal. She had so much potential." Sela didn't care. It didn't matter about the details, anyway. What mattered now was that they had a match. Beth's hair matched the one found at the crime scene and Matt's hair was found at Beth's house. Ted had explained to her that loving two women and being a two-timing cheat was not a crime. Beth visiting Charlee in San Fran wasn't a crime, either. The murder weapon was at the scene with Charlee's prints. There were no signs of a struggle. They would just about need a confession from one of them to solve this murder. One thing was certain in Ted's mind. Beth killed Charlee and Matt knew all about it.

"It doesn't matter about the pregnancy now. We all made mistakes when we were younger. You should have told me, though."

"There was never a good time to bring that up. With Beth

out of the picture completely, I never had a reason to talk about it. All this time, I've been so afraid of you finding out the wrong way."

"I was very upset at first. I've had a few days to think about it, and I just figured what's done is done."

"So Beth didn't give us her blessing."

"Not hardly."

"Oh, well. At least we know who not to send an invitation to. What time is your meeting with Hanson?"

"Two-thirty."

"Good. We have plenty of time." He looked at his watch and tapped the table nervously.

"Aren't you a little concerned that you might just have a kid somewhere in Atlanta who looks like you? A kid who needs his dad and wonders who his dad is? Maybe Beth didn't have an abortion."

Matt knew his answer meant everything to her. She did run a ranch for kids, so this sort of thing was very personal to her.

"Of course, I'm concerned. It's going to be my highest priority now. I'll find out if she's telling the truth and if she is, I will find my child and do whatever I need to do."

Whatever that is. He didn't have a clue what he would do.

"How will this affect our relationship?"

"I love children. Of course, I would love your child if you brought him or her into our lives."

"You are the most understanding person I know, and that is why I love you."

They finished their meal in near silence. They both had so much to think about as their wedding day drew closer and closer.

Sela and Matt waited in the historical home that had been turned into a plush law office for rich people. Matt had dreamed of working in a place like this.

Hanson appeared in the doorway, thin and wrinkled, wearing an expensive black suit and tie and a warm smile. He shook their hands and led them into his office. He had been handling her father's affairs for many years. There had been such confidentiality between them. Now, it was her responsibility to carry her father's fortune to the next generations.

"Please have a seat. Have you been doing all right, Sela?"

"Yes, sir. As well as can be expected, I guess you could say."

"I understand. We won't drag this out any more than we have to. Per our earlier conversation, several people and organizations have been added to your will. I have them all listed here. If you could just look it over and make certain I haven't left anyone out, then sign the bottom." He was all about business. No time for small talk or informal chat.

"Sela looked over the document. She moved over so that Matt could see the page with her. On it, Lily was listed along with several other employees. Altogether about ten million dollars had been divided amongst them. There was several million donated to the Red Cross, Girl Scouts, and United Way. It was to be expected. Matt did not mind the small contributions. "I would like to add in writing that the rest of my estate will go to my husband upon my death." She smiled at him and he nodded.

"That is usually understood, but it never hurts to have it in writing." Mr. Hanson typed the additional sentence at the bottom of the page. Sela signed it.

"Will you sign it as a witness, Matt?" She knew it wasn't necessary, but she wanted him to be as close as he could to the will. She wanted him to have it in his hands and see the words on paper. Everything else would go to him. He signed the bottom, underneath her name.

"I guess that will do it, then. Thank you for coming by. It was good to see you again, Ms. Barnes."

Sela intentionally left her keys sitting in the chair.

"It was good to see you, too, Mr. Hanson. Are you coming to the wedding?"

"Of course, I am. I have my invitation right here in the drawer. Wouldn't miss it for the world." He was an old man, but still very much in the game. He had known Matt as a child and now knew him as a fellow lawyer. He had no opinion of him, one way or the other.

"We'll look forward to seeing you then."

Matt waved and they walked to the parking lot. Halfway across, Sela mentioned her keys.

"Oh, no. I left my keys in his chair."

"Do you want me to go and get them for you?"

"No. I'll get them."

"Meet me at my house. I think I'll take the rest of the day off." He felt like celebrating.

"Okay."

She walked across the long parking lot back to the office. Once inside, she went back to Mr. Hanson's office.

"Here you go, Ms. Barnes." He handed her a revised copy of the will. She looked over it quickly. There were only a few sentences on it. She signed it and tore up the copy she had signed with Matt.

"I'm not sure what all this is about, but I trust you know exactly what you're doing. This is your last will and testament. There are no other copies. This will stands alone. Any previous copies are null and void." He placed it in a folder and put it in a file.

"It's very complicated, but I know exactly what I'm doing. You'll find out soon enough, Mr. Hanson. Thank you."

She didn't knock when she got to Matt's house. She just let herself in. Matt was in the bathroom. She had planned to bug his home and now was the perfect time. Ted had told her just how to do it. It couldn't be that hard. She listened carefully and worked quickly. Matt was still unaware that she was there. She sat on the couch and looked out the bay window, waiting on him. It would be a long day spent with the wrong person.

"You made it." Matt had slipped into some lounging pants and a T-shirt. He looked extremely handsome and it made her despise him even more.

"So what did you have in mind for the rest of the day?" Any other time she wouldn't have asked. She would've simply lain on the couch and been content just being with him.

"No plans. Is that okay with you? I thought we would just be together for a change."

"Oh. That does sound good now that you mention it." She slipped off her sandals and sat on the couch. "After all that food, I'm ready for a nap." Maybe they could sleep the afternoon away, and when they woke up, it would be time for her to go.

"Come here." He pulled her to him, and they cuddled up on the couch. She pulled a blanket over them and felt him pulling her close to him. She had once felt so secure and protected with him. Not anymore.

"Can't we just do this the rest of the day?" He kissed her passionately and she did her best to kiss him back with equal enthusiasm.

"I guess we could." She pulled back a little. "I need something comfy to put on."

"Grab some sweats and a t-shirt from my drawer."

She was already up and headed to his bedroom. He was following her. She slipped out of her dress and plundered through his drawer, looking for something to wear.

"My, what a beautiful body. And to think it's all mine."

"All yours." She smiled.

He wrapped his arms around her waist and slid his hands to her breasts.

"And these are all mine, too."

He attempted to fondle her for a moment and then tried to unsnap her bra. She pulled away slowly.

"My God, Sela. We'll be married in a few weeks. Can I not even touch your breast?"

"It's not that you can't touch my breast. It's where touching my breast will lead. Can you stop after touching my breast, or will you want to touch something else? Will I let you touch something else? I want to wait." She snapped her bra and put on some clothes. He rolled his eyes and went back into the den to wait on her.

"Have you heard anything from Ted lately?

"Not really."

"What does not really mean?"

"Just that there haven't been any new developments. I have heard from him, but not with any news."

He knew she was lying about something. He knew they had found two matches for something. Only what? He couldn't press the issue. He would find out soon enough.

Chapter Nine

Jake stood in the middle of the football field with a whistle in one hand and a football in the other. It didn't feel much like work. He had gotten to know the boys in a very personal way in such a short time. He was enjoying his new job very much. Another perk was that he was able to see Sela, even if it was from a distance. He had seen her headlights come up the drive very late last night, and he figured she had been with Matt. He knew she would have to continue the relationship as she always had, but it didn't make him feel any better. He thought about her soft plump lips and how he had felt kissing her in Atlanta. He wanted her more than he had ever wanted anyone in his life. She made him feel so alive. Sela watched him from the kitchen window. He couldn't see her from where he was working.

She buzzed for a housekeeper.

"Hey, Shannon."

"Hello, Ms. Barnes. What can I do for you?"

Sela rarely buzzed for anyone, but she needed a letter delivered and she couldn't do it herself.

"I need you to take this envelope to Mr. Caraway. He's our newest employee." Shannon looked out the window.

"I know who our newest employee is. Do you think I'm blind and deaf? Everybody is talkin' about Mr. Jake. With pleasure, Ms. Barnes." Her mouth was wet with saliva at the sight of Jake standing half-naked in the distance. His ball cap shadowed his face, but at this point, the face didn't matter. Shannon jumped into her golf cart and drove calmly towards the figure. Jake saw her coming. He pushed his hat back to get a better look at the approaching girl.

"Ms. Barnes told me to give this to you."

"Well, thanks. Everybody, take a water break." His smile made her panic. She turned quickly and left, feeling disappointed that she had not at least asked him how he was liking his new job or something!

He laid the football on the ground and opened the letter.

Jake,

It has been three days and counting since I have seen you (up close, that is). I watch you from my window sometimes. If you are free tonight, maybe we can spend it together. If that's okay, just raise your head and nod yes right now. (I'm watching you from the kitchen.)

Jake laughed out loud. He raised his head and smiled. She waved from the back door. He continued to read.

I'll see you at 7:00, if I can wait that long.
Sela

Jake folded the letter and put it in his pocket. He was on cloud nine.

There were seven long hours left in the day before she would meet Jake. She phoned a longtime friend of hers and asked her to go shopping. She wanted to wear something very special for her first evening on the ranch with Jake.

Sela pulled up and honked. She had known Julie all her life. They had gone to church together since they were kids. She emerged from her apartment with her red hair pulled in a high ponytail on her head. Her earrings were dangling silver and turquoise. Sela couldn't help but think of the earring found at Charlee's. For a moment Julie was a suspect. Everyone who knew her sister was. She dismissed the thought from her mind as quickly as it had emerged. She hated being so suspicious.

"So why haven't I heard from you lately?" Julie's face showed sincere concern.

"I've been so busy. You know, with the investigation and marriage on the horizon."

"I do know. I just wish you wouldn't alienate yourself from your friends the way you've been doing. Without your friends, you don't have a lot in this world."

Sela wondered about her friends. Her true friends had all gone their separate ways after college. Her high school friends had been Beth and Matt. She and Julie had become close friends after Beth moved away, but Julie was busy with a family and two kids now. She didn't like infringing on Julie's family time.

"I promise to do better. How about that?" She wanted so badly to tell her what was going on, but she knew she couldn't.

"I am never too busy for a friend, Sela. I know it seems like with a family, I have everything I need, but that's not true. Everyone needs friendships they can rely on."

"I've been through so much in the last year. I pulled away from everybody instead of leaning on anybody."

"How's Matt?"

"Matt is Matt." She didn't have anything good to say about him.

"That says it all, I guess." Still the self-centered pig he always was. She never knew what Sela saw in him.

"So you really love him." It wasn't really meant to be a

question.

"Yep. I do." She didn't sound too convincing, and lying to her friend was more than she could bear.

"I'm so ready to shop, to tell you the truth. It's been so long since I've seen you. I want to get something special for your kids."

"Oh, Sela, that's so sweet of you."

She knew Julie and her husband worked hard to make ends meet, but she didn't know how much was left over for fun. Their average home and modest cars and lifestyle said there was no room for frivolous spending.

"I really have missed you, Sela."

The two girls walked arm-in-arm into the mall.

The day was spent soaking up the joy of friendship. Julie shared stories about her kids, with love oozing from every pore of her body. Sela imagined her own big family. Hopefully with Jake.

They packed the trunk with dresses, shoes, and accessories. There were toys for each of her kids and a football jersey for Julie's husband.

"This day has been so wonderful, Sela. Therapy for me. You don't know how much I needed a day out."

"Yeah, me, too."

"I really miss these times."

Sela could see that her old friend really meant it.

"I have something for you. My father once said with great wealth comes great responsibility. I want to give you something." She reached into her purse and pulled out her checkbook. Julie watched in wonder. She had no idea what Sela wanted to give her. She wrote her a check for $200,000.

"I want you to have this. For you and your family, and for

you to share with people you know who need it."

It was no joke and Julie knew it. Tears rolled down her face as she accepted the check from her friend and they embraced.

"You have got to be kidding me, Sela. You have got to be kidding me."

"I'm not."

Julie's hand shook as she held the money. "I don't know what to say. I... I..." She began to cry.

"I didn't want to tell you about Brandon, but he has been diagnosed with a tumor on his brain. The doctor's bills have really piled up. I was afraid we were going to lose the house before it was all over. Aubry's working two jobs and we just sold our second vehicle. Last night, I prayed for a miracle and I turned it all over to God. I felt such sweet peace come over me. I felt my heavy burden slip away. God said not to worry. I said 'Father, you have the best for me, so I will let you work it out.' Yesterday I cried as Brandon snuggled up next to me. His tiny little three-year-old body was so helpless. I was so helpless."

Tears flowed down her cheeks as she continued.

"I want the best for my family. I have always sacrificed for them, but a tumor in my baby boy's brain is not something any mother can prepare for."

"You should have told me."

"I couldn't. I knew I would break down. I wanted this day to be fun. I didn't want you feeling sorry for me all day, or thinking you had to do something special for me because you pitied me."

"My father was generous, and I loved that in him. I try to listen for that still small voice that directs me to those in need. The Holy Spirit connected us today."

The two girls hugged and parted with joyful tears.

Lives would be changed forever because of this gift.

Jake dressed in khaki pants and a yellow hemp shirt. His hair was moussed and pushed back from his face. His high cheekbones were accented by his hairstyle. Sela had not yet seen him so dressed. He dabbed a little bit of cologne on his neck and sprayed his shirt. His brown feet showed through his sandals. He turned on his small radio and put the wine on ice. He looked around at the fresh flowers he had picked from the garden. He felt nervous. Jittery, like a first date. He sat on the couch and tried to relax as he watched the long drive from Sela's house to his. He could see a car coming up the drive, but it wasn't hers. Lily pulled around to the back of the house and drove into the carport. Once inside, Sela rose up from the back seat and got out.

"Thank goodness. I thought Lily was coming to let me know you had changed your mind."

"Nothing could have changed my mind. I just didn't want anyone to see me driving up here. Thanks, Lily."

"Do I need to come back and get you later?"

"No thanks. I'll figure it out. Oh. Will you pop the trunk?" She turned to Jake. "I have a surprise for you. Come see."

Jake walked around to the trunk. There was a stereo system much like the one she had seen at his apartment in San Francisco. "The other speaker is in the back seat."

"I can't believe you did that."

"I knew you loved your music. I saw all those cd' s you had. Charlee told me how you loved music, so I figured you were missing it."

"Oh, wow. This is great. I was missing it more than you know."

Jake unloaded it and they waved goodbye to Lily.

"It smells great in here. What are you cooking?"

"I hope you like baked potatoes and steak."

"Of course, I do."

"I'll put the steaks on the grill when you're ready. That's the potatoes in the oven you smell. I've got some salad ready, too." He had worked for an hour on the salad. She felt his awkwardness.

"It's good to be alone with you." She wrapped her arms around his waist. He held her close. "It's good to be alone with you. I've been waiting for this since I got here." She kissed him before he had time to respond.

"You are all I think about anymore. It's like everything revolves around thoughts of you. I wonder what you are doing. What you are eating. Who you are seeing. I know it sounds crazy."

"It doesn't sound crazy." Sela led him to the couch. "It doesn't sound crazy, because when I'm on the phone with Matt, I wish it were you. When it's dark, I wish you were lying beside me watching a movie. When it's morning, I wish I was drinking coffee with you. I've never felt like this before in my life."

Jake thought quickly to the one person he had been in love with. She had been killed in a car crash his freshmen year of college. The pain was there, but it was far away. The love they had shared was distant. He couldn't remember ever feeling the way he felt for Sela. He loved everything about her. It was her strength. The way her voice was soft and caressing. It was her love for people. Her generosity. Her attention to every detail of life. The way her body moved and her hair fell against her face. Her quest for spiritual purity and holiness. Her desire to be a virtuous woman. The way she said his name. He was, indeed, in love with this woman.

The steaks were grilled, and the conversation carried until

very late. The dishes were done, and they retired to the living room.

"I wish I had my stereo set up." The music from the small clock radio could be heard from the other room.

"Any word from Ted?"

"I can't believe I didn't tell you this. He called yesterday and said they had a match for both Matt's and Beth's hair."

"Well, I have some other news. I was waiting to tell you. I didn't want to say anything to spoil our evening, so I didn't want to bring up Matt. Ted called just a few hours before you got here. He said he has something important to tell you. He said to call him as soon as possible."

"I'll call him now. Can I use your phone?" She knew the answer.

"Sure, it's right here." He handed her a cordless phone and she dialed the number.

"Ted?" Her voice was enthusiastic.

"Hey, Sela. I have some news for you. It seems bugging Matt's place has paid off. Last night after you left, Matt phoned Beth. He told her he had news of a match of some sort. He didn't know what that meant. You are being watched and your phone is tapped as well, unless you told him of the match."

"No. I haven't told him anything."

"That's not all. He told Beth to hang on. That the wedding was just around the corner. He told her about you signing the will yesterday. As far as he knows, everything is going exactly the way he wants it. Where are you now?"

"I'm at Jake's. But don't worry, no one saw me. And if I'm being watched, it's someone outside the gates. No one knows I'm here."

"Be extra careful. We aren't sure who we can trust right now.

144

One thing is certain. He is in a hurry. His patience has run out and so has his lover's. I believe he plans to kill you on the honeymoon. They talked about the honeymoon plans and he said he hoped you were in excellent shape because you would be going for a long swim. That's why he doesn't want any cooks or anyone else going with you. I'm going tomorrow to have the entire yacht rigged with wires. He won't be able to make a move without me hearing it. I'll be following close behind. At the first sign of anything suspicious, I'll be there."

"This is really scaring me. This is my life we're talking about. What if you aren't able to get there in time? Is all this worth it? There's still time to call off the wedding and just play it safe. I don't want to lose my life in the process of trying to find Charlee's killer. She wouldn't want that, either."

"Ultimately it's your decision. If you want to call the whole thing off and keep it simple, you can do that. But if you want to take a chance and get the people that murdered your sister, then we can do that, too."

"Let me talk to Jake and I'll call you back."

"Okay. Think about it."

Sela hung up the phone. She repeated to Jake everything that Ted had said.

"I don't think Ted is willing to lose you anymore than I am. He's a professional investigator. He'll be able to detect any sign of you needing backup. Then you can testify to attempted murder."

"I'm just really nervous. For the first time in my life, I'm in love with someone. I feel good. You know? Now I am being asked to go through with a marriage to a possible murderer, who may have plans to kill me on my honeymoon. It's just all so overwhelming."

"Why don't I go with you? There's got to be somewhere I could hide where he would never think to look. Is there?"

"Actually, there is! There's this area at the bottom of the boat that was built for me and Charlee. It's got everything you need down there. There are even windows so that you can see the fish swim by."

"The idea of you sailing off with that creep and leaving me behind was really getting to me. This way, I'll be with you all the time. I'll have it set up to where I can hear Ted and he can hear me. This will be perfect!"

"Then let's do it then."

She called Ted and told him the plan. He thought it was a wonderful one. He was sorry he had not thought of going along on the boat.

When Sela woke up, she felt like she had been in a dream. The night had been so perfect. Her new outfit lay crumpled on the floor as a reminder that it wasn't a dream. She thought about every minute of her time with Jake. She remembered kissing him in the moonlight before mounting her horse and galloping back to the mansion in her new dress. She rolled over and looked at her message light. Matt had called twice already this morning and she had not answered the phone. She saw the message light blinking. She dialed his number at work.

"Hey, Matt. I'm just waking up." She yawned into the phone.

"I hear that. I wanted to ask you something. I talked to the preacher this morning. He's willing to marry us Saturday if we want. We could get the marriage license today, and the blood test, too. What do you say?"

"What about all my plans? What about our friends and family?" She needed to put up a little bit of a fight. The truth was, the quicker she could get it over with the better. She didn't want to involve her friends in the charade. "They will be disappointed if I don't have a wedding."

"They won't even be thinking about this next month. They will be onto something else. Let's do it, Sela. I've finished up with some big clients, I'm feeling good, and I'm ready for a trip."

A trip to jail, she hoped.

"Then let's do it. I'm going for a swim first. I'll be down to meet you in about two hours."

"You got it. I'll be waiting." The palms of his hands itched with excitement.

Sela hoped Ted had heard the news. If not, she would need to inform him immediately. Jake would need to get his things together for the trip, as well. There was a lot to be done in the next few days.

Chapter Ten

Lily sat at her desk, calling every guest on the list to let them know the wedding had been rescheduled. She informed them that there would be no big ceremony, only the preacher and a few witnesses.

Matt sat at his desk making out his wish list in his head. He called Beth.

"Hey. Are you busy?"

"Not really. Just watching the news."

"Looking for your picture?"

"Not funny. What's going on?"

"Sela agreed to marry me tomorrow. The preacher will meet us at the ranch. We'll do a short ceremony in the garden, and then we are off on the honeymoon."

"You're kidding me."

"Nope. I'm not. She didn't seem too worried about the change of plans. She was a little sad about having a wedding, anyway. Her dad not being around to give her away, and no living family members to see her get married sort of had her down. I think she's actually relieved not to have to entertain all those guests."

"Maybe. I guess this is it, then."

"Yeah. I wanted to make sure everything is set. You know where to meet me, right?"

"Yes. Do you have your passport in a safe place?"

"It's in my safe deposit box. Give me at least several weeks from Saturday. I'll have the money by then. We'll be free at last, free at last." He did his best Martin Luther King, Jr. impersonation.

"You know exactly what you're doing, right?"

So far, Matt had not been directly involved in the murders. He was nervous, but he knew what had to be done.

"I know what to do. I have to admit that I'm nervous about this. But I know what has to be done."

"It'll be simple. Swimming accidents happen all the time. Just keep that in mind. She just needs a little help into the water."

"All right. This is it, then. I don't know when I'll get a chance to talk to you again. I have a lot to do today. If I don't talk to you for a while, don't be worried. Just stick to the plan."

"Gotcha."

"I love you, Beth."

"I love you, Matt. Be careful."

"As always."

Jake packed his bags and hopped into the Dodge Ram he had been given to drive while working on the ranch. He was meeting Ted at 1:00 p.m. at the harbor. He would first need to stop by the grocery store and stock up for his trip. He had no idea how long he would be traveling. He drove past security and onto the main road. Ruez watched as he left. He recognized the man from California that Sela had purchased the new car for. He pulled out slowly and followed him from far behind. He picked up his phone.

"Bossman." His Spanish accent rang unexpectedly in Matt's ear.

"What is it?"

"Remember the guy from San Francisco?"

"Yes, what about him?"

"He just pulled out of the driveway."

"Out of whose driveway?"

"Whose driveway do you think?"

"Sela's?" He was puzzled.

"Yes, that driveway. I'm following him now. He's driving a black Dodge Ram pickup truck."

"Don't let him out of your sight. Find out what he's doing here. Find out why he was coming from the ranch."

"I'm already on top of that."

Matt stared out the window. This was odd. Why was Jake at the ranch? There had been no signs of him. Sela had not mentioned him being there. What business could he possibly have there? Ruez would find out. It didn't really matter now. He would be married in less than twenty-four hours and no one could stop that. He had seen the will with his own two eyes. He felt empowered.

Ruez watched as Jake entered Winn Dixie. After less than an hour ,he emerged with a load of groceries. He then went to Dollar General and came out with several bags. Ruez watched from a distance. He followed him to the harbor. It would be difficult for Ruez to enter the harbor area without drawing attention to himself. He would need an excuse since it was a private area. Jake showed a pass at the gate and drove through easily. Ruez stopped at the end of the road and drove down a long hill. There were woods all around. He would have to park his car and make his way through the woods in order to see what was going on. He didn't have time to waste. He drove quickly alongside the harbor and found a public park about a mile away. He was in luck. Through his binoculars, he could see the boats in the distance. He would need to be closer to find Jake. He jogged along the edge of the woods along a path until he could see most of the boats. He saw Jake sitting in his truck. He watched carefully. Another man pulled up beside him and the two got out. They shook hands and stood there talking for a few minutes. The older man led the way to a large yacht parked in one of the spaces at the pier. They greeted someone that worked on the docks and stepped on board. For fifteen minutes, neither man could be seen. Then they emerged. Ruez watched as Jake unloaded the groceries, some luggage, and a few other bags. Ted retrieved a small black satchel from his car and went back to the boat. After about an hour, one man left and the other stayed. Ruez waited patiently for Jake to leave, but he never did. It was getting dark and he had to report to Matt. He called him.

"What's taking so long?"

"You tell me, man. I have been sitting here at the dock, watching the boat for this guy Jake to come out. He's still in there. His truck is sitting here in the parking lot. That other guy, the investigator, he met him here and they're up to something."

"That's it? They're up to something? I'm paying you to tell me that they're up to something?"

"Correction, Bossman. You are not paying me. So far, you owe me a lot of money. So watch the attitude. I'm still waiting on my money. Yes. They are up to something. I can't get past the guard at the front. What do you want me to do?"

"Just keep watching. I have a plan. If Sela knows something she is not telling me, I know how to find out. If he leaves, you go whack him. I don't care how. Just get him out of the picture. Keep watching, though."

Matt called Sela. For some reason, she had decided not to tell him that Jake was in town, and he needed to know why.

"Hey! Are you ready for the big day?"

"Just about. I have a few more things to do before we leave."

"Like what?"

"Like cancel some appointments that I just realized I had forgotten about. And I have to make sure everything on the boat is stocked. I just need to make sure I haven't left something out." Her voice was controlled and emotionless.

"Speaking of the trip, I need to go do some things there myself. I'm gonna run by and get the key if you don't mind?"

"Tonight? It's already so late. Why don't you do it tomorrow." She knew Jake would be down below tomorrow, but she wasn't sure what he was doing as she spoke. Maybe he had decided to enjoy the upper decks tonight. He couldn't be caught there. They were too close to everything. It would cause way too much confusion. She would be asked so many questions.

"I have things to do tomorrow, too. Like get married. I want to get this done tonight. I'll be by in about twenty minutes."

"All right. Come on." She hung up the phone and stepped outside to call Jake on her cell phone.

"Hey. Matt is on his way to the boat. He'll be there in less than an hour. Are you downstairs?"

"Actually, no. But all my stuff is. I was just enjoying this beautiful night. I'll just go ride around for a while. I need some supper anyway. Call me when you've heard from Matt and the coast is clear."

"Okay. That sounds good. Did Ted get the bugs planted?"

"Yep. Matt won't be able to make a move without both of us hearing."

"Okay. Get out of there. Thank you, Jake."

"No thanks needed. I wouldn't have it any other way."

Ruez watched as Jake stepped off the boat.

"Bingo," he said.

He ran back to his car and pulled closer to the edge of the park so that he could see the black pickup leaving. There was only one way back out to the main road. He would have to pass by.

He followed him to a small barbecue restaurant not far from the harbor. He waited until Jake was inside and pulled up beside his truck. Within twenty seconds, he was inside the truck and crouched in the floor of the back seat. Jake would not know what hit him. He couldn't take a chance on anyone interfering with his payday.

Ruez called Matt.

"I'm in Jake's truck. He's at a little barbecue place eating. Don't worry though. He won't be interfering in your wedding plans. I'll take care of him."

"OK. I am at the boat now. No signs so far of anything unusual. I hate to say it, Ruez, but you had better let Jake go. He could have been delivering groceries for Sela. Maybe he decided to enjoy the boat while he was here. Maybe she told him he could spend the night here. He's probably in town for the wedding."

Who knows what he's doing? One thing is certain, though. Sela is not in love with him, or she wouldn't be marrying me. If she knows he was out here, she'll be wondering what happened to him.

"I can't have another death holding up my wedding plans."

"Now you tell me all of that."

"Sorry. I didn't think of it before. Just get out before anyone sees you."

Ruez clicked the phone off. He heard keys jingling in the door. He was a small man. Only about 130 pounds, but he didn't know how long he could go undetected in the floorboard.

Jake slid onto the seat and sniffed. Something smelled funny. There was an unfamiliar stench. He rolled down the window and cranked up the truck. Ruez felt the vibration under him. He froze. He didn't know where he was being taken, but he would have to call someone to bring him back to his car later. All he could do was hope he could get out of the truck before he was spotted. If he was spotted, he would claim to just need a ride.

Matt looked all over the boat. He had suspected there would be security measures, and he was right. Microphones and bugs had been strategically placed throughout the yacht. He couldn't help but wonder if Jake had been the one to do it. What was he doing on the boat? And why had Sela neglected to tell him that he was in town. "Maybe she thought I would be jealous. Or maybe he asked her for a job. Who cares? He probably thought he could weasel his way into Sela's bed since his ticket with Charlee didn't work out. Too late, sucker." His words seemed to echo through the silent yacht. He placed the wine in the icebox and put his guitar in the bedroom downstairs. Sela was always trying to get him to play for her. He had written a song for Beth that he planned to sing to her later, but he would try it out on Sela first.

Jake could feel the presence of someone near him. As he was looking for his phone, he spotted the hip of someone lying in the back. He picked up his phone and called Ted.

"Hey, man. Are you busy?"

Ted noticed the sound of voice was somewhat altered. He had a bit of a country accent.

"Jake?"

"Yeah. It's me all right. I've got the stuff you wanted. I'll be there in about five minutes."

Ted didn't have a clue what he was talking about. Jake was supposed to be hunkered down below, on the Little Princess.

Ruez listened in the back seat. He would have to get out when he stopped.

"Are you all right, man?" Ted knew from experience that something was going on.

"No way." He continued with his southern drawl.

"Do I need to meet you somewhere? At the boat."

"No. I don't mind bringing it. I'll be right there. I'm five minutes away."

"Are you in some kind of trouble?"

"Possibly."

"Is someone with you?"

"Yeah."

"Are you driving?"

"Yeah."

"Okay. I'll be looking for you. I'm at the hotel."

"See ya later then."

Jake sang along with Faith Hill while reaching into the side of the door to retrieve a Colt .45. He held it cocked and ready, should the passenger make a move of any sort. He pulled into the hotel parking lot, up to Ted's door. He was watching from the window. Jake put the car in park and turned off the ignition. He turned around in his seat and held the gun to the man's back.

"There's a gun in your back. Raise up nice and slow. Let me see your hands."

Ruez considered himself a professional. He had spent many years doing all kinds of jobs. If Matt had not interfered, everything would have been fine. He pretended not to speak English. This was his first big mistake.

"What are you doing in my truck?"

"No English. No English." He began to mutter a bunch of jumbled words, none of which Jake understood. Ted saw Jake in the parking lot from his hotel room window and moved quickly to see what was going on. He saw the figure in the back seat and the gun pointing in his face.

"What's going on?"

"I don't know. This guy was in my back seat when I left the barbecue place."

"What were you doing there?"

"Eating. I'll tell you why later. Do you speak Spanish?"

"A little."

"Ask him what he is doing?"

Ted asked him.

"He said he was hiding from some creeps he owes money to. He said they were chasing him, and he saw your truck was unlocked and he jumped in. Said he meant no harm and was scared. I don't believe him. What's that?"

Ted pointed to something in the floor. He couldn't see it completely.

"It's a cell phone. Get it."

Ruez felt his insides shaking. He could not let them get his cell phone. He began babbling irrationally.

"What's he saying?"

"Says he needs to make a phone call. His wife may not be safe. He needs to warn her that those guys are looking for him and that he is okay."

Ruez knew he needed to punch in a number in order to remove the last number he called, which was Matt's.

"Not so fast, big boy." Ted looked at the cell phone. He pressed the redial button. Matt was instantly on the phone.

"Yeah."

"Who am I speaking with?"

"Who do you want to speak with and who did you call?"

Ted recognized his voice.

"Is this Matt?"

"Yeah. Who's this?"

Ted hung up the phone and grabbed the man by the arm and slid him over. He pulled out his own pistol and shoved it into Ruez's side.

"You little shit. You piece of shit jerk. Whatever you were up to is over. Let's go, Jake."

"Where to?"

"Someplace where a man can scream, and nobody can hear him." Ted's voice was gruff and full of anger.

"Someone is about to talk, or experience extensive pain."

He looked at Ruez. His body looked small and fragile all of a sudden. Years of sneaking around, plotting to kill, mugging innocent people, and spying, suddenly seemed nonproductive. He didn't know what Ted had in mind, but it was certainly intended to make him talk.

It was almost eleven when Jake stopped driving. Sitting in the middle of an open range with miles and miles of desert, there was no one in sight anywhere. He had pulled way off the road, and with his headlight off, no one could see the truck or the three men hiding on the other side. Ted pushed in the cigarette lighter. Ruez made a feeble attempt to escape the big man's grasp. He was no match. Jake retrieved some gray masking tape form the toolbox and taped the man's wrists together. He then taped his ankles. They pulled him from the truck and placed him facedown on the ground.

"Now, let's start with the basics. We already know that you're somehow involved with Matt. Correct?"

157

"No English." Ted pulled the cigarette lighter from the dash and placed it against Ruez's neck. The skin sizzled and Ruez screamed out in pain. His body jerked and the smell of burning flesh permeated Jake's nose. He had not expected this, and was not prepared mentally. He turned his face away.

"You work for Matt?" His voice was firm and loud.

"Yes!"

"Why are you spying on Sela?"

"I don't know." Again, Ted pulled the cigarette lighter from the truck.

"Wait!" Ruez had to say something, but he could not risk his portion of the money. "He wanted me to spy to make sure she wasn't cheating on him. He said she had met a guy in San Francisco, and he thought she was attracted to him. He was jealous when she went out there and asked me to follow. He was even more upset when she bought him the new car." It sounded reasonable.

"So what were you doing in my truck?"

Ruez was stumped. He didn't really have a good reason for being there.

"Talk quick."

He couldn't think of an excuse. "I was just spying on you that's all. Just trying to hear if you were talking to Sela. I wanted to…"

"That's a lie. Matt is up to no good. He wants to kill Sela and take her money for himself, and you are in on it."

"I don't know anything about that. I don't know anything except what I was told to do. He paid me five hundred dollars to spy. That's all I know. Please!" He was scared. He had spent all these years without so much as a trace of a loose end. Now he was being forced to either talk or be burned with a cigarette lighter. He felt a lot braver in the shadows. The burnt skin on his neck ached.

"I have plans for you unless you tell me everything you know about Matt." Ted kicked him in the stomach and his breath was forced out as he fell lifelessly to the ground.

"You've got twenty seconds to start talking. That's long enough for you to get your breath back."

"I dunno know what Matt has planned. I was only hired to spy on her. That's all. I dunno any other details." It was partly the truth. He really didn't know how the murder was planned. He had never asked. He planned the others, but not this one. And look where it got him. Facedown in the sand with a scar on his neck and the breath knocked out of him. Matt would pay dearly for this.

"Do you believe him?" Jake asked.

"No, but that's neither here nor there. We've got other more pressing issues right now. Let's go get my car. We'll put him in the truck and take him to the ranch. We'll put him in the cellar and keep him there until we decide to let him go. I'm gonna run a check and see if he is here legally. We may deport him when we're done."

Ruez knew that he would be sent back to Mexico without his $50,000 from Matt. This was turning into an ugly situation.

Matt drove home, and waited for a call from Ruez. No word came.

Ted taped Ruez's mouth shut and stuffed him back into the floor of the back seat. At the hotel, Ted got his car and followed Jake to a remote church parking lot. At the back of the church, Ted popped his trunk and the body was quickly placed inside. With arms and legs taped together, it would be impossible for

Ruez to alert anyone as to where he was. Ted drove him to the ranch and was easily waved past security. Lily met Ted at the side door.

"Is something wrong?" It was late, and Lily knew Ted would never show up unannounced. Is Sela okay? I haven't checked to see if she's in."

"She's fine. I have someone in my trunk who we caught spying on Sela. He was in Jake's truck when we caught him. We aren't quite sure what his role is. He says he doesn't know anything. I am going to see about that. I sent Jake back to the boat. I know Charles has a pretty big cellar. I want to keep this thug in it until we get to the bottom of who he is and what he's really doing."

"Sure. Whatever you need."

Ted opened the truck and picked up the small man as if he were a piece of luggage.

"Do me a favor, Lily. Don't tell Sela. She has enough to worry about without this. The last thing she needs on her mind is knowing that a stranger is tied up in her cellar."

"You got it. Right this way, gentlemen."

Ted placed him on the cold, hard floor. He checked his wrists and ankles. There would be no way of getting out of there. The room was dark. There were no windows.

Ted climbed the long staircase back to the main floor and locked the door behind him.

"Is there a security system that monitors that room?"

"Oh, yes. In my office, there are thirteen monitors. We have cameras all over this place. All I need to do is flip a button to see him."

"Can you show me?"

"Sure." Lily walked him to her office. Inside was a panel of

TV's covering one entire wall.

"I never knew this place was covered with cameras like this."

"Yep. Charles never took security for granted. There he is." She pointed to the TV with the image of Ruez in a ball on the floor.

"He's not going anywhere for a while. Do you have someone trustworthy enough to watch him without reporting us?"

"Of course."

"Good. Let him be in charge of giving him a bathroom break and feeding him just enough to survive on. Make sure he is handcuffed at all times. Most of all, make sure no one sees or hears him down there. I don't know how long I'll be gone, but I've got to stay close to Sela. This guy is probably just a lookout man. I almost believe his story. I just don't know what he was doing in the cab of Jake's truck. Maybe he really is as dumb as he says, and just wanted to hear what Jake was saying on his cell phone. Anyway, keeping him out of the way may force Matt to make some changes that will give himself away. I sure hope this is all over soon."

Lily noticed that he didn't sound as confident as he had in the past.

"I'm praying hard for all of you. Just stay close, like you said. Something tells me that he's planning to do something to her on the boat. He was so insistent on no one coming along."

"I agree. That's exactly what we think. I better get going. Can you handle everything here?" She knew he meant the prisoner.

"Yes. I'm going to call Mr. Phelps now, and tell him I need him to come on down." Mr. Phelps had been her head of security for ten years. A tall, black man in his early forties who was

161

recently divorced and had two teenage daughters. He loved his job at the ranch and loved the Barnes family. Charles had given both of Mr. Phelps' daughters a scholarship. He was a devoted employee and loyal friend. Lily had always been attracted to him from the first day he started working there, but he had been married and they had never so much as engaged in a flirty conversation. Now she relished the idea of him having to spend many hours in her office.

"All right then, Lily. Here's my cell number." He handed her his card. "Call me and let me know what's going on."

"Of course. Thank you, Ted."

Lily called Mr. Anthony Phelps. His nickname was Pony, but as his boss, she'd never used it before. They'd had very little interaction. Pony was on his own to take care of things as he saw fit.

"Hey, Anthony. It's Lily. Listen. I know it's late, but I really need you to come down to the house. I have a very important project I need you on."

Pony looked at his clock. He had been in bed for three hours already. This was highly unusual, but he did not question it.

"Okay, Lily. I'll be right there. He slipped on his clothes and drove down the hill to the house. Lily met him at the door.

"Hey. Come on in." She led him to her office. He followed her silently. In all his years of working there, he had never been asked to come to the house for a project. His curiosity was killing him.

"Have a seat." She pointed at one of the leather chairs against the wall. He sat without losing eye contact.

"What's going on?"

"This." She pointed to the screen.

"What? Who is that?"

"That is our prisoner for now. He was just brought in by Ted. You may remember Ted. Mr. Charles had him over quite often."

"Yes, I do. Big, burly man."

"Well, this is a long story, but I feel that you deserve to know if you are going to be caring for a prisoner in the cellar. It involves Sela and her marriage to Matt. This is all top-secret stuff." Lily's voice was barely above a whisper.

"You can trust me, and you know it."

"I know. That's why I called you." She loved the way his eyes were concentrating so hard on everything she was saying. She loved the way he hung on her every word. Even if it was just because it was the most excitement he had experienced on the job, in all of his five years working there. She began to explain about Matt and his lover. And about the two hair matches. Pony shook his head in disbelief as the plot thickened.

"Sela is getting married tomorrow. All we can do is pray that Ted and Jake are able to catch Matt before it is too late." Lily was tired. Tired of being the strong one. She was always the one masking her own feelings in order to keep everyone going in the right direction. The truth was, she herself needed a good shoulder to cry on. She held back her tears.

"I'm glad you called me."

Lily stared at the floor. She didn't want him to see the weakness that she felt.

"Lily. It's going to be okay." He didn't know if it was or not. He just knew it was the right thing to say. He stood up and placed his hand on her shoulder. "It's going to be okay, girl." It was the first time that he had ever touched his boss. It felt good to be there for her.

Lily felt a tear roll down her cheek.

"Yeah. It is, Anthony. Thanks." She took a deep breath.

"Why don't you just call me Pony like everybody else does."

"If you don't mind."

"I'd love it."

"What do you need to be comfortable in here?"

He looked around at the huge office. There was already every accommodation he could think of in front of him.

"I can't think of a thing."

"If you get tired, take a nap on that sofa. That guy's not going anywhere. Your big job will be tomorrow when you have to take him to the bathroom and feed him. There are some linens in that closet if you need them."

"Thanks."

Lily's room was six doors down. She walked slowly down the hall.

"Hey, Lily?"

"Yes."

"I could use something."

"What's that?"

"Some company for a little while. That is, if you don't have plans just now."

Lily smiled as she walked back to her office. "I don't have any plans. I was just going to go to my room and worry a while. I guess I could use some company, too. Do you want me to make us some coffee?"

"Sounds good."

"I'll be right back."

Lily looked forward to getting to know the man she had only viewed from a distance for so long.

Jake took his place below deck back at the boat. Ted finished his last-minute packing and boarded his own boat just eight piers down from the Little Princess. Sela could not sleep. She tossed and turned as she thought about the preacher pronouncing her Mrs. Matthew Kinsley.

Matt slept like a baby.

Chapter Eleven

Sela and Matt stood before the preacher in the middle of the formal garden near the ranch lake. There were only two witnesses, Lily and a friend of Matt's. Pastor Seymour had been the one to dedicate Sela when she was a baby, and had also preached at both her parent's funerals. He had counseled the family many times over the years, and now he stood ready to perform what should have been a joyous ceremony for Sela. He had been informed that it was only a mock wedding. He was given no details. He signed an agreement not to leak a word to anyone at the risk of causing Sela severe danger and possible death. He did not understand, but agreed just the same. Not even Matt was to know that he was not actually getting married on this day.

"I now pronounce you Mr. and Mrs. Matthew Kinsley."

Sela heard the words, but they meant nothing to her.

"You may now kiss your bride, Mr. Kinsley."

Matt turned to Sela and gave her a heartfelt kiss. Sela responded and smiled. She turned immediately and looked at Lily. "This is it." She took a deep breath and exhaled heavily. Lily knew what she meant.

"Congratulations, dear." Lily hugged her tightly and could feel her body trembling against her own.

"Thank you, Lily."

"I'm praying for you," she whispered in her ear.

"I love you. I'll see you in a few weeks, okay?"

Matt patted Lily's back. "Don't worry. I'll take good care of your baby girl from here on out."

"If you don't, you'll have me to deal with. Do you understand?"

"I understand." They both smiled. He put his arm around Sela's around the waist and guided her toward the house. "This is it ,my dear wife. The day I have so longed and waited for."

"Thank you for being so patient with me."

"I had no choice. You were the only woman for me, so I had to wait. It was worth it. Believe me."

The luggage had already been taken to the boat. Sela and Matt waved from the window of the limousine as they slowly wound down the long drive. Lily stood on the porch and watched. She wondered if this would be the last time she would ever see Sela's smiling face. She could not even bear to think such a thing. With Jake on board and Ted listening to every move, she fervently hoped that Sela was in good hands.

She went inside and poured herself a tall glass of iced tea. She walked into her office and looked at the monitor. Ruez still sat bound up in the same little knot with his feet and hands tied. His mouth was still covered with the silver masking tape. Tony slumped over in a recliner, fast asleep. She watched him for a moment. He had been awake most of the night. She had enjoyed their conversation and was not surprised to find that after they had opened up to each other about many things, she was all the more attracted to him. She smiled as she closed the door and let him sleep. Ruez wasn't going anywhere.

Sela and Matt boarded the yacht with little attention from anyone nearby. He was glad of that. There would be plenty of time for attention later. The last thing he needed was for someone to find out about the marriage and follow them in order to get pictures or some news for the local tabloid. Together they walked around the yacht admiring the flowers and gifts that Lily and some of the others had arranged. It was beautiful. It was full of life just the way it had been when her whole family had been there. Lily had always made sure there were fresh flowers on board when her mother sailed. Now the fresh flowers were a reminder of life and of the love Lily was sending with her.

"Are you ready?" Matt was more than anxious to set sail.

"I sure am. Let's go."

The anchor was lifted, and the ropes were untied, allowing the boat's freedom. Matt could hear his pulse above the sound of the engine cranking. It beat loudly in his ears. His blood pumped like never before. This had been way too easy. Now here he was setting sail with the richest girl in Texas who just happened to be his wife. He had never felt more exhilarated in all of his life. Not a drug on earth had ever made him feel the way he felt at that moment.

"Do you realize we can go wherever we want to go, do whatever we want to do, and not worry about anything for the next few weeks? Just me and you, together." Sela was trying her best to sound excited to be on her honeymoon. Jake listened from down below. Ted listened from the other end of the dock.

"Yep. Just you and me, baby. I have a map right here. Which direction first?" Matt opened the map out on the table and they both appeared interested. The truth was that neither of them cared.

"Why don't you pick and surprise me?" Sela wanted to make everything easy for Matt. Whatever he had up his sleeve, she didn't want to hinder his plan.

"That sounds good." He kissed her on the cheek.

"I am going to change and get something to eat. I'm starved. Are you hungry?"

"Nope. I ate before I got to your house." He was too excited to eat.

Sela put on her bathing suit and a wrap, and retrieved a bowl of shrimp dip and crackers from the refrigerator. She went to the upper deck. At the bar, she made herself an alcohol-free pina colada and settled into a large lounge chair. She could not afford to have alcohol in her system. She had to be one hundred percent alert.

Matt could see her on the monitors. She looked beautiful. Her skin was already golden brown from hours of swimming. Her muscles were firm, and her dark brown hair was piled loosely on top of her head. She slathered herself in oil and slipped on her sunglasses. He had grown fond of her over the years. She was a good person. He wished it had not come to this. He tried to remember back to a time when his mind did not crave wealth and power. He tried to think about the days when he was honest and true love was important to him. He was bitter and unable to think back to a time when he felt loved completely. His father had left him when he was eight, and his mother remarried shortly after his ninth birthday. His stepfather spent years molesting him and threatening to kill his mother if he told. He remembered the last time he saw his mom. After mustering up enough courage to tell his mom about what his stepfather had been doing to him, she refused to believe him and called him a lying little thief. She accused him of taking money out of her purse and trying his best to wreck her marriage. He knew his stepdad had been stealing from her to support his drug habit. That, too, was something he was never supposed to tell. After running away from home several times, his mother sent him to live with foster parents, and by his eighteenth birthday he had been in three different homes. It had been a difficult life, but one he managed to live without anyone finding out the gruesome details of his stepfather. Most people believed his mom ran out on him just like his dad. How ironic that the Barneses had been helping kids without parents, but they never offered to help him. He wondered if somewhere deep inside he might have wanted revenge on those people who said they were helping kids, while letting so many right in front of their noses slip through the cracks.

His good looks and charm kept him on top. Beth didn't care about his lack of family. She loved him and was ready to go to any extreme to be with him. She was the closest thing to love he could remember. Even though her love seemed twisted and unnatural, it was the only love he knew.

Somewhere deep in his heart he believed he could have loved Sela if she had only tried harder to love him. He had grown weary of waiting and wishing. If she had loved him, she would have married him years ago. For Sela, marriage to him was only a means of securing a certain stability that she was lacking now that her own family was gone. He knew that now. He could feel it in her touch. She didn't love him. It didn't matter now. There were no other choices.

He watched her lying so still. How easy it would have been to place the rag over her face. He was nearly twice her size. She would have been out in seconds. It would be harder now that he had discovered the ship was bugged. There could be no signs of a struggle. There were no video cameras anywhere. He had made sure of that. He didn't care if Ted listened to them. That would make his plan even more believable.

He was almost glad the ship had been bugged, for two reasons. They were obviously suspicious of him and this affirmed it. Thanks to them, the microphones would be his ticket to freedom. As long as there was nothing incriminating on them, they had nothing to pin on him.

He had found all the microphone chips last night while searching the boat for anything suspicious. The black briefcase Ruez had reported was the first alert. He had not even thought of Ruez until now. It was late the last time he had talked to him, but it wasn't like him not to check in. What was Jake doing here? That still bothered him. It didn't matter now anyway.

Sela slept. Two hours had passed before she felt a hand on her shoulder. She was startled.

"I'm sorry. I didn't mean to scare you. I've been watching you sleep. You look so beautiful." He squatted beside her and rubbed her arm with the back of his hand. Her skin was soft and smelled like coconut.

"Pull up a chair."

Matt dragged a chair from the other side of the deck.

"Matt, I want to be honest with you about something." She took a deep breath. "I believe in honesty. You know that."

He nodded.

"I haven't been completely honest with you about some things."

"Like what?" Whatever it was he knew it would in no way compare to the lies he had told.

"I want to start from the beginning. When I went back to San Francisco a few weeks ago and met Jake, he was falling apart. I invited him to come back and work for me at the ranch. I bought him a car and offered him a job in one of the homes. He was thrilled with the idea, and he has been working there for the past few weeks."

Matt stared in bewilderment at the goodness of this person

171

in front of him. "Why didn't you tell me earlier?"

"I knew you were jealous of him. I knew that from the beginning. I didn't want to put a strain on us right now."

"I understand. I would have understood if you had told me earlier."

"That's not all. I was told not to talk about the case with anyone."

"Not even me?"

"Yes. But there are some things I think you should know." She was hoping to push him to desperation. Ted had told her it might push him over the edge. "We found a hair at the crime scene. They also found a hair at the hotel where the suspect was staying. Charlee received a call from someone, it was traced to the room where she stayed, and the hair matched."

That explained why Ted had said they have a match. But he remembered him saying they had two matches. What did that mean?

"So now all they have to do is find the person that the hair belongs to, right? But that could take forever."

"Or maybe never. I wanted it to be known that my sister did not kill herself, but I cannot drive myself crazy looking for the killer. I will leave that up to the experts and get on with my life. A life that is really just beginning today." She leaned over and kissed Matt on the mouth. Her lips parted and she felt his tongue. She stopped.

She realized that he would now be expecting her to make love to him. Tonight. Or today. He had waited long enough.

"Now, I want to be honest with you about something. Please understand that I never meant to lie to you. I did get Beth pregnant. She kept her baby, my son. I knew that. I support them and I always have. Sometimes when I told you I had a business trip scheduled I was really going to see my son. It has been so hard keeping it from you. I made a bad decision and I know that now, but I didn't want to leave college and end up being a nobody like the rest of my family. So I stayed here in Texas. I visited every chance I could, but Beth was angry with me for not moving there. I knew I had to tell you at some point. After college I had every intention of moving to Atlanta to be with both of them, but then I fell in love with you. I was so afraid that if I told you I had a baby with Beth you would think our relationship was doomed from the beginning. I was determined to keep it a secret."

Sela stared in bewilderment. Her heart sank. If this was true, then it was possible he had nothing to do with the murders. Maybe he was just visiting his son in Atlanta that weekend she had seen him. Maybe this wedding and this whole plan was a failure. She would be faced with a whole new problem. One that involved being married to the wrong person. Beth could have easily done all of it on her own. He could have bugged the phones out of jealousy.

"So that is why Beth was so angry when I was there."

"Yes, because she hates you. If you had not stepped into my life, I would be in Atlanta with them right now. I didn't love her any more, Sela. I loved you. Love will make you do some really crazy things. I have lied to you. I wanted to tell you earlier. Honest, I did. But I just couldn't. Yes, there have been times when I would say I was going on a trip to meet a client and I would go meet my son, but is that really so wrong? I guess you wondered why I have been driving the same car for four years if I had so many successful clients I was meeting."

"It did cross my mind. I don't know what to say. I don't even know how I feel. You are right, though. I would not have gotten involved with you had I known you and Beth had a child together

173

and continued to be in touch."

"Please understand. I have loved you so much and this has been the hardest thing in the world for me. I have wanted to share it with you. You. My wife. There have been so many wonderful times I've had with my son. But I was so afraid of losing the woman I love. Please tell me you understand. In the beginning, I didn't think it was your business. You had no reason to know. Then, after we became seriously involved, it was too late. Nothing will change, Sela. I love my son and hope you will want to be a part of his life when we get back from our honeymoon. I want him to be a part of both of our lives." He knew her goodness would never turn anyone away. Her deep-rooted sense of forgiveness would pardon him of all iniquity. He knew that already.

"Well, this is the other part of it. He lives with foster parents. As you could plainly see, Beth is in no shape to take care of our son. She is clearly a little insane. She doesn't work and I have had to support her in many ways over the years, as well as support my son."

"He lives with foster parents and I have a ranch for children just a few miles from your house? That doesn't make sense."

I couldn't take him too far away from Beth. She is so fragile and confused. I'm so sorry, Sela. This is complicated, I know. I only wanted the best for my son and his mother. At the same time, I did not want to lose the love of my life. I have been so afraid and dishonest about all of this, I know."

The more he talked, the more he felt himself pinning the idea of a raving lunatic on Beth. He felt greed taking over and fear stepping in. What if he wasn't able to kill Sela and Beth cracked?

Sela didn't know what to say. This was a bit more than the truth; it was a grim realization that she was about to become involved in a triangle with the woman who killed her sister, and she could be responsible for putting to death the mother of her husband's child!

"Is there anything else I should know?" Her words were soft and unassuming, even though her thoughts were charging through her brain like wild animals,

"That I love you." There were times like these that Matt loved Sela in a special way. There was a bond between people when they were being honest with each other, only he could not differentiate between honesty and a lie. He had crossed the line too many times. He had battled his mind for so many years, and in the end, did not know where reality stopped and truth began.

Sela tried hard to read his mind and body language. It was no use. Everything about him said he loved her and that she had been wrong all this time. She wondered if Ted had heard their conversation. Matt knew he was being recorded. He knew that at this very moment that they would be checking to see if he had a son in Atlanta, and if it was a legitimate alibi. It was. Even if the murder was pinned on Beth, there was nothing to implicate him. As long as he was visiting his son, he had a reason for the calls and the trips. He chuckled inside at his ingenuity. What perfect timing to bring out his secret weapon, and it had not even been planned.

"Everybody makes mistakes. Some bigger than others. I do forgive you ,Matt. Things make more sense now."

Sela felt a release of pressure. Somewhere in her heart she wanted all of this to be true. She rubbed Matt's fingers between her own. He was her family now. Not just her boyfriend or fiancée. She could never tell him it was a mock wedding. That was cruelty way beyond anything she would ever do. She had banked on him trying to kill her. Not this.

Ted listened carefully over the headphones. He wasn't sure what to think. Matt was certainly convincing. Jake listened, too. He wondered what emotions were running through Sela's head at this very moment. If all this was true, and Matt was not involved, did this mean that Sela could possibly remain married to him to avoid a scandalous situation and embarrassment? His heart dropped at the thought of the two of them embracing on the deck above him.

"Can I get you something to drink?" Matt stood up and moved toward the bar.

"Just some iced tea, please. Thanks." She watched the muscles in his back move as he strutted across the deck in white shorts that were a little too tight for his large legs. She had always had an attraction for him. She now sensed his vulnerability and felt sorry for him. He was extremely handsome at this very moment.

She thought about how painful it must be to be away from your child, torn between lives and distance. She wanted to comfort him, but at the same time felt angry and betrayed at the lie he had lived. She had seen him leaving Beth's condo and had made certain assumptions that had led her into a bad situation. A trap that had backfired on her.

She watched Matt's every move. She would sacrifice her love for Jake. It was the only thing to do. She had been mistaken about his involvement with Beth. She would get the preacher to give her an official marriage certificate and that would be the end of it. She would have Beth locked up eventually, and they would take custody of Matthew Junior. Her life would go on as planned and Jake could go back to California. There would be no scandal. There would be no broken promises. She was married until death-do-us-part. How could she be in love with someone she had only known for a few months anyway? She tried to shake the images of Jake from her mind. She remembered the will and how she had written Matt out of it completely. It had been cruel, and she would change it as soon as she got back.

Matt brought her the glass of tea. Let's make a toast. He held his glass in front of him. "To the luckiest man in the whole world. Thank you for trusting in me enough to make me yours." He clinked his glass against hers and drank the cold Pepsi.

"I'm just sorry it took me so long." She was truly sorry.

"There's one more thing I need to tell you. Father always had the boat monitored when we were out for security purposes. There were only certain areas he and mom could go to really be alone, if you know what I mean. I had the boat rigged before we came out." She had two reasons for telling him. One was that she had noticed him looking at a microphone under the edge of the bar. He had even run his fingers across it. She knew he was quite familiar with the bugging processes and how to identify them. She knew that if by some chance he did have plans for her, they would be impossible to carry out if he knew he was being listened to. She had a little plan of her own, anyway.

"You did?"

"I did. There are only a few of them, but should some pirates or crazies try to rob us while we're out, it's nice to know that they're being recorded and videotaped."

Matt smiled. Her honesty was killing him. So no one was suspicious of him after all. This was getting better all the time.

Ted listened in astonishment. What was she up to? Had she actually fallen for his story? He slapped the desk where he sat.

"I'd really like to turn the cameras off and get rid of the microphones. Whaddya ya say?"

"I want to be alone with my wife."

177

He pulled her close and she felt his bare chest on her skin. She felt confused. She could feel her body wanting him, but emotionally she was running a marathon. She was exhausted from the drama. She pulled away slightly.

"I know where the bugs are." She gathered up five of the microphones and placed them in a baggy. She put them in a kitchen drawer. She flipped the main switch that controlled the television monitors. "It's just me and you now."

Ted could still hear her. Jake listened as his own chest rose in an unnatural manner. His breaths were deep and extremely controlled. He was losing the woman he had searched for his whole life.

"That's all of them? You are sure?"

"I'm sure."

They stood at the edge of the deck looking out over the water. The waves splashed against the boat. The water was blue and inviting to Sela. To Matt, it was a murderous call to a long drama that had met the final curtain call. He would not prolong this any longer than he had to. He was a liar and a thief, but he had great respect for Sela. He would not make love to this woman and then kill her. A twisted way of sparing her dignity.

"So where are we headed? Somewhere warm, I hope."

"Definitely. I know how much you are longing to dive into this shark infested water."

"How did you guess?"

"It's all over your face. Give us another day and we will be in warm enough waters for you to swim comfortably. We are headed south is all I can tell you."

She smiled. "Do you feel like doing some fishing?"

"Of course."

Together they gathered their poles and tackle boxes. Fishing was something her father had always been very good at. He had taught her well.

Hours passed as the two of them fished off the stern of the boat in style. They reeled in all sorts of deep-sea fish, but kept none of them. They had enough seafood to last them weeks already. As the sun began to set, they realized for the first time in their relationship, that they had spent many hours talking. It was hard to believe that six hours had passed since they had first sat down to fish. With classic rock seeping through the speakers and the feel of the ocean wind on her face, she was invigorated. The hours seemed like minutes. They had laughed like old school friends. Jake and Ted could hear every word, but couldn't figure out how it was possible.

"Do you think the water is warm enough now?"

"Probably."

"Do you want to go for a swim with me?" Ted could hear her plainly, but he wasn't sure where the microphone was located.

"I don't like to swim in a pool. I definitely will pass on swimming with the sharks. You go. I'll watch."

"I think I will." Sela slipped the large hair clasp from her hair and laid it on table beside her shorts. Ted could hear something rustling. Then he heard a thud. The voices became more distant. He knew Sela was going for a swim. Sela felt safe in the water of all places. It was her second home. She climbed down the stairs to the second deck and dove off a diving board into the blue water. She didn't need the bugged hair clasp right now. She needed to clear her mind. There had been too many surprises in the last hour. She needed to digest them all and focus on her future as Mrs. Kinsley, but right now she needed to relax and enjoy the water.

Jake sat confused and alone. His future with Sela was over.

He could hear her confusion slowly being sorted out as she laughed with Matt and discovered the truth about his relationship with Beth.

Sela swam about fifty yards out and floated on her back. The water wasn't too cold. The calm waves bobbed her up and down gently. Suddenly, she heard the engine crank and watched in shock as the boat began to move away from her. Slowly at first and then at full speed. She watched as it pulled further and further away. With a rising sense of panic, she began to swim quickly in its direction, but her efforts were futile. The boat was moving away from her with increasing speed. Over the microphone, Ted could hear the engine rumbling. He could hear Matt humming. Thank God that Sela had not removed all of the microphones from below deck.

Sela's mouth went dry from fear. Heart racing, she screamed loudly in the desperate hope that one of the microphones would pick up her cries for help. Jake lay still on the down-covered mattress, listening to her fading screams. He knew Sela was in the water. He also knew that the boat was moving. He snatched up his cell phone and rang Ted immediately.

"Do you know where we are?"

"Of course, I do. I have your coordinates here. What's going on?"

"All I know is that I heard Sela say that she was going for a swim. She apparently left her microphone on the boat. The next thing I know, we're moving quickly. We're at full speed now and Sela is still in the water! He's leaving her to drown! Get here as quickly as you can and pick her up! She's stranded out there all alone!"

"I'm about forty minutes away from you right now. I had to keep my distance to avoid suspicion."

"Sela can make it as long as she doesn't get bitten by anything. She's a strong swimmer. She can swim for hours. But please hurry!"

"I'm on my way. Full throttle! I can't wait to see how the little snake plays this part out."

"Right now, just focus on finding Sela and getting her out of that water before it's too late!"

As the boat continued to move at high speed through the water, Matt grabbed his binoculars and scanned the ocean in every direction. He looked at his radar screen. There wasn't another boat around for nearly fifty miles. He hadn't planned on doing it this way, but it was just so easy, he couldn't resist. It was less messy and there would be no signs of a struggle. He put the boat on automatic and walked back up to the deck.

"Be careful, baby, that water looks dangerous! You are much braver than I am." He spoke to the small figure, disappearing far into the distance. Just in case there was a microphone left, he wanted to be on record. "Don't go too far! I can barely see you. Sela, are you okay? Sela! Sela! Where are you?" He continued to frantically call her name, just in case someone was listening.

Chapter Twelve

Sela floated on the surface of the calm ocean. The undulating water moved her body up and down. She could hear the sounds of the sea around her, but she didn't bother to look at anything. Her eyes were closed as she floated on her back. She knew there was nowhere to go. Her only hope was to pray that Jake and Ted would realize she that was not on board when they could no longer hear her over the microphone. Or maybe by some miracle, Jake would realize that the boat had left without her.

Sela knew that she was a strong swimmer. She knew that if she continued to float and not waste her time trying to swim, that she would be able to conserve her energy for as long as she needed to. She also knew that she had a very strong survival instinct. She had been through so much already; she would get through this, too. Adrenaline kept her alert and strong. Her thoughts gave her courage. A sense of peace settled over her. She would make it. She knew deep down that she would be rescued. All she had to do was remain calm and wait. She had no idea how long she had been floating when she suddenly heard a boat in the distance. From the position of the sun, she guessed she must have been in the ocean for at least an hour. As the boat came closer, she could see Ted standing on board, waving and calling to her.

"I'm okay!" She waved back at the boat and began swimming in his direction. She wasn't even tired or winded. She had gotten such an adrenaline rush from the whole scenario that she felt as though she could have swum a mile if she had to. In a very short space of time, she had gone from being in love with Jake and faking a marriage, to believing she was mistaken and thrust into a lifelong commitment with Matt. She had thought plenty while floating alone in the big open space. Matt had left her to die. He had proclaimed his love for her and then left her to die. He was a real psycho. Why had she never seen the signs? Her father had seen something she had not seen. If he had been alive, she was sure it would have never gotten to this point. He would have told her. She would have listened. She felt her family with her. With every stroke she made, she felt renewed strength.

"Here!" Ted threw out a life ring in Sela's direction.

"I'm okay," she repeated. She didn't grab the life ring.

"There's a ladder over here." He pointed to the side of the boat. She swam over and climbed up.

"For someone who's been floating in the water for almost two hours, you don't even look tired."

"It's what I do best remember?" She shook her hair and squeezed the excess water from it. Ted watched in amazement. She didn't seem upset or nervous at all.

"Let's go in here."

Sela followed him to a cool room down below. Neither of them said a word for several moments.

"What took you so long?" She smiled. Ted felt immediately at ease. She had a way of making people feel at ease, even in the most tense situations.

"Girl, you had me scared to death! Did you actually believe all the garbage he was filling your head with?"

"I wanted to." In another way, she wanted it all to be lies because of Jake. "I wanted to believe that he wasn't the monster we thought he was. I saw something in his eyes today that I've never seen. It was a vulnerability that he has never shown. He looked hurt. He was wounded inside, and I don't know why. When he started opening up about his son, I thought that was why he was hurting so bad. I thought for a minute that maybe I was somehow to blame. I was always saying that I was in no way ready for children. Maybe I had forced him to lie. Does he even have a son?"

"I don't know yet. You can't force anyone to lie. That's a choice we make on our own, Sela. Why did you remove the microphones?"

"I saw him looking at two of them. I watched him from under my sunglasses. He was searching for more of them. I was afraid that he knew we were on to him. If he thought we were monitoring him, his plan might have been spoiled. I hid one in my hair clasp. My plans were to keep it on me at all times."

"That makes sense. This was not his initial plan, you know. He had no idea you would go for a swim just now."

"No, but he knew I would eventually, I guess. I never dreamed he would just leave me, though. I figured he would try to poison or drug me and dump me in the water, leaving me for dead. I was watching his every move. He brought me a glass of tea earlier and I just kept putting it to my lips like I was sipping it. I am so relieved it all happened this way." She was shaking as she spoke. Ted held her tightly for a few moments.

"It couldn't have worked out better for us, really. You didn't risk getting poisoned, and he thinks that you're lost at sea. I wonder how long he will go before reporting you missing?"

"I can't wait to see."

"I need to let Jake know I've got you. He was the one that realized you were still in the water after the boat cranked."

Ted called Jake.

"Yeah?" Jake's voice was heavy with worry.

"I've got Sela, and she's completely fine. She was swimming in the ocean like a mermaid when I found her."

"Thank God. Can I speak to her?"

"Sure." Ted handed her the phone.

"Sela. My God, I thought I lost you. Are you okay?"

"I'm fine. Tired, but okay. You were all I was thinking about on that boat. I was so confused." Sela realized she was saying some very personal things in front of Ted and blushed. Respectfully, Ted left the room to allow her some privacy. He had known they were attracted to each other from the beginning. Sela lit up like a schoolgirl when Jake was around.

"Those moments when I thought we had made a mistake about Matt were the longest minutes of my life. I thought I was going to stay married to Matt and lose you." The reality of what was happening hit her and she began to cry. She didn't like to cry, but she couldn't stop herself. She wanted to feel Jake's arms around her. She had experienced the ultimate betrayal and now she needed comfort. She could begin not fathom the mind of a betrayer. She still felt shocked and numb from the entire experience.

"I'm right here thinking about me and you. About us being together. About me loving you forever. I will see you very soon. I don't know where we are headed, but we are moving fast."

"I…" She hesitated. It had been so long since she had felt love. "I love you, Jake." She immediately felt embarrassed. She didn't wait for a response. "Are you comfortable?" She was just like her mother. Always wanting to make sure everyone had everything they needed. Even if there was nothing she could do.

"I love you, too, Sela. And yes, I am as comfortable as I can be without you."

"Have you looked in the side pocket of your bag?"

"No. Why?"

"I asked Ted to put a letter in it last night when ya'll were getting things set up."

"Then let me go read it." His heart leapt.

"Bye. I'll see you soon!"

Sela smiled at the thought of Jake lying in the bed she had shared so many times with her sister, holding the love letter she had written. It had been so many years since she had written a letter to anyone.

Jake opened the letter slowly. He wanted to savor every second of the delight that was washing through him.

Dear Jake,

Right now, you are probably lying on the bed wishing you could come up and see the sunshine. I wish you could come up, too. I wish I were sharing this trip with you. I have thought about you every day since the day we met. I think about your smile and your kiss. I have never felt this way before. When we are together, I feel so peaceful. Like there is no one I would rather be spending my time with.

This situation I am in is really crazy. I don't know what's going to happen on this honeymoon. I'm nervous and somewhat afraid, but knowing you are down below watching out for me is so very comforting. I can't wait to see you when this is all over.

Love, Sela

Jake smiled and laid the note on his chest. It said everything he wanted to hear. He fell asleep with the delicate scent of jasmine and rose filling in his nostrils. The petals were inside the envelope.

It was around two in the morning when Jake heard Matt talking to himself. He couldn't understand him completely, but he could hear his voice. The words were muffled, but it had been enough to wake him from his light sleep. He could hear footsteps and then, after a moment, they would stop. He sat up in bed and listened more intently. He picked up his phone.

"Ted, you there?"

"Yeah, I hear him."

"Just making sure."

"Ten-four."

There were several minutes that passed before Jake heard the distress call being placed to the Coast Guard.

"This is Matt Kinsley. I have an emergency! Come quick! I believe my wife has drowned." His words were convincing and voice shook with feigned fear.

"Where are you, sir?"

Matt gave his exact coordinates as the person on the other end of the line took notes.

"We copy and we are on our way. We have a boat in the vicinity. He should be arriving in the next forty minutes."

"Forty minutes could be too long. It's so dark. I can't see anything. She's not answering me! It's too dark for me to see her." His voice sounded legitimately frantic.

"Hang in there, sir. They will do all they can. Do not try to get in the water. Just keep yelling for her. Remain calm and wait for the rescue crew."

"I've got to do something! I can't just stand here while my wife drowns!"

"The best thing you can do is wait for the rescue group. Please, sir. There is nothing you can do in the water but put yourself at risk."

"Please hurry. You've got to save my wife!"

Sela listened through the headphones. She could hear every

word he spoke through the mics they had placed on the yacht. She couldn't speak. Her heart raced. He had left her alone in the water to die.

Jake smiled at the foiled plan and sheer lunacy of it all. His life had never been this exciting. He couldn't wait to see the look on Matt's face when he saw Sela alive and well.

Matt stood by the rails and peered into the dark water, yelling for Sela. He would yell for her with his last ounce of energy if that's what it took to be convincing. The Coast Guard arrived within twenty minutes and found Matt hanging over the rail, throwing up. Several of them climbed the ladder and stood in support of the grieving husband. They had done the drill before. They began to circle the area, shining their large spotlight into the water. They saw nothing for several minutes. They continued to circle. Matt stood in his bathing suit, wrapped in a towel, watching. His hair was wet and there were small puddles of water where he had tracked across the boat. One of the rescue workers spotted a bathing suit bottom floating in the water.

"Over there!" He pointed to something in the water.

"What is it?" Matt stretched his neck to see.

They pulled the bottoms from the water. "Is this hers?" They knew the answer.

"Yes. We were swimming. We're on our honeymoon. Just got married. Sela wanted to swim. She's a good swimmer. We decided to go skinny-dipping. She took off her bottoms. When she went under to take off her top she never came back up. I thought she was just kidding around. I didn't even feel nervous at first. She's a very good swimmer." He was deliberately talking gibberish and trying to sound nervous. It was working.

"So is this the area where you last saw her?"

"Yes, sir. Right about there. She just never came back up. I got out of the water because I thought maybe I could see her better from up here. I shined this flashlight everywhere, but it was no use. That is when I called for you."

"We will continue to look for her until we believe there's no hope."

"No hope? She's only been gone for an hour!"

"An hour is a long time in this water. I'm sorry, sir. We'll do all that we can." Divers were already in the water, searching below. The water was dark, and it was impossible for them to see very far in front of them. They knew the woman was dead. Finding her body was the priority now.

Another hour passed and still there was no sign of Sela.

"Sir, I am afraid we've done all we can do. You'll be asked to make a formal police report and take your boat back to its point of origination where a report will be filed there. Someone will escort you back."

"Thank you. I know you have done your best."

Matt cried for many hours on the trip back to Corpus Cristi. He actually felt real tears of deep sadness, but he couldn't quite put his finger on why. He went below deck and let the coast guard escort steer him home. It was dawn when he arrived at the dock.

Upon arrival, Matt was greeted by several police officers. It was their duty to file a report and investigate the accident. Questions were asked that seemed to insinuate Matt might have killed his wife. He didn't care. He had heard the drill over and over in his own court cases. He knew there was no way they could prove anything. Sela had willingly jumped into the water for a swim. He couldn't help it if she swam too far away and he couldn't find her. He had done all he could do. He called for help.

"We were married yesterday. It was just a small ceremony. It was the first day of our honeymoon," he sobbed. "We had so many plans. It can't be ending this way." He ran his hands through his hair. He wiped his face with the back of his hand. He felt the tears still streaming. It was all over. He was a very rich man.

"I'm sorry, sir. We have to ask these questions." He could hear the cop saying something, but he didn't know what it was. "Did you hear me, sir?"

"What was it you said?"

"How did it happen?"

"Sela is a great swimmer. She kept asking me if I thought the water was warm enough to swim in. I told her yes. She swam for a while by herself and then I got in with her. We decided to go skinny dipping and she went under to remove her bathing suit and never came back up. I thought she was playing around and then I started panicking. That was the last time I saw her." He sobbed.

"Get some rest, sir. They may have something else they'll need from you tomorrow. This is all I need from you for now."

"Thank you."

Chapter Thirteen

Matt tossed and turned in his bed. He was much too anxious to sleep. He knew the police were searching frantically for any clue to help them close their case. He knew they would search in vain. There weren't any clues. Another perfect murder. He felt invincible. Only one more day and they would officially declare Sela dead. A funeral would be held. He would grieve and then collect the money. He would need to get away from the pain of his dead wife and would start over somewhere else, never to look back on the state of Texas again.

Ted saw the patrol boat in the distance.

"You better get down. Here comes the patrol." Ted watched through binoculars, as the boat got closer.

"Hello, sir!" The young guardsman yelled across the water. Ted could hear him.

"Yes, sir."

"We have been looking for a girl that was lost at sea late last night. If you wouldn't mind keeping your eyes open as you travel this direction. We're pretty certain that she's dead by now, though. No way someone could have survived all night battling these waves."

"I'll keep my eyes open."

"Thanks." The boat sped off.

Jake remained in the secret room until there were no signs of any movement from above. He then gathered his belongings and headed back to the mansion. He went directly to his house. He took a tablet from the drawer and wrote a letter to Lily.

Lily,

It is all over. Sela is safe. She is with Ted. You will get word soon that she was drowned at sea while swimming after dark. Matt left her in the water to die, but Ted managed to rescue her. I'll explain more later. Ted wants to see what Matt has planned. He wants to see if he runs off with Beth, as we suspect he will. We will probably go through with the funeral. I don't know who is still listening, so that's why I wrote this. Couldn't take a chance, you know.

Jake

He would give her the note as soon as he could get to her, but he didn't know who was watching so he needed to find a way to discreetly let her know what was going on. He picked up the phone and dialed her number.

"Hey, Lily."

"Jake." She tried not to sound startled. He was supposed to be on the boat with Sela. "You forgot to sign that check you gave me. I know it's late, but would you mind signing it tonight? I'm headed out of town early in the morning."

Lily knew something wasn't right. She knew what he was doing.

"Sure, son. Come on down. I'll meet you at the back door."

Lily waited for him in the kitchen.

"Here you go, Lily." He handed her the note.

"Sorry, Jake. I was just so busy I forgot to sign it. Where are you headed?"

"Just up to San Antonio for a few days."

"Be careful."

"Thanks."

Lily opened the letter and read the words quickly. She breathed a heavy sigh of relief. She walked to her office and looked at the little guy on the monitor. She felt the need to inform him of what his boss had done. She opened the door and descended the stairs with confidence.

"I just thought you might want to know that the person you were working for is just about to be convicted of murder. Seems he left Sela to die in the ocean. The only problem was that you underestimated her. Somebody picked her up and rescued her. I'll be sure to keep you posted, little fella."

His eyes were scared. He looked completely drained. His cut of the loot had just gone up in flames. It was all over. There was no other possible way of getting his hands on the money. Matt had blown it. His blood boiled. After so many years of working on this, it all just blew up in his face. Now he sat, restrained with duct tape, in the basement of the home he was supposed to have been scouting. Things certainly looked bad for him. He grunted from underneath the tape placed over his mouth.

"I'm sorry. I didn't understand you. You'll have to wait for Anthony. He may be able to understand you more clearly. I don't speak grunt."

With that, she turned and headed back up the stairs.

The police called early the day after the accident, as expected. They needed Matt to fill out some paper work and sign some things, as well as go over exactly what had happened once again.

Matt arrived at the police station at around 10:00 a.m. He was informed that the search had ended and there was no sign of his wife. There was nothing more that could be done. Once more

Matt felt the obligation to shed tears and continue the grieving husband routine. Papers were signed, condolences were given, and he left feeling like a very rich man. He almost had a spring in his step as he walked to his car. He had to watch his body language more carefully. He would also have to help Lily plan a funeral immediately.

From his car he called the mansion.

"Lily?"

"Matt?"

"Yes, Lily. I'm afraid I have some very bad news." He considered telling her in person, but then that would a waste of his time and he was tired. "Something has happened to Sela."

"What Matt? Is she all right?"

"No, she's not all right. She went for a swim last night. She was joking around with me. Going under the water and trying to tease me. She went too far out. I yelled for her to come back, but she didn't listen. She went under and never came back up. They looked for her all night. They said it was impossible to find someone in those waters after so long." He wasn't crying. That was for the ones that counted. Lily was just the housemaid who had gotten a lucky break all of her life. It was time for her to hit the road. He was running the show now. He waited for Lily's sobs. They did not come. "Are you there?"

"Yes. I'm here. I'm shocked, I guess. I don't know what to say."

"We've got to plan a funeral. There will be no body of course, but I figured you knew who to contact and what she would like. Spare no expense, of course." It was the first time in his life he had ever used that phrase. Lily cringed at the sound of it.

"Of course, Matt. Only the best for my daughters."

Matt hated that. They were not her daughters. It made her sound like part of the family. Someone who would get part of his share of the estate. She would be given a million dollars, and in his mind, that was a great deal more than she was worth.

"Let me know when you have the details worked out. I'll be at home for the next few days. When word about this gets out, I'm afraid it will be all over the newspapers. I can't deal with that right now."

"Sure, Matt. I'll let you know." Lily thought about the ceremony. She knew that Sela would not expect a big formal funeral. She wouldn't let her friends sit through such a mockery. She thought for about ten minutes and called Matt back.

"I don't think Sela would want a funeral. There's no body. There won't be a viewing. Let's just consider her buried in the ocean where she was more comfortable anyway. We will each grieve in our own way, but putting an empty casket in the ground is no good to anybody. Do you understand what I mean?" She knew that he did. He didn't care.

"You're right, Lily. It's just all so painful. I just want to get away from it all. I understand now why Sela went to South Carolina to make a new start. It's an awful feeling of total loss that surrounds you every minute. I want to leave this town. In the next few days, I'll be dividing the estate and going over her will. There's a lot that we need to cover. I know you'll need money to keep the ranch going, but I don't plan to continue supporting the ranch. I know that's difficult to hear. Let me know what you need to keep things going for the next six months. Meanwhile, we'll need to figure out a plan for relocating these kids."

Nothing surprised her at this point. He was a real monster.

"I'd like to be present with you when you meet with Hanson."

"Of course. You're more than welcome to be there with me. I may set something up tomorrow if you don't think that's too soon."

"Of course not. It's a lot of money, and it needs to be handled properly and in a timely manner."

"I agree." Lily hung up the phone in total shock. Nothing could have prepared her for the evil oozing out of this man's pores.

The next day Matt was decked out from head-to-toe in new clothes and shoes. He wanted to look the part of a billionaire. When he arrived at the office of Mr. Hanson, Lily was already seated in a big burgundy leather chair with gold studding. She sat respectfully with her head and shoulders slumped as if she were in great pain. Matt entered the room slowly.

"Mr. Kinsley."

"Mr. Hanson." They shook hands and nodded at one another.

"Please, take a seat. I'm so sorry to see you on this sad occasion. It's never easy going over a person's will. Feelings are often hurt, and families sometimes split up forever. I trust you are both somewhat aware of what is in the will."

"I am, indeed, aware. Sela and I were just here a few weeks ago."

"Yes, but there have been some changes I'm afraid. Changes which you are most likely unaware of." He stared pointedly at Matt. He had never been put in such an awkward situation. He now understood why Sela had cut him out of the will. She must have expected something like this. But why had she not protected herself?

"What sort of changes, sir?"

He opened the yellow file on his desk and read out loud. "I, Sela Barnes, do in good faith and of a sound mind, leave all of my money and assets to my second mother, Lily Booker. To my husband I leave nothing. He will understand why."

Matt sat motionless. His mouth was slightly opened, and his hands lay loosely across his lap. This was a sick joke.

"Mr. Hanson. I find this highly unprofessional and utterly sick. You, of all people, should know the pain that we are going through. Yet you take an opportunity like this to crack a joke at my expense?"

His words were deliberate and direct. "Sir, this is no joke. I have a copy for you here." He handed Matt a copy. He scanned the words.

"This can't be her last will. I was here with her the day she bequeathed nearly everything to me. Lily was to get one million dollars. I saw her sign it." His eyes bulged with hate.

"Yes, you did. On that day, she came back in and signed another copy. It was this one. I don't know why. That is between you and Sela. She said that you would know the reasons. I am not here to pass judgment on either you or Sela. I didn't understand why she did this. Mine is not to understand. I do what I am asked to do. This document is legal, sir. My secretary and I both witnessed it. It is notarized. You were married less than forty-eight hours. There is no way you can fight this."

"But guess what, Matt? Sela isn't dead."

Matt swung his head around to face Lily.

"That's right. She was picked up shortly after you left her to die. You wanna know something else? You weren't even legally married. This was a setup. Everyone was in on it but you. Yes. Even Pastor Seymore." Lily recounted the wedding vows in her head.

Matt stood up and reached across the desk. His veins were exploding as his heart pumped blood faster than he could process it. He grabbed the older man by the neck and raised him to his feet.

"I could break your neck right now!" he screamed. His fingers gripped Hanson's neck.

"And what good would that do?" Lily spoke to his back.

"Shut up!" He backhanded her across the face. Blood spilled from her mouth. Lily felt the pain shoot through her jaw. Blood dripped down her dress.

"Matt, you must calm down. This will not help you in any way." Hanson could barely speak through the grip Matt held on his neck. Matt shoved him violently into the chair and it slid into the wall. Enraged, Matt didn't quite know what to do next. He frantically looked back and forth between Lily and the lawyer. They had somehow done this to him. He could just feel it. Sela would never have done something like this. Someone had manipulated her somehow.

"You did this." He pointed his finger in Lily's face. She did not move. Before she could speak, he grabbed her by the hair and lifted her out of her chair. She did not fight. In an instant, his arm was around her throat, and he was dragging her from the office. A police officer was waiting outside for Matt, but he was caught off guard by Matt's rage and unprepared for it. He was really just a security guard. He reached for his gun but froze as he watched Lily being dragged from the office.

Lily's legs barely reached the ground as Matt dragged her roughly through the lobby. Her screams were muffled by the large hand that covered her face. Lily bit hard into the bottom of his hand and clawed at his skin. He was unfazed.

"Don't anybody come near me or I'll snap her neck!" His words were full of vicious intent.

"Let go of the lady, sir." The police officer pointed his gun at

Matt without getting any response. Down the steps and to his car he dragged her. She knew she had a better chance of surviving if she didn't get into the car, so she fought hard. She tried to struggle long enough to give other officers time to get there.

Matt wanted to kill. He would kill. There was no doubt about it. Lily had robbed him of his whole life's work. She had stolen his dreams and she would pay with her life. His own life was already over. He had nothing left to live for. Lily's body went limp. He tried hard to control her dead weight. He opened his car door and tried to reach the gun he kept under his seat. Lily saw the opportunity to escape. She kneed him as hard as she could between the legs and ran as he doubled over in the seat. By the time he was recovered enough to look around for her, she was gone and he knew there would be no chance of catching her.

He got in the car and sped away. The police were only seconds behind him. He ran through the red light and up a small side street. He couldn't think. Confusion and panic set in. Beth was waiting on a phone call. She was waiting on millions of dollars and a ticket to a new life. It was all they had planned for.

He stopped in the alley, looking at the high brick wall that surrounded him. Police officers had arrived, and they, too, surrounded him. Soon he would be charged with murder. And then what? There would be investigations. They would find out his job was a sham. There were no real clients. There had been only a few to keep him looking busy. His credit cards were maxed out, and he had a double mortgage on his house. He pulled his pistol from the console and placed it against his head. Blood spattered the windows, even as the police yelled at him to get out of the car.

Paramedics arrived shortly after and dragged Matt's lifeless body from the car, loaded it onto a gurney and headed to the hospital. He wasn't dead yet, but close to it. He was placed in intensive care. Rumors began to spread that he had committed suicide or that he was only being kept alive by a machine. No one in the media knew the truth yet.

Two weeks had passed since Beth had heard from Matt. She knew some time would need to pass before they could make contact. She was prepared for that. But something felt very wrong.

Chapter Fourteen

Sela sat talking to Ted on the boat, formally known as "Ted's Trooper." They talked about everything from divorce to starfish. She realized why her dad had thought so much of Ted. He was a very loving and compassionate man. The days she had spent with him on the Trooper had been some of the best days since her dad's passing. It was a much-needed time of relaxation, even if it did come under unusual circumstances. She had gotten to know Ted in a way she never expected. He now felt like family. He had helped her through some very rough times in a professional way. But now, on a more personal and emotional level, he had offered her the sort of guidance and leadership that only her dad had given her. It felt good getting to know him.

"Look at this!" Ted turned up the local news and watched in amazement at the report.

"Another tragic turn of events surrounding the Texas billionaire's daughter, Sela Barnes. Two weeks ago she drowned while going for a swim on her honeymoon. Her husband, Matt Kinsley, would have been the only living family heir to the large fortune accrued by the late Charles Barnes. But today, Mr. Kinsley shot himself in the head. Police say they were called to Nolan Hanson's Law office after Kinsley became enraged after learning he had been excluded from his wife's will. He then attempted to kidnap Lily Booker, a longtime employee of the Barnes family. A police chase ensued and ended when Mr.

Kinsley shot himself in the head."

Neither of them spoke. They could not believe what they had just heard. They had previously discussed how shocked Matt would be to find out that he had no inheritance, but neither of them expected anything like this. There was still no connection to Matt concerning Charlee's murder. There was no actual crime in an unmarried man having two women. He didn't know Sela was still alive. Had someone told him? He had pulled off a perfect crime. Why would he have ended his life? All of this was running through Sela's mind. Surely no one had told him she was alive.

"Lily. I need to see Lily."

"We'll head back home, but let's not forget we still have a murder to solve."

She knew it wasn't over yet. "What do we do now?"

"We have to see what Beth is going to do. As of right now, all we know is that she visited your sister. There's no weapon with her prints. Without a confession or some reason to lock her up, we're just spinning our wheels. We need more time. We need something more solid. I need you to do something for me."

"Whatever you need."

"When we get back, I need you to change the way you look. Can you do that? I don't want anyone recognizing you yet. We can't afford to have this whole story out in the public right now. Let's just keep it simple. As simple as we can. Let me do everything from this point on. You just stay low. Take a trip or something."

Sela thought about Jake waiting on her back home.

"I can handle that."

"I'll have you home by midnight. Just leave everything to me and don't worry about a thing, okay?" He placed his big arm around her shoulder, and she relaxed.

"Thanks, Ted. I'll be below if you need me." She wanted to sleep. Just sleep until this whole thing was really over. When she woke up, she wanted to be lying next to Jake. That dream wasn't too far away.

Jake stretched out on the couch and set his alarm for 12:30 a.m. He wanted to be at the dock when Sela arrived. Ever since Ted had told him that they were headed home, his stomach had been tied in knots. But now, Sela was safe. Sela loved him. They would soon be free to do whatever they wanted from now on. No more secrets. He drifted into peaceful sleep.

Sela stood on the deck watching the harbor lights get closer and closer. Her hair was pulled up tightly in a cap and her large eyes were hidden behind the dark glasses that Ted had loaned her. She wasn't wearing any makeup and she looked refreshingly young. Jake watched the boat from his truck. It docked safely and the precious cargo he had so longed to see, walked quickly down the pier to where he was.

Her footsteps quickened the closer she got to him. She didn't remember the pier being so long. At last, she reached the man she loved. The man she had waited so long to hold in her arms.

He held her tightly in the dark. The pier was dimly lit, giving them a sense of privacy. She kissed him over and over, their lips pressed perfectly together once again. She felt his tongue touch hers. Gently at first and then more passionately, more demanding. She could't stop. He led her in the direction of his truck, and they leaned against it. Again, she kissed him. He held her face and stroked her neck. His hands caressed her shoulders and moved down her back. His touch sent a thrill of excitement down her spine. The hair at the base of her neck tingled. Her body became heated with want and desire. He filled her senses. She was utterly lost in this complete moment of passion. She heard him whispering her name over and over. She loved the way it rolled from his tongue, the way it sounded in her ear. She knew without a doubt that she had never felt such desire before.

"Jake, do you have a passport?"

"Yes, of course. Why?"

"Is it with you?"

"It's in a briefcase under my seat along with some other important papers. Why?"

"I want you to go away with me. Right now."

"Now? Where do you want to go?"

"Ted said I needed to keep a low profile. He said I would have to stay out of sight until he's finished with Charlee's case. Let's just leave right now. We'll take the Princess and just stay gone. We can do whatever we want. I don't care where we go. The Princess is stocked with everything we need. My clothes are there. I wouldn't be surprised if Matt didn't leave his suitcases there. They're probably full of brand-new clothes. Whatever you need, we'll stop and buy."

"I'll have to call Lily and tell her to find someone to fill in for me."

"There are plenty of people around there to help out."

"Then let's do it."

Jake dug under his seat and retrieved a tattered leather briefcase with his important documents inside.

Hand-in-hand they met Ted at his boat. He smiled as they approached.

"We're going to leave on the Princess right now. Let us know when it's safe to come back. I have no idea where we're going yet, but I'll keep in touch with you."

"That sounds like a great idea. Do you have everything you

need?"

"It's all on the yacht."

"What about money? You can't very well use your bank accounts right now."

"We can use Jake's credit cards." Jake nodded in agreement.

"You've got my number if you need anything. Otherwise, I'll keep you posted. Don't worry about a thing. You two just have fun and be safe. I've got all of this under control."

Sela gave Ted a big hug and a kiss on the cheek. Her kiss was cool against his face. He felt such a fondness for this sweet girl. He didn't have any children, and knew he had lost out on one of life's greatest gifts by working so hard and giving up on the notion of having a family life. He smiled as the two boarded The Princess and waved goodbye to him through the darkness.

Sela cranked the ship and eased it out of its parking place. She looked around at this place where she and Matt stood together two weeks before. She felt nothing. There was no pain that she could recreate in her mind. She felt Jake's arms slip around her waist. She felt his breath against her neck. Right now, the only thing on her mind was being with the man she loved.

In Atlanta, Beth was getting antsy. It had been more than three weeks since Matt and Sela were married and let on their honeymoon. It was time for Matt to check in. She had heard nothing from him at all. He'd had more than enough time to do what had to be done. She was worried now and losing patience. Could there be any possibility that he was leaving her out of the plan? She picked at her sandwich. Her appetite had vanished in the last week, and she had already lost nine pounds. She picked up the phone and dialed his number. His answering machine came on and she hung up. She tried several more times. He was sure to guess who it would be. He never called back. She googled the Corpus Cristi news and saw the headlines "Texas Billionaire Drowns at Sea". Where on earth was Matt?

Morning came just as it had every other day, and still Beth lay alone in her bed with no word from Matt. She looked at the empty vodka bottle on her nightstand. Her head pounded. She simply had to go and see him. There were only a few things she needed to take care of before she left. She tumbled out of bed and stumbled to the kitchen. She popped a few Tylenol extra-strength and chugged a glass of water. She packed up some boxes with clothes and keepsakes, and sat down to write a letter. It was very short, but she didn't need to say much. She dug through her address book for the address of the one person she could call in case of an emergency. She carefully wrote the address on the boxes and loaded them into her car. On her way out of town, she stopped by the post office and mailed the boxes to the Mexico address.

With her suitcases packed, she headed west. She would be in Texas by nightfall. She could sense that something had gone terribly wrong, and felt sure that Matt was in some kind of trouble.

Ted watched as Beth's Jeep Cherokee eased out of the driveway. She was on the move for the first time in a week. At a safe distance behind her, he followed. She wound her way through Atlanta's busy traffic, made a stop at the post office, and then headed south onto I-85. After about four hours, he guessed where she was going. She pulled into a gas station and pumped some gas. He filled up beside her, getting a good look at her face. The face of a murderer. A face as lovely as he had ever seen. She wore very little makeup, and he suspected she was wearing a long dark wig. Her glasses did little to hide the large blue eyes the hotel worker had described. Under the frumpy clothes, he knew she had a gorgeous body. He had seen her in her shorts, retrieving the newspaper from her yard in the mornings. She felt his gaze on her and nodded shyly in his direction.

On the interstate again, he stayed far enough behind to see keep her in sight, yet not draw attention to himself. After four more hours, she exited the interstate and pulled into the parking lot of Ruby Tuesday's and went inside. He grabbed a sandwich at Arby's next door and continued to watch her from his car. He could see her eating through the large windows. He needed a quick bathroom break, and this was the perfect time.

Beth watched from the restaurant window as Ted emerged from his car and went inside. She had been watching him since she first stopped to get gas. Initially, she had hoped that perhaps Matt had sent him with a message for her, but she quickly realized that he was not a friend. It was no coincidence that he had exited with her both times. She was sure of that. She motioned for the waitress.

"I need to pay."

"Do you need a go-box?"

"No. This should be enough."

She handed the waitress a $20 bill.

"Keep the change."

She walked quickly to her car and got inside, locking it carefully. She quickly pulled out of the parking lot and on to the main road, glancing carefully behind her. Whoever he was, she was going to make sure that he would have a very difficult time finding her here. She drove about ten miles into the country and pulled onto a small dirt road. It would be dark soon, so she would just wait.

Ted had been only a few minutes in the bathroom. But when he came out, she was gone. He assumed she had finished her dinner and had gotten back onto the interstate. He pulled onto the highway and hit the gas. He wouldn't need to go all that fast to catch up with her. She kept within the speed limit and he knew she could only be minutes ahead of him.

Ted had been watching her for nearly a week, and now she was gone. Just like that. He was angry with himself. He was doing 89 miles per hour. When he realized he was not catching up with her, he began to wonder if she had stayed in the small town somewhere. Maybe she was going to spend the night in a hotel. He had already driven twenty miles, and still she was nowhere to be found. He turned around and headed in the opposite direction. He would search every hotel in the town until he found her Jeep.

Beth leaned the seat back and rested. She didn't need to sleep a long time. Just long enough to regroup. When she awoke, it was dark. She drove out of the woods and back to the interstate. Whoever was following her had definitely been given the slip. From here on out, no one would follow her. She would make sure of that.

At 1:00 a.m. Beth pulled into The Hampton Inn. She wasn't sure exactly where she was, but she knew that she could drive no more. Paying cash, she checked in under her new ID. Margaret Denise Fletcher.

The next morning, Ted drove on to Corpus Christi. He knew that was where she was going. He recounted all the facts in his mind. The San Francisco police were looking for a tall blond who was wanted for questioning in the murder of Charlee Barnes. Beth was connected to the murder scene. Matt was connected to Beth. He now had motive for the two of them. With Matt's attempt to murder Sela, along with the news about Matt's affair, he felt he had enough evidence to arrest Beth. Now he had let her slip through his fingers. He should have arrested her long before, but he was hoping for one more incriminating piece of evidence. It was time to turn the information he had over to the federal investigators. He was done trying to be a hero. He needed help.

"Yes, Ma'am. We can do that for you."

Beth nodded at the car salesman with pleasure. "Great."

"This is a fine Jeep, Ma'am."

"Yep, but it is so bad on gas. I just want something small for a change."

"I understand. You'll be happy with this Miss Margaret. It gets thirty-two miles to the gallon on the interstate." His southern charm was at its best and wasn't hard to see through. Just give me the keys, she thought to herself.

"Sounds good."

The paper work was filled out in the name of Margaret Denise. Beth exchanged keys with the salesman. She drove away in a GEO Prism. No credit check had been done. There was no need. With the cash back from her Jeep and the low-priced GEO, she had just about broke even. She only had to put a few thousand dollars with it. But she was on the road again.

Chapter Fifteen

Beth sat in the parking lot watching the men and women in fine dress suits enter and leave. For two hours she scanned the parking lot outside the office where Matt worked. She wasn't exactly sure what she was looking for. It just seemed like a good place to start. She picked up her cell phone and dialed the work number. The familiar voice answered on the other end of the line.

"Mr. Matt Kinsley, please." She usually disguised her voice. This time she did not.

"I'm sorry, ma'am. Are you a client of Mr. Kinsley?"

"Yes, I am."

"I'm sorry to tell you this, but Mr. Kinsley is no longer with us. I'm sorry you were not informed. We thought all of his clients were notified." The polite secretary offered no further details.

Her heart fluttered, but she did not speak.

"He's been gone for more than two weeks now. I am so sorry that no one has contacted you. We went through his files and notified his clients. We let everyone know that we would still be glad to work with them in any way possible."

"Gone? Passed away? As in dead?" The words she spoke were only words. She knew he could not be dead.

"I was told not to divulge any more details. I'm sorry."

"Can you at least tell me if he is dead? That's all I am asking."

"From what I have heard, he committed suicide, ma'am." The lady whispered so that no one could hear her.

"When did this happen?"

"It's been several weeks ago, now. It was such a shock."

Beth tried to sound distraught.

"Of course. How awful! And it was my understanding that he was to be married shortly." Beth shook her head sadly.

"He was married. His wife drowned on the first day of their honeymoon. It was all over the news."

"This is so tragic. My regards to his family."

Sitting back inside her car, she felt completely stifled. She could hardly breathe. She drove quickly to the library and pulled up newspaper articles from the previous weeks. There it was. She read intently as the photo of Matt smiled cruelly at her.

"Today, Matt Kinsley, the recent husband of Sela Barnes, shot himself in his car in the alley behind SouthTrust Bank on 29th Street, as police officers looked on. The recent loss of his wife, Sela Barnes, a local billionaire, along with the recent news that she had eluded him from her will just prior to their honeymoon, left him outraged. Upon finding out that the will had been changed, he attempted to take a hostage, a longtime employee of the Barnes family, Lily Booker, to whom the money and entire estate had been left."

She did not read far enough into the article to see that he had not died, but was taken to the hospital and placed in intensive care. It was enough that there was no money and she believed Matt was dead. It was true. No wonder he had not made contact. They had banked everything they had on this. Now it was over. She knew he was dead. There would be no way to fake the police finding the body. She had to move on to plan B. In her mind ,she had already worked out another plan. She had been unsure if Sela would ever marry Matt to begin with. Her plan B was already in place, and she would be out of the country by nightfall.

Beth drove slowly back to her hotel. She was in no particular rush right now. There was plenty of time. She gathered her things and drove to the mall. She purchased a very large purse, sunglasses, and a hat. It was the first time she had been back to that mall since she was a teenager. She had been with Sela then, shopping for a Christmas gift for Matt. They had spent hours there together. Now Matt and Sela were both dead.

She wondered where all the craziness had begun. She remembered joking around with Matt about wishing they were as rich as Sela. She remembered being in her parent's basement when he said that they could be rich if he married Sela and then killed off her entire family. It was just a stupid comment. Something neither of them thought about again, until Sela's mother died. She remembered Matt saying, "one down and three to go." It still meant nothing to her. Then one day they were watching The Learning Channel when they learned of these huge oil fires and how dangerous they were. Matt said it would be easy to die in an explosion, and that's when the murders were planned. Her mind was crammed with all their plans. She could see Charlee with her big white smile, sitting across from her drinking tea. She was a picture of goodness, with a heart for every living creature. Time for goodness was over.

Beth pushed the images from her mind and moved swiftly to her car. She drove to an area of town that was known to be poor .She parked her car near a rundown park and watched as a group of young men played basketball on a worn-out court and with a rim, but no net. She waited until the game was over and watched the boys and men begin to disperse. She pulled her car up beside the curb and slowed to a stop. She called several of the men over. Four of them stood in a group nearby, and one man leaned forward.

"I'm about to rob some banks." She pulled the gun from under her leg and pointed to the black bag. She spoke deliberately.

"Damn! You serious?"

"If anyone is interested in making a quick $10,000, get in."

"You some kind of undercover cop or something? You think we're fools?"

"Look, if I were a cop, I couldn't do anything to you until the bank was robbed. And then that would be a serious set-up. Cops don't do that. All I need is someone to drive me. You wait outside and when I come out, we drive away. I have it planned to perfection. You'll make a quick $10,000. I have two stops I want to make. So in the end, you're $20,000 richer for simply driving me. You can come right back here with the money in your pocket. An easy day's work."

"No way, man. You crazy." They were laughing at the thought of going from basketballers to bank robbers, just like that.

"Your face will never be seen."

"I'll do it." The voice was deep and slow. It had come from the back of the group of boys. Everyone turned and looked at him.

"Are you crazy, man? You gone go to jail and be sandin' rocks for the next twenty years 'cause this woman comes outta nowhere askin' you to do some stupid shit."

"He's not going to jail. I promise you."

"I'll do it. I ain't afraid. What do I do?"

"Just get in. I'll tell you the rest as we go. Can he borrow your hat?" She pointed to one of the guys.

"Yeah, sure."

She handed him the hat and he put it on.

"Pull it down low." He did what as instructed. "Now you get in the driver's seat." They got out and exchanged places.

"Yo momma gon' kick yo butt, James!" They were laughing and pointing at him. "You ain't for real, are you?"

James didn't say a word.

"So your name is James?"

"Yep."

"How old are you, James?"

"I'm nineteen."

"Okay. Well, listen. Don't be nervous. Just do exactly what I say. Do you know anybody who will help us?"

"I think so."

"Then let's go get him."

James drove around the corner to a car wash where several guys were washing cars by hand. He yelled out the window.

"Hey, Rod! Come here, man."

Roderick dropped his brush and came to the window.

"What up, Jimmy Jo?"

"This lady here and me we need you to help us do something."

"Whaddya need?"

"We need you to help us go rob a bank or two."

"Yea, right. Rob a bank or two? Say what?"

"He's serious. I need another driver. Someone who will wait for us so we can change cars. There's a lot of money in it for ya."

"Do I have time to think about it?"

"No. We need you to tell us now. We've got exactly one hour before we hit."

Roderick listened to the woman talk. He had stolen some beer from the local drug store, but he didn't consider himself a criminal. This was crazy. He felt a rush of adrenaline.

"I don't like it."

"Then don't do it. See if anyone else over there will help us."

"Wait a minute." He needed a minute to think. "What are we gonna do?"

"Just drive this lady. We ain't the criminals she is. All we are is two guys who gave a lady a ride."

"Sounds harmless."

"Then you'll do it?"

"Yeah, I reckon."

"Get your car and meet us back at the park where you guys play basketball. We'll be near the court."

Both boys listened carefully as Beth explained exactly what was to be done.

James waited in the parking lot as Beth entered the bank. Wearing a tan safari hat pulled down rather low on her head, she knew that she couldn't be recognized under the sunglasses. Carrying her black straw purse, she concealed her loaded weapon until it was time. Keeping her head low, she avoided the cameras and stood at the teller window, confident and bold. She pulled her gun from the purse and pointed it at the clerk.

"Get your hands where I can see them and give me your money quickly and I'll spare your life." The woman paused briefly and looked in complete disbelief at what Beth was asking. She didn't care about the money. She was thirty-four years old and didn't make much above minimum wage. This job was not permanent, and she was not going to risk her life playing the hero.

"Move quickly!" She yelled at the other tellers. "Everyone, get your money out of the drawer and lay it in front of you. If it's not there when I come by, you die!"

One teller quickly hit the panic button before she began getting out her money.

"Yes, ma'am!" She began putting the money in the bag

quickly.

"Faster! And get that stupid look off your face. Smile while you still can."

Her drawer was quickly emptied in less than a minute. Beth ran to each window, filled her purse, and then ran out of the bank. James pulled the car up to the door quickly and they sped away.

"Good God, lady. You did it."

"Just get to Rod quickly. Every cop in town will be looking for this car in the next two minutes."

Rod waited just around the corner. Beth's car was stashed, they loaded up in Rod's Mustang, and headed ten miles away to AmSouth Bank. In the back seat, Beth pulled a long blond wig from her purse. She put on a Braves ball cap and handed the two guys their money. Now, do the same thing. Only this time we don't have another getaway car. We'll drive as far away from here as we can and then I'll buy a new car later."

"Wait a minute. I don't wanna be looking over my shoulder every day. My car will be the one they're looking for. I don't think so. I got you out of there, now you are on your own. I didn't realize MY car was going to be the one parked outside the bank."

"It's not. Just put me out around the corner. When I'm done, I'll come around and you can pick me up where you dropped me off. How about that?"

"That's fine."

Word had already spread about the robbery. Police were looking for the GEO that someone had spotted leaving the parking lot.

Beth entered the second bank as before. Following the same procedure, she left with her bag fully loaded with money. She ran from the bank, down the street, and behind a building. There, she took off her wig and cap and pulled a large pink sack from her black purse. She emptied the money quickly and stuffed her wig and cap into the black bag. Under her loose-fitting blue dress was

216

a black mini skirt and red halter-top that formed tightly to her body. She slipped off her clogs and put on some black sandals. She tossed everything into a big brown dumpster and walked slowly back out to the main road and down the block to meet Rod and James. They sat motionless in their car watching nervously as the blond bombshell came closer and closer.

Beth got back inside the car. "Let's go. Head towards Mexico." She dropped $20,000 dollars over the seat. "I think this belong to you. Thanks guys."

James took his $10,000 and handed Rod the other $10,000.

Two hours passed before anyone said a word.

"Listen guys. No one ever saw you. They saw a young white female in frumpy clothes. That's it. You got off scot-free." That was Matt's favorite way of putting it. He certainly didn't get off scot-free. "If you don't mind, just drop me off at the next hotel you see. I'll rent a car, and the rest is history."

They didn't answer. This had been the wildest ride of their lives.

"Take care of yourself. And do me a favor. Keep the details to yourself. I know you're going to want to brag and stuff. Your friends are gonna start talking. Just deny it all. Nobody has any proof. Keep it all between yourselves. Leave the details about me out of it. Like where you took me and all that. If you start talking, we will all go to jail. Right now, we are just three people who are richer now than we were this morning. Keep it that way."

"Yeah. Sure. Good luck, lady."

Beth waved as they left the EconoLodge parking lot. They had dropped her off at the back of the hotel. No one witnessed the drop-off, so she was safe.

Chapter Sixteen

Ruez sat behind bars at the county jail. He had been hand-delivered by Ted after a background check showed that he had warrants in several states, including Texas. Warrants for robbery, conspiracy to commit murder, and assault & battery. There would be no need for Ted to try and pin additional murders on this man now. He would have plenty of time for that later, and he knew exactly where he could find the guy. Right now, his focus was Beth. He had tried once again to be the hero, but this time he let the suspect slip right out of his hands. He had seen it too many times before. He knew a person was guilty, but there wasn't enough proof. He didn't want this to happen with Beth. He told himself that he had good reasons for trying to handle it all on his own. He picked his teeth with a toothpick as he sat at the red light, contemplating his next strategy. He could hear his police scanner faintly in the background.

"Attention all units. We have new information on the bank robberies. Someone reported a black Ford Mustang parked on the 1400 block of Madison. Two black men were seen driving away with a white female, approximately 6 feet tall, blond, weighing around 130 pounds. They were seen around four-thirty. This just in." The information was repeated.

Ted had been inside Applebee's eating lunch and having a beer when the robbery had occurred. He knew who it was immediately. It was time to tell the police everything he knew.

Ted recounted the facts to the chief of police.

"So what you're saying is that Matt Kinsley murdered his wife and his girlfriend from Atlanta, and Beth is the one who robbed the banks." The police chief looked doubtfully at Ted.

"That's what I know happened. There's a lot more to the story."

"Do tell."

"Sela is alive."

"Say again?"

"Sela Barnes is alive. Matt tried to kill her on their honeymoon. Sela did go for a swim, and he left her there to die.

"Whoa. Are you kidding me right now?"

"I know. It's mind boggling."

"To say the least!"

"We suspected he was going to try something on the honeymoon, so we had the boat rigged with wires, and someone was on board to protect her should she need it. After Sela jumped in the water to go for a swim, Matt left her. The person we had on board reported to me what was happening, and I went to pick her up. I found her floating in the water nearly two hours after he left her to drown. Sela suspected he was only trying to marry her for her money. That's why she had the will changed, leaving him nothing. He had been having an affair with his high school girlfriend for many years. We found evidence that she was in Charlene Barnes' apartment the week she was killed. I've been following this girl for a week in hopes that I could gather more evidence on her. I followed her from Atlanta all the way here. But I lost her. My gut tells me that she was the one who robbed the banks. If we can't pin Charlee's murder on her, we can possibly pin conspiracy to murder Sela and the bank robberies."

"And why, sir, were you trying to do all this without

assistance?"

"Initially, the police ruled it a suicide. Sela tried convincing them otherwise. They had evidence of an open-and-shut case. There was a suicide note, no forced entry, no evidence of foul play, and there was a gun at the scene. Sela hired me. I'm a private investigator. We work alone most of the time. I didn't want to risk getting too many people involved and blow it before I had any real proof. Forgive me if I don't have that much confidence in police investigations. I've seen my share of mishaps."

"You could have contacted the FBI."

"I did. They put out a sketchy description on America's Most Wanted of a woman who was staying at a hotel in San Francisco when Charlee was killed. They said she was wanted for questioning only and that she was not considered a suspect. At the time, we didn't know who she was. It wasn't until later that Sela put two-and-two together and we started investigating her. They haven't done any investigating on their own."

"So where is Sela now?"

"She's on a ship somewhere in the gulf. She's traveling with the person who helped save her life when Matt left her to drown."

"Wow. This story is going to bust CNN wide open. Can you get in touch with her? I need to get a statement from her."

"Yeah. I can." Ted dialed her number. "Sela?"

"Hi, Ted. How are you?"

"I'm good. I'm down at the police station. They know everything now. We're nearly positive that Beth has robbed a couple of local banks. I'll give you more details later. Right now, the police chief needs to hear that you're alive and confirm that I'm not making all this up."

"Sure, Ted. Thanks." He handed the phone to the officer.

"Hello?"

"This is Sela Barnes, and yes, Matt Kinsley tried to kill me. I went for a swim, and he drove off in the boat. He left me to die." The words did not even sound real coming from her mouth. "Any other details you need?"

"Okay, Ms. Barnes. As you may expect, we have never handled a case like this. I'm not sure what else we're going to need from you. When I find out, can I call you back at this number?"

"Of course."

"Thank you." The chief hung up the phone. "Unbelievable. In all my years on the force I've never seen anything like this. What a twist of events! So you knew Matt was planning this?"

"Yes, but I wanted to see if he was going to join up with Beth. She's the one we believe is responsible for the recent bank robberies. She and Matt thought he had been added to Sela's will. It's a long story, but he wasn't. He just thought he was. When Matt found out he'd been double-crossed by Sela, he shot himself. Then Beth went to plan B. Maybe she believes he's dead. I'm not sure. It was me who leaked all the information about his 'suicide' to the press."

"Wait. You mean he's not dead? Even I believed it."

"The rumor is that he died at the hospital and was cremated at his family's request. Would you believe he's had no visitors at the hospital? There were a few calls on the first day, from people he worked with. The operator was told to tell them he was no longer with us. We have someone guarding his room. Not that anyone has even pursued an interest in him, living or dying. Sad really."

"I find it a little odd that there were no visitors."

"Yep. That's what they've said, anyway." The sergeant

shook his head.

"Sounds like he wasn't a very likeable guy. What about his family?"

"No one has contacted us."

"I guess it's pretty easy to spread a rumor that you're dead if no one is looking for you."

"Yes. The reason I wanted everyone to believe he was dead was that I wanted to see what Beth would do when she believed that Matt was dead."

"Well now you know. Rob a bank!"

"We've got to find her. She's a very dangerous woman."

Within minutes, the Georgia police surrounded Beth's house and searched everything. Her computer was seized, as well as boxes of other items. It wasn't hard to see that she had a long-standing love affair with Matt and that she had left in a hurry with no plans to return.

A nationwide search was put out, and everyone was looking for Beth. Matt's house was also searched, and many items were taken in to police custody.

Beth starred at the ceiling of her hotel room as she lay stretched out crossways on the bed. If Matt could only see her now. It wasn't a fraction of the money they had counted on, but it was a start. $140,000 would go a long way in Mexico. She pulled her purse up on the bed and dug around for the slip of paper with a very special address and phone number.

She called collect to Mexico.

"Gerardo? It's me. Beth."

"Beth, dear. I received so many packages with your name on them yesterday." The Spanish accent was thick but completely understandable and beautiful.

"Do you remember what I told you?" She sounded so sincere.

"Yes. That if ever I received a package from you that you had changed your mind and decided to be with me here in Mexico City. It's true? Yes? You are coming? What changed your mind after all these years?"

"I'll explain it all when I see you, my love. It's true. Will you come get me?"

"Yes, of course I will. I'll call the boss and see what I can work out. How soon do you want to come?" Gerardo didn't have a boss, but he had never told her what a wealthy boss he was.

"Immediately. Don't tell anyone that you're coming to get me or anything about your plans. I'll explain it all. It's a little complicated. Call me when you know your plans." She gave him the number where she was staying at the EconoLodge.

Gerardo was used to giving the orders, not taking them. But with Beth, it didn't matter. He had loved her from the moment they had first met.

"You're not in Atlanta anymore? I tried to call you after the first package arrived, but the number had been disconnected. I didn't know where to reach you. I don't have a cell number for you. Only the landline. I have been so worried. Is there trouble?"

"Yes. It's a long story. Just come quickly. I've had a run of bad luck, to say the least. I can't explain it right now. I just need to be with you, Gerardo. I've always known in my heart that being with you is where I needed to be." She did her best to sound desperate for him, not desperate to leave the country.

"I'll be there quickly. Remain safe and I'll be there tomorrow. There are a few things I must do, my love. Will you meet me at the airport or where?"

"I don't have any money. Nor any transportation." She lied

about the money, but she couldn't take a chance on being seen somewhere. They were looking for her everywhere by now.

"I am staying at the EconoLodge in a little town outside of Corpus Cristi. It's called Linden. I'm in room 224."

"How did you get there?"

"I'll tell you when I see you. Is that okay?"

"Of course, it is."

"I'll be waiting for you tomorrow, Gerardo."

"I'll be there."

Beth recalled the first time she had ever met Gerardo. She was a junior in high school, vacationing in Cancun with her family. He was fifteen years her senior and was very much enamored of her. They had only known each other five days when he proposed to her and begged her to go back with him to Mexico City. She was extremely attracted to him, but was in love with Matt and had no plans of marrying a stranger and leaving the country. Right now, that sounded exactly like what she should do. Start over in Mexico and lay low.

It had been three years since she had seen Gerardo. He had visited her in Atlanta during Christmas and begged her to return home with him. He promised her a life she could only dream of. They had communicated through letters and e-mails since then. Matt had no idea, of course. Gerardo was only a backup plan. She had joked repeatedly about surprising him and just showing up in Mexico. She had kept him optimistic for all these years and now it was going to pay off.

She didn't know about his financial status. She had questioned him in different ways, but it was always the same answer. He was a computer salesman, and he made enough money to stay comfortable.

An all-points bulletin was put out on Beth. There were pictures of her all across the internet. The search was on for the frumpy brunette, or the glamorous, tall blond. It would not be an easy task finding her. James and Roderick listened to the breaking news reports over the radio. They laughed at the crazy, fine lady with the long legs they had dropped off at the EconoLodge

Beth had not had a good meal in more than twenty-four hours. She, too, watched the news reports and was afraid to leave her room. She ate chips and crackers out of the vending machine, and wondered what was taking Gerardo so long. She wondered if he would still come if he heard the news about the robberies. Her name was now being plastered across the TV stations, over and over again. If he had to wait at the airport for long, he would surely have seen the reports. Her thoughts were interrupted by a knock on the door. She peeked from behind her curtain and saw the dark-skinned man standing erectly with his hands behind his back. So handsome. His chest was much broader than she remembered. He smiled sweetly. She opened the door and fell into his arms.

"Oh, Gerardo! I was beginning to think you had changed your mind and you weren't coming for me. What took you so long?"

"And what would make you think that? Nothing could have stopped me." He held her shoulders and focused on the face he had so longed to see. The face he had dreamed of since the first time he had laid eyes on her.

"I want to leave as soon as possible. Can we leave now?"

"Have I no time to sit down and take a small break?"

"Of course. Are you really tired? I'm sorry. I'm not thinking clearly.

"I was a little tired before I saw you. But now that I see you, I have much more energy."

"Then let's go. I am so ready to leave this hotel room." She felt her accent change slightly in his presence.

"I understand."

She gathered her bags and he took them from her.

"Shall we stop for something to eat?"

"Do you mind going through a drive-through?"

"If that is what you want."

"I would love an Arby's Beef 'n' Cheddar with some curly fries and a Jamocha milkshake."

"Then let's find an Arby's for you, my love."

Gerardo got on the interstate heading north, not south. They had been driving about thirty minutes before Beth realized it.

"You're headed north."

"Yes. To the airport."

"I thought we were going to drive to Mexico."

"Why would you think we would drive when we could fly so quickly?"

Beth knew she could not show her face at the airport.

"Because I remember saying that I wanted to drive and not fly."

"Is there any particular reason?"

"Well, by the time we wait in the long lines and go through security, plus an hour at baggage check, we could already be there. Besides, we could enjoy the scenery on the way."

"My dear. We are not going to wait. I have a private jet waiting for us. We will load the jet and touch down in Mexico in about one hour from now."

Beth didn't know what to say. In all the years they had corresponded, he had never let on that he had money.

"A private jet? Whose private jet?"

"It is my private jet, my dear. Also, I have something for you. Reach into the compartment there and get that passport."

She opened the passport. There was her picture on a Mexican passport. Her name was Elizabeth Garcia.

"What is this?"

"I did not want any trouble at the airport. This way everyone will think you are my wife and we will never have to go through a long customs interrogation of any sort."

"When did you think of this?"

"Look at the date."

It was dated two years earlier. She was speechless.

"I took a picture you sent me several years ago and had one made. It's easy when you know the right people. I believed in my heart that you would join me. I kept every letter and printed every e-mail."

"I kept your letters too," she lied. She could barely remember what his letters said. She had never thought twice about leaving Matt before. She had only enjoyed having a pen pal. She knew she had probably led him on, but she never really thought she would see him again.

"I don't know what to say."

"You need to say nothing. I made the passport on faith, and indeed it was faith that has brought us together."

She needed to get rid of the extra passport in case someone searched her bags. She would stick it down her pants once they were on board the aircraft.

"So as of right now I am Elizabeth Garcia, a Mexican citizen?"

"That is correct."

"That sounds so good." She put her arm around his shoulder

as they drove the rest of the way to the airport.

They were greeted in Mexico City by a limousine driver, who ushered down a long drive, up to a pair of iron gates attached to two imposing brick pillars. Beth caught her breath at the sight of a huge mansion surrounded by an immaculate lawn and beautiful gardens. Beth could not believe her eyes. The driver pressed a button and the gates slid open to bid them welcome. She stared in amazement at the well-kept secret Gerardo that had never revealed to her.

He was many times over a millionaire. In front of the mansion, she sat speechless. She thought of the many years she had planned and schemed and worked to obtain this kind of wealth. She had completely alienated herself from everything and everyone she knew, including her own family, in her single-minded quest to become a wealthy person. Now, with just single a phone call, she was instantly without want. She knew that.

"Why didn't you tell me you had all this?"

"I was afraid that if you knew, you may come to just be a part of the money, like so many other girlfriends I have had. I wanted you to come because you wanted to be with me. And that is what you did."

"So what is it that you do?"

"Come. We can discuss all of this later. I have something very special prepared for your arrival."

A butler greeted them at the door. His name was Fernandez. He greeted them with a firm handshake and pleasant smile.

"I have heard many wonderful things of you. I am so glad to finally meet you. You are every bit as lovely as Mr. Garcia has said."

She smiled bashfully. He led them through the foyer and into a magnificent dining hall with a table bigger than she had ever seen. It was filled with fruit of every kind and and a mouthwatering array of Mexican dishes. She was so hungry. There were roses everywhere. The sight and smell of everything was overwhelming.

"Do you like?"

"Oh, this is the best welcome I could have ever imagined. It's wonderful."

"Then let's eat."

Soft music floated down from the high ceiling and engulfed the room around her. After so many weeks of hell, she felt like she was in heaven, sitting at the master's table. She had never seen so much food on a table in all her life.

After dinner, they retired to the den. On the wall was a massive five-foot tall oil painting of two people on a beach. She took a closer look, and immediately recognized the place where she had first met Gerardo in Cancun. She was the woman in the painting. She was in awe.

"That's where we met. Is that me?" She didn't need to ask.

"Yes, it is you. I had it painted several months after we met. I never wanted to forget that feeling of when I met you there that night." He was caressing her arm. This was all so unexpected. "I never gave up hope that I would feel you in my arms again."

It was such a beautiful painting, but something about it made her cringe. It seemed a bit obsessive to view a picture of herself from the dinner table every single day.

She didn't know how to respond to Gerardo's touch. It felt foreign to her. It had been so long since another man had touched her body. She knew she should feel guilty about enjoying herself so much after what she and Matt had been through together, and how it had ended for both of them. But she didn't feel all that guilty, really. After all, he was gone, and this was all too good to be true.

Gerardo showed Beth to her room.

"This will be your room until you decide you wish to share a room with me." She peeked into the room. She saw four large boxes that she had shipped the week before. The room was fit for a queen, with rose gold and pink decor. There was a beautiful hand-painted mural covering the entire ceiling, and gorgeous Spanish tiles and gemstones imbedded in the walls.

"I want to be with you tonight." She held his hands and kissed him softly on the mouth.

"Then come with me, my dear Elizabeth." He led her down the hall and into a large master bedroom suite. "This will be our room tonight." He smiled and led her to the bed. Tonight, she would put everything behind her and focus on making Gerardo feel like he was the most important thing in the world to her. This would be her new life for a while, and she needed him to completely trust her. She slipped off her dress, and pulled Gerardo onto the bed.

Chapter Seventeen

After two weeks at sea, Sela and Jake knew that it was time to go home. They both had responsibilities to the kids and the ranch that they couldn't shirk any longer. Sela knew everything was in good hands with Lily running the place in her absence. Still, so many of the kids were old enough to have heard the news about her. She knew it was time to set things straight. The charade was over. She was alive, and that alone was going to be shocking news to everyone.

Sela had dreaded going home, and back to the ranch, so much. She knew that her unexpected return would put her in the public eye. She would have to answer so many questions from the press. Her life was going to be the splattered all over the headlines for the next few weeks. She was also worried about how things would go for her and Jake. Would he want to go back to San Francisco and continue in his field of study? Would he be content in Texas helping her out with the children? She knew he loved her, but since she had never experienced true love, she wasn't quite sure what a person would do for love. She knew that she would do anything for him, except leave the children again.

She watched the stars twinkle overhead in the night sky as she heard the sounds of the shore getting closer. Sela steered the yacht into the dock with the help of a familiar face on the pier. It was tied down and they were given the "all clear" sign for.

Sela was the first to speak after the long silence on the way to the shore.

"I knew I would have to face the rest of the world at some point. I just didn't know it was going to be this hard."

Jake did not respond to her comment. He was thinking carefully about what he was about to say.

"I could not have dreamed of a better person to share the last two weeks with. I could never get tired of hearing you laugh and feeling you near me. I want you to be my wife, Sela. I know this is sudden and we have only known each other for six months or less, but will you marry me, Sela?" He knelt down on one knee and looked into the face that had taken him by surprise on the day she had met him for the very first time at the airport.

"Oh, Jake. Yes, I will marry you. Oh, yes, I will!" She felt tears running down both cheeks. She cried because of her happiness and her sadness, too. She cried for her father and mother and Charlee. She cried with joy for the new family she was about to create. Jake held her and felt her sobs. He let her cry. When she finally wiped her face, he spoke.

"When do you want to get married?"

"Let's do it this Christmas! Let's have a Christmas wedding. It's my favorite time of the year!"

"December twenty-third."

"Sounds perfect." Nothing could describe the emotions she felt at this moment. Mere words were not enough to convey what she was feeling. When you know it's love, it doesn't take years to be convinced. It had taken her two years to finally agree to marry Matt. Now, in just a few short months she knew she was ready to be the wife of Jake Carraway! She spoke the words out loud.

"Mrs. Sela Carraway!" Jake smiled and they embraced.

Hand-in-hand, they walked down the long pier to Jake's truck. It had been sitting there for two weeks.

"It won't be so hard facing the rest of the world, as long as we're together." He squeezed her hand a little bit tighter, and she squeezed back.

"I'm ready," she whispered.

Lily greeted them at the door with hugs and kisses.

"Come on in! I have been missing the fire out of you, girl. I can't wait to hear about y'all's adventure!"

"I can't wait to tell you about mine and Jake's time off the coast of Mexico. It was absolutely fabulous. We even went to a bullfight in Mexico City. Don't worry. I took lots of pictures." Her mind went briefly to the bullfight where she thought she had seen Beth sitting with an older guy in the VIP section. The impossibility of it all had made her look quickly away from the woman.

"I hope so! I've got some pretty exciting news of my own. I want you to meet someone. Well, you already know him, but he has a new title around here."

Pony came from around the corner of the kitchen and greeted Sela and Jake. "This is my fiancé, Anthony." Lily grinned with complete glee.

Sela's mouth dropped wide open. "You're kidding me?"

"Congratulations! I'm so excited for you two. When did this happen?" She wrapped her arms around Pony and kissed him on the cheek. She had known and loved him for many years. He was great with the kids, and he did so much for the ranch.

"Tonight. Not too long ago."

"Lily, I am so excited for you! Guess what?" She grabbed Lily by both hands. "I have some wonderful news of my own. Jake asked me to marry him tonight, too. Of course, I said yes!"

Jake and Tony watched indulgently as the two ladies exchanged more hugs and kisses.

"I have an idea, but it might be crazy. Would anyone object to a double wedding?" Sela looked at everyone's expressions. Pure love in the room.

"I would love a double wedding!" Lily looked a Tony. "What do you think?"

"I've never even heard of a double wedding, but I'm in as long as I get to marry this lady." Tony grabbed Lily by the hand and kissed it.

"Jake?" He smiled. He didn't care how they were married, just as long as they were.

"Sounds good to me!"

"Then it's settled. We're all getting married!"

Jake pulled Sela in close to him and Tony pulled Lily close to him on the couch, as the two couples exchanged stories and discussed wedding plans.

After a lengthy goodnight, they all parted ways and left in separate directions. Each one spent the remainder of the night thinking sweet thoughts of the coming wedding.

Weeks passed, as Sela and Lily kept the ranch running. Together, they organized a gigantic wedding that included white horses and white doves. It would be the party of the year. Since every child old enough to ride at the ranch had a horse of their own, they would all be included in the ceremony. Each child would decorate their horse and parade them behind the wedding couple's carriage. It seemed no one could speak of anything else these days.

Meanwhile, Beth stayed hidden away in Mexico City. She had left without a trace, leaving behind no clues. It was a case that baffled the authorities on all levels.

One month had passed since her arrival, and already the

language barrier and culture shock were beginning to cause her great grief. With Gerardo working long hours, she was forced to shop and entertain herself alone. She was finding out rather quickly that without love, the money wasn't very much fun. She could buy anything, but why did she need to?

She sipped her coffee outside on the veranda and listened listless to the early sounds of autumn. Leaves rustled and fell to the ground. Winter would be here soon. And then spring and then summer. Would she still be sitting alone on this veranda? She had tried to make trips into town, but paranoia got the best of her. She felt the locals' eyes as they followed her. She stuck out in the Mexican crowd like a sore thumb. She was tall and blond and always turned heads in this town. But she refused to live under a disguise. Gerardo would not like her hair dark.

She felt her heart palpitating erratically. It was another anxiety attack. She was stressed. There she sat with access to millions of dollars and her body ached for passion and love and adventure. She missed Matt, but thoughts of him filled her with such anger. He had fouled up their carefully made plans, and then left her to pick up the pieces. Her mind was muddled with conversations they had had.

"What went wrong? Why did you leave me here to sort through everything on my own?" She slammed her fist into the table and the coffee cup rattled in the saucer.

"I'm not dead, Beth. I am not dead!"

Beth turned to look at the person who had spoken. There was no one behind her. Her heart began to pound. She had heard the words so clearly.

"Why are you here in Mexico City? Whose place is this anyway?" Beth grabbed her head and ripped at her hair. She was going crazy. She couldn't possibly have heard his voice. Matt was dead. She pushed her chair out violently and ran up the stairs to her room. She opened one of the boxes she had mailed ahead of her arrival for the first time. She pulled out a photo album, and thumbed through pictures of her and Matt. Her eyes swelled with tears and she screamed out in pain. Within minutes, Fernandez was at the door.

"Excuse me, ma'am, but I thought I heard a scream. Are you all right?"

"I'm perfectly fine. Thanks."

He closed the door.

"I'm not dead Beth. It was a trick, so that I could get away."

"This is not real!" What if every detail had been planned so perfectly to fake his death and now, she sat in Mexico going crazy? What if Matt was waiting for her in Germany?

Gerardo sat at his desk working as he listened to the news of the one million dollar reward for information leading to the arrest of his precious Beth. CNN World News had kept the story going since the bank robberies had occurred. The latest development was the million dollars in reward money posted by Sela Barnes. He had been following the report over the last month. He seethed. He felt broken-hearted and disrespected. Two things he would not tolerate.

He hated being used, and Beth was doing just that. She needed an escape and now she would pay for what she was doing. He had loved her and invested his emotions in her for many years. She had kept him hanging on, but for what reason?

He was unable to love another, though he had dated many girls. The American southern girl had haunted his memory and heart for too many years. She had led him on with her letters, saying she wanted to be with him. She had made passionate love to him in his bed. He had dreamed of the moment for many years. Well, now she would be his forever, whether she liked it or not.

James picked up the phone and called his buddy.

"Have you seen the news today?"

"No. I'm working dude. What's up?"

"A million dollar reward for information leading to the arrest of that crazy lady we dropped off at the EconoLodge. I don't know about you, but that sounds pretty good to me."

"Hell yeah, it sounds good!"

"Here's what we say. That this lady asked us for a ride. We were on our way to a friend's house and she was walking down the road with a suitcase. She said she was heading south and needed a ride. We dropped her off at the EconoLodge and that's all we know. Nothing else. We stick to that. We had no idea she was the robber."

"What about the black men that drove her from the bank? What if somebody points a finger at us?"

"How could they? It could have been anybody. I kept my hands in my sleeve, so I know my prints ain't nowhere in her car."

"Well, my fingerprints are all over the steering wheel. Shoot. Maybe you should just go and say you gave her a ride. Don't even mention me."

"Naw. I don't think so. We're trying to analyze this too much. Let's just go say we saw the woman walking and she asked for a ride. That's it. We took her to the motel."

"When do you get off work?"

"Now, if I am about to make a million dollars."

"That's half a million each."

"Yeah, yeah. I get off at four. Meet me here."

"All right."

James and Rod sat in two separate interrogation rooms, answering one question after another. They told the officers that they had spotted the woman hitchhiking. The story just didn't make sense.

"Son, witnesses said she left the first bank with a black man about your age. We have video. He picked her up at the front door. The getaway car was found. We have DNA samples and fingerprints from the black man's hair that was found on the seat. Would you mind if we took a hair sample?" James squirmed. He knew what would be found.

"All right, I was scared. That's why I lied. But I didn't know this woman." His voice was squeaky now. "She asked me to give her a ride to the bank. Said she had an account at SouthTrust and AmSouth. I had no reason to doubt her. She didn't say she was going in to rob the bank. I waited on her and gave her a ride. She said she would give me a hundred dollars. I needed the money."

"Who's car was it?"

There was silence. He should have thought his answers through before he just barged in with a story.

"It was her car."

"You drove her car, but she said she needed a ride."

"Yes. But I drive my momma and grandma all the time when they have errands to run. I thought she wanted me to drive her around like I drive them. You see, they don't like to walk far, so I always wait for them by the front of the store. That's what I thought was goin' on here."

"How did you meet this woman?"

"She came up to us on the basketball court and asked if anyone was interested in driving her around for a few extra bucks. We thought maybe she was some rich white woman who wanted herself a chauffeur."

It sounded plausible.

"In a GEO Prism, you thought she was a rich white woman? How much did you say she gave you?"

"Fifty dollars."

The officer made a note of the discrepancy. "Then what?"

"I took her to the bank. She got in and told me she had robbed the bank. I was scared. She had a gun. She said she was heading south. She told me to drive. We drove for a few hours without talking. We made it into Linden, and she asked me to drop her off at the EconoLodge. She thanked me with ten one hundred dollar bills."

"Do you still have the bills?"

"Yes, some of them."

"I need you to bring them to me. I need them today."

"Yes, sir."

"Why didn't you report this?"

"We were scared. Didn't know what we had done, really."

"Look guys. I don't believe all of your story. What I do believe is that you didn't know this woman, and you got involved in something you didn't wake up and plan to do. This woman is a killer. She's wanted for at least one possible murder and now the bank robberies. You guys got lucky. She could have killed you."

"She did have a gun, you know."

"Yes, I know. The DA is pushing for you guys to be charged with accessory to the bank robbery, but I am not going to charge you with anything yet. I trust that you've told me everything you know about this incident."

"We have. We're victims in this, too. How could we have seen it coming?"

He realized he was taking it a little too far and needed to quit while they were ahead.

"If I need you boys, I'll call you at this number." He looked at the formal report.

"What about the reward?"

"The reward comes when the woman is arrested. That's why it says. "Information leading to the arrest." We'll follow-up on all this info and be in touch. That's all."

They left the station, filled with the hope of that million dollar reward.

"It went well, don't you think?"

"I guess it did in the end. It looked pretty bad there for a minute."

"I know what you mean. We need to find that crazy woman and collect us some money."

"I wouldn't know where to start."

"We could start at the hotel."

"She's done been gone from there by now."

"Well, somebody might know somethin'."

"We can't do no better than the police. They'll get her, and I'll be drivin' a Porsche this time next month."

"Ooooh."

"I don't know what I'm gonna do with my half."

The two boys spent the next hour discussing what they would do with their reward money.

It was confirmed that a woman fitting Beth's description had stayed at the hotel. Phone records showed that she made a call to Gerardo Garcia at 6:30 p.m. Finding Gerardo Garcia in Mexico City wouldn't be easy, but not impossible. She wasn't as slick as she thought. Mexican authorities would be notified that she was there, and she would be arrested and extradited back to America when found.

Beth packed her things back into the cardboard box and put away the album. She looked at the passport Matt had made for her. She would have a much happier life in Europe somewhere. She just couldn't blend in here no matter how hard she tried. She would stick it out long enough to soak some money out of Gerardo, and then she'd be gone. She would take as much jewelry as possible, then sell it later. She certainly couldn't live the rest of her life on what she had gotten from the banks. Not in Europe, anyway.

Gerardo contemplated his first painful move. He knew what it would be.

Chapter Eighteen

The table was set for two, with a lovely arrangement of candles and flowers. Red wine was poured, and sweet violins could be heard from the music chamber, as two men dressed in black played for them.

"Are you enjoying your dinner?"

"Very much so." She smiled sweetly.

"Are you enjoying our time together?"

"It's exactly as I had hoped it would be. You've been so kind and generous to me. I don't know how to thank you."

"Why shouldn't I be kind and generous? I have wanted you in my life for so long. I have spent days and nights thinking of only you. Now you are here with me, and I want it to be forever. It will be forever, right? You are not planning to leave me, right?"

"As long as you will allow me to stay." She did not look at him, but she could feel his gaze upon her, burning her skin. She wished the conversation had not gone in this direction. She found it difficult to digest her food.

"Elizabeth, why did you come to me after so long? What changed your mind and made you come now?"

She had already rehearsed this question a thousand times in her mind.

"I want to be truthful with you. When I met you, I was in a serious relationship. I was not sure what I wanted from you. All I knew was that I did not want to let you out of my life completely. That's why I continued corresponding with you. Matt and I weren't doing so good together. Then one night, he told me that I had been acting as though I was preoccupied with someone else. We argued a while, but it was that moment when I knew I wanted to be with someone else. Until that moment, I didn't even realize how much I wanted you in my life. The someone else I had been preoccupied with for so long was you, Gerardo. I was in Texas with Matt at the time. He got so angry! He went nuts. I ended up driving back to Atlanta. I packed my boxes and mailed them to you. I felt like I owed it to Matt to give him one last goodbye. I didn't want it ending so badly with him. I drove back to Texas to tell him goodbye, and he was gone. When I went into his office, I left the keys in my car and it was stolen. I know it all sounds so crazy. I took a taxi to a nearby hotel and that's when I called you." She watched his face anxiously, for any signs of belief or disbelief. His features remained impassive, expressionless. She continued.

"I've felt so desperate and alone for such a long time. I needed you. You were the one person who I knew in my heart, could heal me in so many ways. Gerardo, you have been a rock for me over the years. Your letters and phone calls have kept me sane."

"What about your home in Atlanta? You are just leaving it?"

"I was renting it with a friend. She will stay there. Most of the furniture belonged to her. I told her I was starting over and that she could have whatever she wanted of the things I left behind. She said she would clean it out for me and what she can't sell, she will give to the Salvation Army." It was all a lie. She had walked away from all her things. Matt had bought her the house a year ago with money he had stolen from Sela. She would check on it at some point, but that was not her concern at the moment.

"Thank you for coming to me after so many offers." Gerardo

smiled, but it did not feel friendly. Her scalp tingled and she cringed inside, as he stared at her in silence for an uncomfortably long time.

"My dear, you have not seen my wine cellar. I have many bottles of the finest wine. It is something I am very proud of."

"Let's make a toast." Beth tried hard to lighten the mood. It was time to drink and be merry.

"Of course."

"To new beginnings and time not wasted." She held her glass high as they looked at each other in classic form, clinked glasses, and drank the toast.

"I have one as well. To honesty and sincerity. May it forever be the rock of our relationship." He watched her carefully as she drank the drugged wine he had placed before her.

"Cheers."

"Cheers." Drink up, my dear. The drug would make her hallucinate for many hours after it was taken.

It didn't take long for Gerardo to begin to see the effects of the drug. Beth was shaking her head as if to clear something from her mind. Her speech had become slurred and now and again she would blurt out the words "stop" and "no." He didn't know what she was seeing in her mind, but he knew the drugs were working.

"My dear, are you feeling all right?"

"I feel sick. I'm not able to finish dinner. I'm so sorry."

"It's fine. First, I wanted to show you my cellar."

Beth couldn't be less interested in his cellar at this point, but she didn't have the strength to resist him. He grabbed her by the shoulders and lifted her to her feet.

"Follow me."

He escorted her down a long flight of stairs and into an underground floor. At the end of the long hall was a door.

"There is my wine cellar."

He moved slowly and deliberately. He knew what was to come. He turned on the light and revealed rows and rows of wine. The walls were thickly padded and the temperature was very cold. He closed the door and shoved Beth to the ground from behind. He pounced on her, hitting her in the face until she was barely conscious. Ripping her shirt open he bit her breasts until they bled. He then forced himself on her. Afterward, she lay lifeless on the cold floor.

"I will not be made a fool of by anyone. Including the woman I love."

He stood up and wiped his mouth with the back of his arm and left, locking the door behind him.

"Do you think that I am a fool? That I don't know what you did in Texas? I don't know what game you are playing, but I'll find out. Until next time, my dear."

Beth lay on the floor, unable to move. Above her, she could see Matt. He was grinning from ear-to-ear. In his hand, was a torch and a handful of money. He lit the money and laughed out loud. Beth reached for him. "Help me, you fool. What is the matter with you?"

Charlee stepped up next to him. "No one can help you. Not even God himself. You will burn in hell when this is all over. But for now, see what you did to me?" She ripped the rotting skin from her body and dangled it in Beth's face. "Do you see what you did to me? Do you smell what you did to me?"

The drugs that Gerardo had put in her drink continued to create images in her mind that she could not control. She was helpless.

Sela finally received some news about Beth's whereabouts. After nearly six weeks of following leads, packages that were sent, and phone calls that were made, the police were en route to Mr. Garcia's home. It was about 8:00 p.m.

The front gate security officer rang the home of Mr. Garcia and Fernandez answered.

"Ola." The conversation was completely in Spanish.

"The police are here to see Mr. Garcia. They have questions they need to ask him concerning a missing woman. Beth Newberry."

"Mr. Garcia is already in the bed. They will have to come back later."

The message was relayed.

"They cannot come later. They have a warrant to search the house and ask him some questions. He must cooperate."

Gerardo could hear the conversation. "Tell them it is okay. Fernandez, you and Julio take everything that belongs to Miss Elizabeth and put in the secret room. I want no sign of her here. Are the dishes removed?"

"Yes, sir." He wasn't sure what was going on, but he knew not to ask questions.

"Good. Move quickly. I will stall the police."

He picked up the phone to speak with the gate attendant.

"Let me speak to one of the officers."

"Yes, sir."

"This is Gerardo Garcia. How may I help you?"

"We need to speak with you concerning a wanted felon by the name of Elizabeth Newberry. We have airport records showing she was on a private flight with you on October 28, flying out of Dallas, Texas. She used a fake passport at the airport."

"This is correct. I know nothing about her whereabouts,

though. She told me she was in some kind of trouble and asked me to come get her. I did. We had dinner together and went our separate ways. That was over a week ago."

"We need to come in, Mr. Garcia. We have a search warrant. She is a very dangerous woman."

Fernandez nodded. Everything had been moved.

"Okay. Give me one moment."

He instructed the security guard to allow the officers to pass through. The thick iron gate swung slowly open. Gerardo watched the headlights move closer and closer. He didn't care. They would never find his cellar or the secret room. It had been used so many times in emergency situations. The secret was another one of his genius moves at the mansion. There were many secret paths and tunnels, should he ever need them.

The officers entered and immediately began asking questions.

"Like I said, she told me she was in trouble. I never knew what kind of trouble. I later found out she had robbed some banks or something. Possibly she has committed murder, from what I understand. She is not here. She said she was passing through. Possibly headed to Europe at some point.

"Did she give you any idea about where in Europe she might go?"

"No."

"You said she did stay here with you?"

"Yes. But only for a few days.

"How long have you known Ms. Newberry?"

"About six years."

"Exactly when did she leave?"

Gerardo looked at Fernandez.

"It was Thursday morning, a week ago. I left for work and when I returned in the evening she was gone. She left no letter and gave us no information about where she was going. That is all I can tell you." His accent was elegant, and his voice was full of authority.

"We need to search the premises. Maybe she left behind some clue as to where she was headed. Where did she sleep?"

"Up here."

He led her to the room Beth had occupied for the last month. What a close call. If he had waited just one more day, he would not have been able to inflict torture on the woman in the way that he had planned. She would have been in the hands of the authorities. Now she was all his.

As a wealthy business owner in the country, his chances of being in serious trouble were slim-to-none. Still, he knew he needed to go through the routine. He could have picked up the phone and had the police thrown out immediately, but he was morbidly interested and excited by the whole thing. He could still picture the look on Beth's face as she lay violated in his basement. He would teach her to never betray his trust again.

He explained to the police officers how they met, and their continued connection through letters and over the internet. He had no reason to lie, and they believed him. They were satisfied with what they had found out from him. There was no reason for any further questioning.

Beth didn't know what day it was or how long she had been in the wine cellar. She was barely conscious and was close to hypothermia. It must have been several days. Maybe weeks. She drank another one of the bottles of water that had been left for her. No one had checked on her. She knew that much. She opened a bottle of wine by shoving the cork through with a pen that was attached to a pad on the wall near the door. She drank a few sips of the wine.

She had not noticed the phone on the other side of the wall until this moment. With the little energy she had gotten from the water, she stood up and picked up the receiver. The line was dead.

She knew someone would be coming to the cellar at some point. If she could just maintain enough strength to attack whoever came down, she could make her escape. She had no idea how long she would have to wait, but she knew she was a survivor. This would not be the way she left this earth!

"Ola, my dear Elizabeth. How are you doing down there?"

The intercom system could be heard loud and clear. Beth jumped at the sound of the booming voice.

"Push the red button near the phone if you wish to talk back to me. Have you missed me?" He waited for an answer. "I'll be back to see you soon. You just get yourself all cleaned up and looking good for Papi. We will pick up right where we left off. Surely you remember where we left off, don't you?"

Beth trembled with fear. This man was a monster. A freaking monster. She gave no thought to the monster she was herself.

"Oh. I'll bet you are thinking how cruel I am. Well, think of yourself. You are the cruel one." She could hear him breathing on the other end of the line, but she did not dare speak back.

"The police were here looking for you several days ago. Seems your felonies have caught up with you. I told them you left weeks ago. They believed my story of, course. Would you believe they even searched the place looking for you? Like I would lie or something. Lying is for losers, right honey? Lying is for murderers and thieves, not lovers like me and you! When did you plan on telling me you didn't really love me?" He was angry and agitated. She wondered if he would be down soon to take out his frustration on her. How long had he known about what she had done?

"You know what, dear Elizabeth. I have almost had enough of you. And when I am done, you can rot in hell. Or should I say in my wine cellar."

His laugh was horrifying. She knew that he meant it. How long could she survive down here in the cold? When had she eaten last? Gerardo flipped the breaker, and the basement light went out. She knew he would be back. She would be ready for him.

"I hope you are not afraid of the dark."

She couldn't see anything. Not even her hand in front of her face. She was living a nightmare. She would die in her nightmare unless she thought of something fast. She felt her way over to the bottles of wine and pulled several from the shelf. She went to the wall and felt for the red button. She pressed the button and smashed a bottle of wine on the floor. She pulled one after another from the shelves until the lights came on and she heard the key in the door turn. She knew he would not be able to stand his precious bottles of wine being wasted.

The door swung wide open, and Gerardo stepped inside. In his hand was a long carving knife. Beth jumped from behind the door and jammed a broken bottle into the side of his neck and twisted it. He yelled and fell to the floor, grabbing her arm and pulling him down with her. She wrestled with him as blood gushed from his neck. She fought to keep his hands from chocking her. She picked up another bottle of wine and hit him as hard as she could over the head. The bottle didn't break like in the movies, but rather made a dull thud against his head, immediately followed by the sound of his skull cracking. She dragged herself up the stairs. She could barely walk. She had no energy left to escape the house.

Gerardo pulled the glass from his neck and held his hand against the oozing gash. He climbed the stairs and opened the door. He stood staring at her as his neck gushed a stream of blood. He walked toward her with the large knife in his hand as she screamed. She managed to crawl weakly down the hall. He fell, unable to move. Blood puddled on the white marble floor around him.

At the top of the stairs, Fernandez watched as the brutally beaten woman crawled across the floor. She was covered in blood. He did not move towards her until he was sure his boss was lifeless.

"Please, help me."

She collapsed on the floor at his feet.

"Miss! Mr. Garcia! What happened to you? Where have you been? What have you done to Mr. Garcia?"

"Gerardo raped me. He drugged me and beat me and left me in the cellar to die." She could barely speak. "I don't know why. I don't know what's happening."

He remembered his boss telling him to stay away from the cellar until further notice. He didn't know why. Now he did.

Fernandez called the ambulance and covered her body with a blanket. She was cold and shivering. She lay there, motionless. He felt for her pulse. She was alive, but he was sure that she was in shock.

The emergency medical technicians arrived within twenty minutes and quickly revived her.

The police questioned Fernandez.

"What happened here?"

He would not lie. He was too afraid to lie.

"All I know is that this woman came up the stairs like this. She told me Mr. Garcia had raped her and that he had left her to die."

"Who is the woman?"

"She is the woman the police were looking for last week. Mr. Garcia met her many years ago. Her real name is Beth Newberry. I have seen her picture many times on the news in the last weeks. I could not go to the police because I was afraid of Mr. Garcia. You can see that you do not want to cross him."

"So you knew that the girl was here, and you lied to the police."

"No, I did not know. I knew that she was staying here and then I didn't see her any more. Mr. Garcia told me to stay away from the cellar until further notice. I do as I am told around here."

Beth could not understand a word of what they were saying. She had heard her name though, and that was not good. Her running days were over. She knew that. It was all over.

She was placed on a stretcher and taken to a local hospital. Gerardo was taken in a separate ambulance. He was in critical condition, but still alive. He would be charged with many things, including aiding and abetting a fugitive, lying to police, rape, attempted murder, and anything else they could think of to charge him with. There had been rumors about his treatment of women for years. No one would come forward because they were afraid of the consequences. This was all they needed to put him behind bars for a long time.

An armed guard was placed outside Beth's room and when she was able to travel, she would be transported back to Texas where she would be charged with armed bank robbery and murder.

The phone rang and James turned down the TV.

"Yeah."

"Is this James?"

"Yeah. Who is this?"

"Sgt. Patrick. I have some news for you. Beth Newberry was transported to the county jail this morning. Looks like you boys will be receiving a right hefty reward in the next few days."

"You kidding?"

"No, I'm not. Your tip led us to Mexico City where she was found several days ago. She had been badly beaten, raped, and nearly killed. It looks like you guys probably saved her life by coming forward when you did. If you want to come by the office, I have a check from Ms. Barnes in the amount of $500,000 for each of you gentlemen."

"Are you serious? Don't joke. This is unbelievable. Talkin' 'bout a change of luck. Are you for real? Hallelujah!"

"I'm not kidding you. I'm going to see what I can do to get the charges against you two dropped. This girl manipulated you guys, just like she manipulates everyone."

"Yes, sir. Thank you. I'm forever grateful to you."

"So when will you be down?"

"Just as soon as I can get a ride."

"I guess the first thing you're going to do is buy a car."

"You got that right, sir." The boy chuckled.

"Are you going to pass this news on to your buddy, or should I give him a call?"

"I'll call him. I'll see you soon. Thank you!"

"James dialed Roderick's number.

"Dude. What up?"

"Nuttin' much."

"I just got a call from Sgt. Patrick. I guess you won't be workin' at the car wash tomorrow."

"They got the girl?"

"They got the girl, and we got a check waiting at the station. Come get me, dude!"

"Today is the last time they gone see me with a dirty rag in my hand. We rich!"

"Yeah, we rich."

"Come get me."

"I'm leavin' right now."

Headlines about the scandal flashed across the screen for weeks. "Murder Plot Foiled By New Fiancée." "Secret Lover Saves the Life of Sela Barnes On Her Honeymoon." "Ex-best Friend Has Affair with Sela Barnes' Husband and Plots to Kill Her On Her Honeymoon." Every newspaper ran the juicy news story.

Sela was invited to speak on many talk shows. She tried to explain everything in detail. Jake sat beside her during every interview to show support for his future wife.

"What would you say to your former best friend right now if she were watching?" Larry King asked his guest. Sela had pondered that exact question during the past few months.

"I guess I would tell her that I had always loved her and that I miss the times we shared together. I have never had, nor will I ever have, a friend who was as special as Beth was to me. I would have given her anything she asked for.

"Do you think you will ever ask her why?"

"No. I have resolved to never think of her or this awful experience again. It's over. She'll pay for what she's done. It will take a while for me to recover, but thank God for the man beside me. He is so perfect for me. I never really knew love before him.

I realize that now." She looked at the man sitting next to her. How close she had been to making the biggest mistake of her life.

Sela and Jake held hands as she spoke of the tragic loss of family, friends, and her trust in her former fiancée.

The interviewer continued, "So what would you tell anyone out there who is feeling a little anxious about who they have agreed to marry?"

"Pray hard for clarity. That's first. If you feel in your gut something isn't quite right, it probably isn't! Listen to your friends and family, because sometimes they can see things that you can't."

Beth sat in jail staring at the bars and the thin mattress that she would grow to hate during her long stay. She could hear the clanging of keys and footsteps moving in her direction.

"Let's go." The officer opened the door to her cell, but she did not move.

"I said let's go!" He repeated the command louder and stepped in her direction. Grabbing her by the arm, he raised her to her feet and placed the handcuffs on her wrists.

"You are in a heap of trouble, little lady." He received no response, as he led her to the courtroom. "You sure don't look like the typical criminal. They won't treat your kind too nicely in a place like this."

There were dark suits everywhere, and the room was full of reporters. She took her seat as she stared down various individuals in the room. The judge spoke after several minutes of paper shuffling.

"You have been charged with the murder of Charlene Barnes, conspiracy to commit the murder of Sela Barnes, and armed bank robbery. How do plan to plea? There is a load of evidence against you, I might add."

"You left something out." She was thinking about Mr. Charles Barnes.

"What did I leave out?"

"You'll have to figure it out on your own. Not guilty, your honor." The court room gasped in unison. The judge pounded his gavel.

"You are looking at the death penalty. Do you realize that?"

"I already have the death penalty." Her lips barely moved.

"You'd be crazy not to plea bargain and plead guilty." The voice sounded so familiar. When she looked up, she could have sworn Matt was in the room.

"Matt? Is that you?" Her eyes danced with new life.

"Excuse me?" Barker Leverette, her assigned lawyer looked confused. "What are you doing?"

"For a moment I thought you were someone…" her voice trailed off. Her thoughts went to Matt. He had left her to deal with everything alone. She hated him.

Barker looked at the battered woman in front of him. He had handled some crazy cases in his life, but this one was the highest profile case he'd ever had. Secretly, he wanted to drag it out a bit. She could hear the words being spoken around her, but chose to shut out every word.

Barker spoke quietly in her ear.

"I thought we agreed that you would plead guilty."

"I changed my mind. It's a woman's prerogative."

She would never plead guilty. She would fight until the bitter end. It would be her only form of entertainment until she could come up with something else.

"I'm sorry, Your Honor. This is new. My client wishes to plead not guilty, so we will move forward with jury selection and a trial."

Beth smiled at the shocked faces around the courtroom. She loved having all the attention on her, after living in the shadows for so long.

She was escorted back to her cell. After several hours, a handsome young guard jangled his keys unnecessarily before he opened the cell door. It was definitely an attempt to make her watch him. It was then she began to plot her next move.

Sela had one more thing she had to do. She stepped inside the elevator and pressed the button to the eighth floor. She entered the room and saw Matt lying motionless in his hospital bed. His neck and face were partly bandaged, and he had lost a lot of weight since she had seen him last.

"Matt, can you hear me?" She touched his hand to gently wake him. He slowly opened his eyes and look hopelessly into Sela's.

"Can you hear me?" she repeated. She knew he could. The doctors had said that he would make a full recovery. He was lucky he had not been able to hold his gun with a steady hand.

"I have something for you." She pulled out a syringe and stuck the needle into his IV tube. "Your girlfriend is in jail. She was beat-up and mangled pretty badly when they found her in Mexico with an old lover. Maybe you've heard of him? Gerardo Garcia? Remember? She met him our junior year of high school. Anyway, she has confessed to nothing, although we have enough evidence to put her on death row. As for you, you are on your death row. I'll be back to see you every two weeks with a new injection that paralyzes you from the neck down. Maybe the doctors will figure out what's keeping you paralyzed or maybe they won't. Since you can't speak, I guess you won't be telling anyone anytime soon. It takes weeks for it to wear off, so if you don't see me for a while, it's because I am on my honeymoon with Jake."

Matt looked terrified. He was at her mercy now, and there was nothing he could do. He felt for the buzzer to ring the nurse.

"Are you looking for this?" Sela held the device in her hand. "Would you like for me to call the nice nurse for you? I'll bet you would. Let's just give that medicine I gave you a few more minutes to work." She put the buzzer just out of his reach.

"Well, that's all the time I have for now, Matt. I'm sure you'll be looking forward to our next visit. By the way, we've located your son. You weren't lying about that, after all. He's three years old, so your timeline is a little off, but you'll be pleased to know that he has been invited to live on the ranch. He'll be arriving in early January. We found him in the foster system in Georgia." Sela flipped her long brown hair as she left the room. Matt lay there, scared to death. He had no way of knowing she had not actually inserted any drug into his IV tube and that she would never be back to see him. She had only pretended to insert something to scare him. It was a cruel ploy, but it was her own form of justice being served.

After four months, Matt regained his strength enough to stand trial. He was convicted of attempted murder with the help of a very nervous and illegal Puerto Rican named Ruez. Matt was sentenced to twenty-five years in prison.

Beth was sentenced to death for the killing of Charlene Barnes, and will live the rest of her life on death row.

Sela stood there, on the most important day of her life, wearing the most beautiful white gown that money could buy. With a

258

sequin and pearl bodice that fit tightly around her waist, her hourglass figure could not have been more perfectly accented. The modest plunge in the neckline showed a mere glimpse of her rounded breasts, and her hair flowed in curls down her back. On her arm, Ted smiled with pride.

"Are you ready for this?" He looked at the blushing bride.

"I've never been more ready in my life." She squeezed his arm. "Thank you for giving me away. Daddy would be so pleased."

"Please consider me your godfather, Sela. I've known your family for so long. Sharon and I never had any kids. I was selfish and stayed gone too much. She would love to have you be a part of our lives. Give us a chance to be the grandparents we could never be."

Sela smiled. "I would love to."

The music started and the flower girl headed down the aisle. Sela looked behind her at the beautiful woman who had invested so many years in her life.

"You look beautiful." She mouthed. "You do, too, Mr. Booker." Lily's father, an eighty-five-year-old veteran, smiled a pearly white smile as he escorted Lily down the aisle.

Sela and Ted started down the aisle.

At the end of the aisle was Jake. His eyes gleamed with pleasure. He had never seen a woman so beautiful in all his life. His eyes met Sela's, and he felt the old familiar flutter he had felt the first time their eyes had locked at the airport. Behind her waltzed Lily, as radiant as she had been in her youth. Tears streamed down her cheeks as she walked down the aisle toward her husband-to-be.

As the vows were spoken, Lily and Sela could not restrain their emotions any longer, and they began to weep. They were bonded together through laughter and tears, and now on this special day, they would forever share this memory of matrimony. True love had been a long time coming, but for both of them, it was well worth the wait.

Two hundred children gathered to see the wedding. Horses were decorated with red and yellow poinsettias draped around their necks. Each couple was helped into a golden carriage only seen in fairy tales, as guests cried and laughed at the awesome spectacle. Horses pranced in rows carrying the couples to the front drive where limousines waited to take them to the airport. Sela and Jake would spend two weeks in Aspen, Colorado before making their way to San Sebastian, Spain for a week.

Lily and Anthony would spend two weeks in Cancun and two weeks in Aruba.

The children, ranging in ages from two to eighteen, waved as Sela and Lily and their husbands disappeared down the driveway and on to the main road. Sela blew kisses to the children and waved until she was out of sight. She felt ashamed of the way she had left them and moved to South Carolina. She had so many big plans for the ranch once she returned from her honeymoon. She would start gymnastics and music classes. She would build a theater and offer dance lessons for those that wanted it. She would turn out the most well-rounded kids in Texas!

She blew kisses to the kids as they cheered and threw confetti into the air. Through the crowd, Jake could see the little boy whose parents had been shot at the football game. He pointed to the kid. "Randy!" The boy smiled. "When I get back, I'm going to help make you the best quarterback in Texas. You'll be playing for the Dallas Cowboys one day!"

The young boy's face gleamed as tears welled up in his eyes. His prayers were finally being answered. He raised his head toward heaven and spoke to his lost father. "I'm gonna make you so proud, Papa. One day you'll be so proud."

Matt sat in his cell, reading. It had been one year since he arrived at the prison, and things had happened there that he dared not repeat. He had never gotten a letter or heard from a single friend, but this day would be different. This day would bring hope.

Dear Matt,

I hope this letter reaches you. All I want to say is that it's not over until we have no breath left to breathe. I still love you, even though you tried to leave me alone in this world. All we have is each other. We can still be together. I have a plan.

Love forever,
Beth

Matt smiled. She always had a plan. Her failed plans had gotten them both into this mess. Maybe her new plan could get them out.

- Ruby Harper old lady took to police station
- Charles Barnes - her father - deceased
- Shes from Corpus Christi texas
- mother died breast cancer 15 yr ago
- Charlene sister only sibling - archeologist - SF
- Ruez stole her purse + necklace
- Matthew - fiancé
- Lily - Seta's long time nanny
- Beth - HS friend now Mat's affair - helped killed Charlene
- Jake Caraway friend of Charlene in SF
- Teddy investigator old family friend
- Hernandez - maid
- Julie current good friend gave $200,000
  (her son, 3, Brandon dog brain tumor - aubrey husband
- Phelp's Sela's security guard
- Hanson - Lela's attorney